Zane

THE MCKADES OF TEXAS

KIMBERLY LEWIS

ISBN-10:0-9852752-2-7
ISBN-13:978-0-9852752-2-8

Printed in the United States of America

Edited by: Jennifer Pitoniak

Cover Design by: Kimberly Lewis

Cover images purchased from Dreamstime.com

www.kimberlylewisnovels.blogspot.com

For my husband, Rob.

ACKNOWLEDGMENTS

I would like to take this opportunity to thank all of the people who contributed to helping me with this novel. To my dear friends— Ashley, Megan G., Jenn, and Megan D.—I would not have been able to do this without you. I appreciate you taking the time to give me your honest opinions and suggestions. To my fellow author, MK McClintock, thank you for your time and guidance. Your kindness and willingness to help other authors is extraordinary. To my mother, thank you for all of your sacrificed spare time. Your love and support is absolutely priceless and I am lucky to have such a wonderful parent. To my wonderful editor, Jennifer Pitoniak, you are an absolute pleasure to work with and I am truly grateful for all you have done for me. Your honesty and dedication is indescribable. And last but certainly not least, my husband, Rob. You came along at a time in my life when I doubted I'd ever find a decent, trust-worthy man. You showed me what real love was all about—trust, respect, and friendship. Thank you for your support and for being there when I needed you most.

Kimberly Lewis

Chapter One

My mother always warned me that guys like him were nothing but trouble. I should have listened. I should have gotten out before things got so bad, but like every other woman in my position I believed he would change. Now I realize how stupid and naïve I was, but not anymore.

I did it! I finally did it! After months and months of putting up with his never ending bullshit I finally got the courage to leave. Never again will Vince Machetto be able to hurt me. I must admit I feel a little drunk with power right now. I am finally a free woman and answer to no one. But as I sit here in this musty motel room the adrenaline that pulsed through my body from my abrupt escape is slowly starting to fade away. I knew that the fear of the situation would eventually settle in but, to be honest, I didn't expect it to happen so soon.

There are a number of thoughts running through my mind right now. For one I know that what little money I was able to take from Vince's safe before I left will only hold me over for so long. I have no idea what I'm going to do for money after that. For the past few years I've been nothing but Vince's girlfriend, or should I say "property." And at twenty-four years old I should have some sort of job experience, but I don't. So I'm pretty sure that finding a job is going to be very hard. But I think the thing that scares me most of all is the one thing I really don't want to even think about. And that is, what if he finds me?

Kellan Anderson quietly closed her journal and gently laid the pen down on top of it. She ran her fingers through her damp, dark brown hair and watched as water droplets fell onto the comforter. With a sigh, she flung her legs over the edge of the bed, grabbed her journal and walked over to the dresser, placing the items in her duffle bag. Her reflection from the attached mirror on the dresser caught her attention and she gasped. Carefully, she raised her fingers to the tiny cut beneath her right eye. Four hours ago it was just a little red, but now it was swollen and starting to turn black and blue.

"Damn you, Vince," she cursed under her breath as she gently pressed her fingers to her cheek.

She dropped her hands to her duffle bag once more and rummaged around for a pair of shorts or pants, or anything she could find to put on over top of her bikini underwear. Finding a pair of soft velour pants, she slid them up and over her hips, tying the drawstring tight as she slid into a pair of flip flops. She grabbed her room key, the ice bucket provided in the room, and headed out the door towards the vending area.

There was a warm breeze blowing through the summer night as Kellan closed her eyes, leaned her head back, and enjoyed how wonderful the air felt as it grazed over her skin. With her filled ice bucket in hand she opened her eyes and started to walk back to her room. But just as she was about to turn away, she caught the sight of a strangely familiar car sitting just outside of the guest services office.

Trying to hide in the shadows, she crept slowly down the corridor towards the car. When she got to the corner of the building she stopped and pressed her back against the wall. Taking in three long, slow breaths to calm herself, she slowly peered around the corner to see if anyone was in the office. For a moment she felt paralyzed. Her biggest fear was happening right before her eyes. They were here and there was no doubt in her mind that they were looking for her. Panic swam through her body and made her limbs go numb. She couldn't let them find her; she *wouldn't*. Going back to that monster and his prison was not an option. Carefully, she laid the bucket of ice on the concrete walkway, took one last look around the corner and ran.

"How did they find me?" she whispered breathlessly as she fumbled with the key and the lock.

Once she managed to get the door unlocked, she threw it open, quickly stepping inside and locking it behind her. She grabbed her purse and duffle bag from the dresser, and then ran over to the nightstand where she had left her cell phone charging. And that's when it clicked. Vince's buddies had tracked her to this motel by her cell phone. The son of a bitch must have had some sort of GPS tracking device in it.

The footsteps outside of the room snapped her attention back to the present. She could hear Sal and

Tony's muffled voices from outside the door and her eyes frantically darted around the room. Remembering the window in the bathroom, she ran to the room and attempted to quietly but quickly open it. She stuck her head out and looked both ways before tossing her bags on the ground, then sliding her body through the small opening. Keeping to the shadows, she made her way around to the front of the building and saw Sal knock on the door to her room while Tony kept watch.

Just then she saw Sal reach for something from the back waistline of his pants. When Tony followed and did the same action she realized that she needed to get out of there and fast. Thoughts swirled in her mind about every possible escape route. But all of them revolved around her getting to her car which was, unfortunately, sitting right outside of her room. Kellan leaned her head against the wall of the building, knowing that she had been caught and that there was no way she was going to get away this time. But just as she started to believe that this was the end she noticed the bright shiny red Mercedes Benz sitting at the gas pump across the street. She watched and held her breath as Sal and Tony burst through the door of her room and then she took off in a full run across the street.

The owner of the car walked into the gas station and began to browse through the aisles while his lady friend stepped outside of the car and lit a cigarette. Kellan carefully snuck around the hood as to not be seen and peered in through the driver's side window. Surely her guardian angel must have been looking over her tonight because the keys were still in the ignition. Quickly, she opened the door and started the car.

"Well it's about time!" The lady dropped her cigarette to the concrete and ground it out with the toe of her shoe before turning towards Kellan. "I want to go home and... Wait, you're not my boyfriend," she said with a confused expression.

"I'm really sorry!" Kellan yelled over the roar of the engine and pushed the gas pedal to the floor, squealing the tires on the pavement as she sped away. She glanced in the rearview mirror and saw the lady's boyfriend come racing out of the gas station in her direction, but she was too far away for him to do anything about it. She turned her attention back to the road and attempted to calm her breathing.

"Oh my God, oh my God, oh my God."

Kellan stared blankly out the windshield for a few minutes shocked by what she had just done.

"I just stole a car," she whispered in disbelief. "Shit! I just stole a car!"

She slammed her fist down on the steering wheel and let out a long string of curse words.

"Oh, I am so going to hell for this," she said, propping her left elbow on the door and resting her head in her hand. With no game plan and no idea where she was going, Kellan made the first turn she came to knowing that the only thing that mattered right now was getting as far away from New Jersey as possible.

****

A thick cloud of steam seeped out from underneath the hood of his truck, making it impossible to see the road in front of him.

"Oh, this *cannot* be happening!"

Zane McKade carefully pulled his truck off to the side of the road and slammed the gear shift into park.

"This day just keeps getting better and better," he mumbled under his breath as he exited the truck. He walked around to the front and lifted the hood, leaning back as he did so the hissing steam wouldn't hit him directly in the face.

He sighed heavily. "Perfect."

As he removed his off white cowboy hat from his head he began to wave it back and forth through the thick cloud. When the steam had somewhat cleared he replaced his hat and went back to his truck for an old rag or something that he could use as a barrier between his hand and the hot gasket. The late afternoon sun had quickly heated the inside of the cab, making it stuffy and unbearably hot. Sweat beaded up on his forehead and he impatiently wiped it away with the back of his hand.

Zane stepped out of the truck empty handed and slammed the door shut. Cursing under his breath, he removed his cowboy hat long enough to maneuver out of his t-shirt. This would just have to do. The sun was hot on his bare shoulders as he wrapped his shirt around his hand and carefully unscrewed the gasket. Leaving his shirt hanging off the side of the truck, he made his way back to the horse trailer. The large bay stallion inside pranced nervously, causing the trailer to rock back and forth.

"Settle down," Zane instructed the horse. "We'll be on our way soon."

He opened the side door of the trailer and entered a small room that was usually used for housing his tack. It was fairly empty though, aside from a few lead ropes and a cooler; the cooler being exactly what he was looking for. He crossed the room towards it, knowing that there were at least ten or fifteen bottles of water in there as of the other day. He lifted the lid and…

"Son of a!" Zane slammed the lid of the empty cooler down and kicked it. The horse began to prance again and Zane exited the trailer to calm it down.

He had just stepped out into the blistering heat when he saw it; a slight flicker of light down the road. Zane adjusted his cowboy hat on his head and narrowed his eyes.

"Thank God," he said when he noticed that little flicker of light was actually a car coming towards him. He stepped away from the horse trailer and waved his hands above his head, trying to flag down the driver.

"Hey! Hey!" Zane yelled as the bright red sports car flew past him. "Dammit!" He kicked dirt in the direction of the speeding car and walked back to the front of the truck to retrieve his shirt. "Stupid city slickers," he mumbled as he slipped it over his head and went back to the truck cab for his cell phone.

If someone had replaced the bottles of water they'd used then he wouldn't have to call for help right now. And if people in their fancy foreign cars would stop when a stranded man was flagging them down he wouldn't have to call for help either. And, of course, if he wasn't stuck in the middle of nowhere his cell phone would have signal.

"Well, this is just great!" he said, flipping the phone closed and shoving it into his pocket. He removed the keys from the ignition, pocketing them as well as he made his way back to the horse trailer. Town limits were at least a couple of miles away and he was going to have to walk it. But he couldn't very well leave the horse locked up while he was gone, so it would have to come with him. Zane entered the small room of the trailer again and grabbed a lead rope. A sudden thought popped in his mind, and he contemplated it for a moment before deciding *"What the hell?"* and grabbed another lead rope. He entered the main area of the trailer, hooked one of the ropes to the stallion's halter and backed him out onto the side of the road. He took the other lead rope and attached it to the other side of the horse's halter, creating a makeshift bridle and reins minus the bit.

"All right," Zane said, speaking to the horse. "We've got to get to town and it would be a hell of lot faster if you would cooperate."

The horse blew out a burst of air through its nostrils and shifted sideways.

"Don't be like that," Zane said. "Come on, calm down."

Zane gently rested his hand against the horse's neck and gave him a few pats. The horse settled and Zane smiled. "See, it's okay."

He tossed both ends of the lead ropes around the horse's neck and grabbed onto its mane as he effortlessly lifted himself onto the animal's back.

The stallion sidestepped nervously and Zane calmed him once more with a gentle pat and soothing words. He clicked his tongue on the roof of his mouth and gently nudged the horse to walk.

Needless to say, his day had gone from bad to worse. Everything that could have possibly gone wrong had. His truck has overheated, he was stranded in the middle of nowhere, he was completely ignored by that sports car's driver, *and* he had no cell signal. Oh yeah, and now he was stuck riding a horse bareback into town; a horse he didn't even know up until an hour ago when he picked it up. So with the way his luck was going today, there was a pretty good chance that this thing would toss him somewhere between here and town. Zane would probably crack his head on the asphalt and lie there lifeless until someone drove by and found him; that is if the buzzards didn't find him first. As all the possible scenarios of the bad things that could still happen to him ran through his mind, he couldn't help but think about the driver of that stupid red car.

Chapter Two

The bell over the door rang as she entered the tiny diner. The urge to cringe quickly followed as the handful of people in the room turned to gawk at her. Kellan quickly dipped her head and looked for a place to sit; one that would be as far away from her audience as possible. There was an empty booth in the corner, so she quickly made her way towards it and slid to the center of the seat. The waitress was at the table no sooner than she had sat down, placing a menu in front of her along with utensils wrapped in a napkin.

"What can I get you, sweetie?" the waitress asked as she smacked on her chewing gum and pulled a pad of paper from her apron.

"Just a cup of coffee please," Kellan said.

The waitress nodded, giving her a thorough once over before taking the menu and heading back to the counter. Kellan stared out the window into the parking lot and sighed. She was literally in the middle of nowhere. This tiny diner sat right on the outskirts of town with nothing surrounding it but trees and a field of crops. The "Welcome to Buford Texas" sign she had passed on her way into town had the quirky little message at the bottom that "If you lived here, you'd be home by now." She had rolled her eyes as she drove by it and continued down the unlined paved road that seemed to be the only way in and out of this godforsaken place.

"Here you go, sweetie," the waitress said as she placed the cup of coffee on the table in front of Kellan.

"Thank you," Kellan replied quietly, keeping her head down.

"You're welcome, hun." The waitress lingered for just a moment, looking to Kellan with questioning eyes. "Say you ain't from around here, are you?"

"What makes you say that?" Kellan asked, looking up at the woman through her large sunglasses.

Apparently, the waitress was heading up the "ask a bunch of nosey questions" committee. She glanced around the room and adjusted the sunglasses on her face. She could see the prying eyes of the other diners glancing in her direction as the waitress continued with her intrusive questions.

"Well, you don't see many people around here dress in something like *that*." The waitress motioned towards the skin tight blue dress Kellan was wearing.

She shifted uncomfortably in her seat.

And you don't see many cars like that around here either," the waitress said, pointing out the window at the bright red Mercedes Benz. "You one of them Hollywood starlets or something?"

Kellan had to laugh. "No, ma'am, I'm not."

"Oh," the waitress said. "Well, honey, you sure had me fooled. Where you from?"

Kellan stiffened and fought back to urge to throw out *"It's none of your business."* "I'd rather not say." The tone of her voice was a little harsher than she meant for it to be. All she wanted to do was stop in and take a break from driving, and now she was stuck playing twenty questions with a stranger.

"Didn't mean no harm. Just trying to be friendly that's all. My name's Belle and this is my place," the waitress informed her. "If you need anything else you just holler. Okay?"

Kellan smiled and nodded as the older woman walked away. She sat there in the silence of her corner booth and spun the coffee mug in a circle. She hadn't planned far enough in advance to know what she would do next. With a deep sigh, she lifted the mug and took a sip of the steaming hot coffee. Moments later the bell rang over the door once more as another patron entered the diner.

"Woo-wee, Belle! What'd you do? Go out and get a new car?" the man asked as he walked up to the counter and slapped his hand down on the laminate.

Kellan jumped slightly at the man's rather boisterous entrance, nearly spilling her coffee down the front of her dress. That being said, she had spilt some on the table and she reached now for some napkins to clean it up.

"Willy, you old fool! You think I could afford that kind of car from selling people bacon and eggs seven days a week. You've done lost your mind," Belle said, joining in on Willy's joke.

"Well, hell, if it ain't yours then whose is it? We got a movie star here or something?" he drawled.

Belle tilted her head to the corner booth toward

Kellan. Willy's gaze followed and when his eyes landed on Kellan they looked like they were going to pop out of his head. He turned to look at Belle once more and she gave him a shrug.

"That your car out there, sweetheart?" Willy asked, taking a seat in one of the counter stools and turning it to face Kellan.

She sighed and nodded her head. "Yes."

Were all small town people this annoying? Once she had time to rest she would get as far away from this place *and* these people as possible.

"It's one of them Mercedes Benz's ain't it?" Willy asked.

"Yes," she told him flatly.

"Man, I sure would like to have one of them one day. Can't you see me, Belle?"

Belle rolled her eyes. "And just what would you do with a car like that?"

"Why, I'd use it for hot dates of course," Willy said with a grin. "I'd be driving pretty girls around all day." He glanced over at Kellan and winked.

She ignored his obvious attempt at flirting and noticed when he smiled at her that he had a small hole where one of his bottom teeth was missing. *What a hick.*

"You'd be driving pretty girls away, Willy. None of them are that stupid to get in a car with the likes of you. Especially seeing as you're old enough to be their grand-pappy," Belle told him. "You just stick to driving your old rusty truck out there." Belle placed a mug on the counter in front of him and poured him some coffee. "I haven't seen you in ages, Willy. Things going good at your place?"

As Kellan listened to Willy fill Belle in on his activities for the past few months, she couldn't help but think of how much she hated being in that diner. She didn't belong there. She belonged in the city, at high society parties, and front row at fashion week. This place was like a foreign planet to her. She'd heard of small towns in the country before but never visited them; never wanted too. She was happy with her comfortable lifestyle and enjoyed having everything she ever wanted. Of course, living a life like that had also cost her. She reached up and touched her sunglasses to make sure they were still covering her eyes.

God, this place was awful. The people were nosey, overly friendly, and not to mention loud. And what on earth was that smell outside? She thought that the country was supposed to have the cleanest, freshest air. It was a strange combination of dirt and some kind of animal; cows she assumed. Either way, it was horrible and she would never understand how someone could live here all the time and breathe that in. She took another sip of her coffee as she stared out the diner window and...

Oh good God! Was that really a man riding a horse up to the diner? It was official; she had died and gone to hillbilly hell. She watched as the man reined his horse towards the tree line where he dismounted and tied one of the ropes around a low hanging branch. He began to walk towards the diner, looking weary as he wiped the back of his hand across his forehead, but stopped halfway. He was staring at something; the look on his face changed and was now that of pure anger and irritation. She saw his jaw flex and wondered what had gotten him all riled up. The man continued walking then, his pace more brisk than before.

"Well if it ain't my lucky day," Belle said as Zane strolled through the door. "How's my favorite…" She let her sentence trail off as she took in his appearance. "Zane, no offense, sweetie, but you look terrible." With her eyebrows narrowed, she glanced around him and out the large window to the parking lot. "Where's your truck?"

"Four miles out of town on the side of the road," he said curtly. "I had to ride the new horse here."

"A horse?" Belle asked. She was about to continue questioning him but he abruptly cut her off.

"Whose red car is that out there?" he asked, pointing out the window.

Belle glanced toward Kellan. It was the slightest movement, but Zane quickly picked up on it and followed her eyes. He had been wrong in his accusation. It wasn't a guy but a woman. But her being a woman didn't hide the fact that four miles ago she had blown past him as he desperately tried to flag her down. He didn't care. He was pissed and he was going to let her know it. Taking in a deep breath, Zane turned and crossed the room towards her.

Kellan saw the man coming her way and a nervous feeling began to grow in the pit of her stomach. She hadn't noticed it when he rode up, but he was *incredibly* good looking. The man had to be a least six two, with long muscular legs leading up to narrow hips that angled into a *very* masculine upper body. He looked like an athlete. He looked…solid. And although his pale blue shirt was soaked with sweat, it somehow added to his overall appeal. He stopped at her table and glared at her. Only then did she realize that this man was not coming over for friendly chit-chat and her mood shifted.

"Is that your red sports car out there?" Zane asked, tilting his head and jerking his thumb towards the parking lot.

"Yes," Kellan told him. *What's it to you?* She stared up at him, waiting for him to continue. But when he just stared back, his deep blue eyes shooting daggers at her, she decided enough was enough. "Is there something I can help you with?"

Zane's jaw flexed. "You could have four miles ago."

"What?" She was utterly confused as to what mileage had to do with his apparent anger towards her.

"I don't look familiar to you?" He stared at her, his eyebrows coming together in frustration.

She looked the man over from head to toe. "No, I'm sorry you don't."

Zane let out an exasperated sigh. "How about now?" He raised his arms above his head and waved them just like he had done when he was trying to flag her down.

He looked completely ridiculous and she fought back the urge to laugh at him. But the more she looked at him she realized that he did look strangely familiar. *Oh my...* He was the man on the side of the road next to the pickup truck just outside of town.

"Oh," Kellan said. "Yes, I do remember you now. I'm sorry I didn't recognize you with your shirt on." She loaded her voice with sarcasm and crossed her arms over her chest. If he was going to have an attitude with her, then she was going to give it right back.

Zane's eyes narrowed. "Well, would you care to explain why you just blew past me like that?"

Kellan laughed, quietly as to not draw attention. "Why did I blow past you? Hmm, let me think. Um, maybe it has to do with the fact that you were partially naked and in the middle of nowhere."

Well damn. He hadn't thought about that. He'd been all riled up thinking that some *guy* just ignored him. Now, thinking about it from her perspective, he could see why she didn't pull over to help him. As it was though, his built up anger from everything that had transpired today got the best of him and he continued with his rant.

"I was *not* half naked," he said, his voice low as he briefly glanced around the room to see if anyone could hear them speaking.

"Look, *cowboy*." She said the word as though it were an insult and not an affirmation of what he obviously was. "I'm sorry you're having a bad day, but don't come over here and take it out on me. I had a good reason for not stopping earlier and I'm not going to apologize for looking after my own safety. You could've been a murderer for all I knew."

Zane knew that he should just man up and walk

away, but he just couldn't do that now after her snarky "cowboy" remark. Why'd she have to go and say it like that anyway?

"Look, *princess*," he said with the same tone she had used. "This ain't Hollywood. Take your sunglasses off. You're inside and you look like a damn fool."

Kellan's jaw fell in disbelief.

Zane smiled, feeling triumphant that he got in the last word. He turned and started to walk away from her.

"Screw you, *cowboy*!" she yelled after him, saying the word exactly as she had before. "And that horse you rode in on."

And—*Whoops!*—now everyone in the diner had turned to look at them.

Zane turned around to face her with amusement on his face. "Very original, *princess*." He turned and headed for the counter. "Can I use the phone?" he asked Belle.

Kellan could feel everyone's eyes upon her, so she quickly pushed herself from the booth and entered the bathroom. Her hands were shaking as she turned on the faucet. That guy had some nerve walking up and berating her like that. Vince use to do that sort of stuff all the time, but she never talked back to him like she did with that cowboy. What on earth possessed her to stand up to him in the first place? As the thought passed through her mind, she couldn't help but think that she didn't care about why she had decided to do it. All that mattered was that she *had* done it and that maybe from now on she'd be able to take care of herself. She pushed her sunglasses back on her hair, creating a make shift head band so she could splash some of the cold water on her face. She grabbed a few paper towels from the dispenser and dabbed them across her skin. The bruise surrounding her eye was fading, but she decided not to take any chances and adjusted her sunglasses back in place.

The cowboy was nowhere in sight as she stepped back into the diner's main area. She sat back down at her table, looked out the window and saw that he was standing next to his horse.

For such a good looking guy he sure is irritating.

Her gaze continued across the parking lot and she stopped at her car. The bright red Mercedes Benz was parked next to an old faded blue truck with rusted out rims. She sighed. There was no doubt that she was bound to stick out no matter where she went in that car. Everywhere she went people would be looking to see who was driving such a beautiful automobile.

Damn that car. Why did I have to steal a Benz?

A sudden thought popped in her mind at that moment. It was crazy and absurd, and a part of her wondered if it would even work. *Only one way to find out.*

She got up from her corner booth and walked up to the counter where Willy was sitting and talking to Belle. Kellan took the barstool next to him and placed her cup of coffee on the counter.

"You really like my car?" she asked Willy.

He gave her a confused look but quickly recovered. "Hell yeah I do!"

"Is that your blue truck?"

"Sure is, sweetheart," he said. "Don't worry I didn't hit your pretty car when I pulled in."

"Wasn't worried about that," Kellan said smiling. "Fact is I happen to like your truck and was wondering if you would like to make a trade."

Willy's mouth dropped and Belle looked at her like she was up to no good before walking away from the conversation to help a customer at the other end of the counter.

"You serious?" he asked in disbelief.

"As a heart attack," she told him with her most serious face and dangled the key on her finger.

Willy looked from Kellan to the key.

"Why would you want to trade your shiny new car for my old rusty truck?" Willy asked, his eyebrows furrowing in suspicion.

"Well, I was thinking about getting rid of it anyway. To be honest with you, it's just too much car for me to handle," Kellan told him, adding a hint of flirt to her voice. "But I'm sure a big, strong man like you would have no problem controlling all that horse power." She smiled at him and hoped that her lie had worked. Turning on the sexy had never failed her in the past in regards of getting what she wanted.

Willy took in a raspy breath and blew it out slowly. "As much as I'd love to trade you vehicles, sweetheart, I just wouldn't feel right about it," he told her.

"I understand," Kellan said, nodding her head. "What if I were to sell it to you? And you could, in return, sell me your truck?"

Willy chuckled softly as he took a sip of his coffee. "I know I may look like I got money," Willy said, clearly making a joke, "but I ain't got *that* kind of money."

"I'll sell it to you cheap," Kellan said. "Say a hundred bucks?"

Willy gave her an incredulous look. "You really are being serious aren't you?"

She nodded and waited for his answer. The smile on his face sent a feeling of victory throughout her body.

"Well shit, I'm not gonna say no to that. You got yourself a deal, hot stuff!" He stood up, reaching in his back pocket for his wallet, and pulled out the cash. He handed over five twenties to Kellan and slapped two dollars down on the counter for his bill.

"Just let me grab my bag and it's all yours," she told him.

"Hot damn, I'm gonna take my new car for a drive!" he said as he strutted out the door.

Kellan followed him and removed her bag from the backseat. "Well, here's the key," she said, dropping it in Willy's waiting hand. "And here's the money for the truck."

She started to hand him back the hundred dollars he had given her for the car, but he waved her off. "No, you keep it."

After a few rounds of her offering him the money as he refused to accept it, she decided to just thank him for his generosity and slipped the money into her purse.

He went to hand over the key to his truck to

her, but hesitated briefly. "I almost don't feel right about letting you take my truck," he told her. "The damn thing is so old and temperamental."

"I thought we had a deal?" Kellan asked, cutting him off.

"We did, but—"

"But now you've changed your mind?"

"Well, no…"

"Okay then, that settles it," Kellan said with a smile and laid her hand on the faded hood of the truck. "All it needs is some love, and I'll be sure to give it plenty."

Willy smiled, shook his head and muttered something about him being a sucker for giving pretty women what they want. He handed the key to Kellan and walked around to the driver's side of the Mercedes. Gripping her duffle bag in one hand, and the key to her new but old truck, Kellan walked back to the diner.

Willy fell into the driver's seat and roared the engine to life. He pulled out of the dirt parking lot and onto the pavement where he floored the gas pedal, making the tires squeal down the road.

Unable to help herself, Kellan looked over at the cowboy. He was standing with his horse, looking at her with questioning eyes. He probably would have left the animal and stalked over towards her but, before he had a chance to a pickup truck with a horse trailer attached pulled into the diner's parking lot. The cowboy removed the horse's rope from the tree and walked it around to the back of the trailer as another man stepped out of the truck to assist him. She rolled her eyes and walked back into the tiny diner. As she sat on one of the barstools at the counter, she couldn't help but notice Belle's questioning glare.

Belle leaned on the counter and spoke quietly enough so that only Kellan could hear her. "What are you running from, sweetheart?"

Chapter Three

"What makes you think I'm running?" Kellan asked.

"You practically just gave a hundred thousand dollar car to a dirty old man with stained clothes and red suspenders," Belle said, crossing her arms over her chest. "I don't care how charitable people say they are. No one in their right mind just gives a car away like that if they ain't running from something."

Kellan didn't know how to answer the older woman, so she just sat there staring at her coffee cup.

"Let me guess," Belle said, a teasing smile spreading across her face. "You go by the name of the *Lipstick Bandit* and you're on the run because you robbed a bank. And *that* was your getaway car."

Kellan laughed and looked at Belle. She seemed like such a friendly woman, almost motherly. Heaven knows she would have confided in her own mother in this situation; had her own mother still been alive. As she looked at Belle's warm smile, she all of sudden felt the urge to spill her whole life story. And who better to talk to about this than a stranger? People did it all the time with bartenders, so would it really be any different talking to a waitress?

"No, I'm not a bank robber," Kellan told Belle.

"I just…" She let out a long sigh then looked around the room to see if anyone was watching. Slowly, she lifted her hand to remove her sunglasses. Using that same hand, she shielded her face from anyone who might decide to sneak a peek.

"Oh, honey," Belle said with a quiet gasp as she looked at the fading bruise around Kellan's eye. "Who did that to you?"

"Doesn't matter now," Kellan said as she dipped her head and stared at the counter.

"Well, I'm sure whoever the bastard is he's got another thing coming to him," Belled told her.

"Why do you say that?" Kellan asked.

Belle smiled and laid her hand over Kellan's. "People don't get away with stuff like that forever. What goes around comes around. He'll get his in the end."

Kellan's gaze fell to Belle's hand upon hers, and for a moment the simple gesture almost made her want to cry. It had been so long since anyone had touched her with such tenderness. "Thank you, Belle."

"Anytime, sweetie." Belle gave Kellan's hand a gentle squeeze then pulled back. "Now, are you just going to sip on coffee all day or would you like something to eat?"

Kellan's stomach growled at the mention of food. "I guess I'll take a burger and fries… If it's not too much trouble."

"Too much trouble?" Belle laughed. "Hun, you're in my diner. That's what I do." She turned and walked back to the open window that separated the dining area from the kitchen. "Hey, Ches! I need a burger and fries…"

It felt like a huge weight had been lifted from her chest. Sure she hadn't gone into detail about Vince and the yearlong abuse she endured while with him. But just letting someone in on the secret she'd kept for so long felt wonderful.

"Here you go, sweetie." Belle placed the hot plate of food in front of Kellan.

The aroma coming from the plate made her stomach growl even more. She hadn't realized exactly how hungry she had been until that very moment. Without hesitation, Kellan began to devour the food.

"Slow down, sweetie," Belle told her with a soft chuckle. "You're going to make yourself sick eating that fast."

"Sorry," Kellan said around a mouth full.

Belle filled a cup with soda and slid it in front of Kellan as well. "This will wash all that down better than that coffee will."

She thanked her and took a deep drink from the cup, halfway emptying it before placing it back on the counter.

"Sweetie," Belle started, but hesitated for a moment. "I know this isn't my place and all, but you kind of seem like you're wingin' this. Do you have any kind of plan as to what you're going to do?"

Kellan finished chewing her food and swallowed. "Not exactly," she said sheepishly. "The only thing that's been on my mind is getting as far away from…where I came from."

"Don't you have any family or friends that can help you?" Belle asked.

Kellan shook her head solemnly and took a bite of a french fry.

Oh, this poor thing. Belle truly and honestly felt bad for the young woman. No family, no friends, and no one to help her out when she obviously needed it.

"Well you do now," Belled told her.

Kellan looked up from her plate of food and stared at Belle with a confused expression. "I'm sorry. What?"

"I'm going to help you," Belle said, then held her finger up to Kellan silently telling her to hold on just a minute. Belle took care of ringing up a customer and handing him his change. "Thanks Charlie, I'll see you tomorrow." She waved at the man and headed back to Kellan. "Okay, we'll need to get you a place. There's a motel across town that you can stay in for a while. Only until I can make a few phone calls to find out if there's anything available for rent. You'll need a job and you've already got a vehicle…"

"Hold up," Kellan said, raising both of her hands to stop Belle from her rambling. "Why are you doing this?"

Belle sighed softly. "Look, you seem like a very nice girl and you obviously don't have the help that you need. I've seen too many stories in the news about women who have gone through what you're going through. Their stories didn't end well and I can't help but think it's because they didn't have someone to help them."

"I appreciate the offer, Belle, but I'm not planning on staying here."

Belle cocked her head to the side. "Why on earth not, dear?"

Maybe because it smells like cow poo outside. But even after her inner snark ran through her mind, Kellan couldn't help but wonder if Belle was on to something. Vince would never suspect her to come to a small town like this let alone stay in it for any length of time. He'd look for her in cities and highly populated places, not Hickville, USA. She hated to admit it, but Belle was right. And the more she thought about it, the more the idea started to appeal to her.

Kellan leaned forward and rested her elbows on the counter. "Go on, I'm listening."

"Well," Belle said. "Like I was saying, you're going to need a job. And it just so happens that the bar on the other side of town is looking for a waitress."

A waitress? Kellan never in a million years pictured herself serving other people drinks or food. People did that sort of thing for her. But then again, things were going to have to be different from now on.

"I might be willing to stick around," Kellan said. "What's the bar called?"

"The Rusty Spur," Belle told her as took care of ringing up another customer who was leaving. "There's your change, sir, and you have a wonderful day now."

"What time do they open?" Kellan asked her.

"Bar don't officially open till seven," Belle told her. "But you can probably get in there around six to talk to someone."

"Who do I ask for?" Kellan asked as she poured ketchup onto her plate.

"Ask for Red. I can call ahead of time so he knows you're coming," Belle told her.

"That would be great," Kellan said. "Thanks, Belle."

"No problem, sweetie," Belle said. "Now who should I tell him to be expecting?"

"Oh, sorry. My name is K-" She stopped mid sentence. Maybe it wasn't such a smart idea to use her real name. If she was truly going to do this hiding out thing, she needed to come up with an alias. After contemplating if for a brief moment she decided to just abbreviate her last name and replied, "Andi."

"Candy?" Belled questioned in a disbelieving tone.

The look on Belle's face made her chuckle. There was no doubt in her mind Belle was thinking that with a name like "Candy" and the way she was dressed that she was a stripper or a hooker.

"No not Candy. *Andi*."

"A girl Andi," Belle said with a somewhat confused look. "Well don't that beat all." Belle shook her head slightly and chuckled as she walked over to the cash register to help another customer.

Andi, a.k.a. Kellan, finished eating her food and reached in her wallet to pull out cash to pay for the meal.

"Don't even think about it. It's on the house," Belle said as she took Andi's plate.

Andi looked at her and smiled. "Thank you. Well, I guess I better go get a motel room and change my clothes before I head off to The Rusty Spur."

"I think that's a good idea. No offense, sweetie, but you look like a street walker in that outfit," Belle stated rather bluntly.

"Thanks," Andi said sarcastically and looked down at the skin tight blue dress she was wearing. She couldn't help but smile as she thought about how spot on she was with Belle's "hooker" assumption. "You don't hold anything back do you?"

"Never did and never will. Guess that's why I never got married. No man could ever deal with my smart mouth," Belle said with a chuckle.

Andi laughed with her and then grimaced when she remembered what was in her duffle bag. "Well, this is really the only kind of clothes I have. I wasn't exactly sure where I was going so I kind of just threw what I could grab in a bag."

Belle looked her over from head to toe. "You're about a size four, ain't ya?"

Andi eyed her suspiciously. "Yes, ma'am."

"About five foot five?" Bell asked.

"About that," Andi agreed.

"I think I might have some clothes that would fit you just fine," Belle offered. "My niece is about the same size as you and left some clothes at my house for the church charity. I'll give you the address and you can stop by around five-thirty and we'll get you taken care of."

"Wow, that would be great. Thank you very much, Belle." Things were certainly looking up for her. A few days ago, she would never have imagined that she'd make friends with a fifty something year old woman, be applying for a job in a redneck bar as a waitress, and looking for residence in Buford, Texas. It was funny how just a half an hour ago she was cursing this town and everything about it, but now she'd be calling it home; well, at least for a little while.

****

"I look ridiculous," Andi stated as she stared in the full length mirror at the hand me downs Belle had given her to wear. The red spaghetti strap top, boot cut blue jeans and old worn out cowboy boots were the last thing she envisioned to wear when going for a job interview.

"That dress you were wearing earlier was ridiculous. This is practical and you'll fit in just fine wearing it. No one will ever suspect that you're an out-of-towner." Belle continued sorting through the clothes on the bed and placed them in a box. "I think this should hold you over for a while," she said, closing the lid and pushing the contents toward Andi.

"Thank you for everything, Belle. I honestly don't know what I would have done if I hadn't met you," Andi said, smiling at her.

Belle placed both of her hands on Andi's shoulders and gave them a gentle squeeze. "Don't mention it, sweetie," she said then gave Andi a puzzled look.

"What?" Andi asked.

"Hmm," Belle said with pursed lips. "We need to do something about that shiner."

Andi walked over to the mirror and traced her fingers over the bruise that surrounded the outer corner of her eye. "I left my make up bag back in Je-, where I came from," she quickly corrected herself.

"I think I've got something that will work," Belle said and walked out of the room. Moments later she returned with a small bag and handed it to Andi. "I'm sure there's something in there that you can use to cover it up."

"Thanks, Belle."

"No problem, hun," Belle said. "Well, I'll leave you to it then."

Andi watched as Belle left the room, and then she started to empty the small bag. She pulled out a bottle of foundation and started to apply it to the bruise, then continued to do the rest of her face. It didn't quite match her skin tone but it would have to do until she could buy some of her own. She decided to go ahead and finish off the look with a coat of mascara, a little blush, and a dusty rose lip gloss. Once her makeup routine was complete, she ran her fingers through her dark brown hair and toyed with it trying to decide if she should pull it back or keep it down.

"This ain't a beauty contest, girl. What's taking you so long?" Belle teased from the other room.

"Coming!" Andi responded and let her hair fall

loosely down her back.

Chapter Four

"Oh, you have *got* to be kidding me." Andi took in the appearance of the building and grimaced. This place looked more like an old shack with its weather beaten tin roof and worn wood siding than the local beer joint. There was absolutely no way that this was the place Belle was talking about. Her eyes trailed up to the faded sign that read "The Rusty Spur" and she scoffed.

"You got the rusty part right."

She was baffled and bemused; and not just from the appearance of the building, but more for that fact that she was actually going to be asking to work there. A slight fluttering motion stirred around in her stomach, and she wondered if she was more nervous about getting the job or whether the building would collapse on her.

She let out a long sigh and fell back into the driver's seat of her newly acquired pick-up truck. The faded blue Ford was at least ten years older than her and, in her opinion, had seen better days. Rust covered the bumper and surrounded the bottom edge of the doors. The dark blue vinyl on the bench seat was cracked in places, exposing the foam interior. But the radio worked; that was a plus. To say the least, this ill-kept vehicle was a far cry from the bright red Mercedes Benz she was driving around just a few hours ago.

This wouldn't be so bad. She'd make the best

of it while she was here. If things worked out like she hoped, Vince would eventually stop looking for her. Until then she was stuck in this little off the map town.

"Well, here goes nothing." She turned the ignition off, and when the engine sputtered and backfired she jumped letting out a startled squeal. She placed her hand over her heart and frantically searched the dash board for any indication as to why the truck had just made that horrible noise. "Oh shoot, I hope I didn't break it."

A light tapping sound on the driver's side window caught her attention and she spun around quickly to see who it was. An older man with white hair and a cowboy hat was standing there peering through the window. Cautiously, she rolled the window down halfway. "Yes?"

"You need help with something?" the man asked.

"No, I'm fine. Thank you", she replied and started to roll the window up.

"You sure?" he asked. "'Cause if you're having trouble with your truck I can take a look at her for you."

Andi sighed and realized that this overly friendly prying nature must be the norm for country folk. But if she was planning on staying here for any length of time she'd have to get use to it sooner or later. "No, I think my truck is fine. I'm just going to the bar."

"Bar don't open for another hour," he stated.

"I know," she said. "I heard there was an opening for a waitress so I'm here to see Red."

The man gave her a once over and stared at her with a puzzled look. "You ever waitressed before?"

"Yes," she lied, but wondered to herself what business it was of his.

He eyed her suspiciously then reached for her door handle. Instantly she became nervous and froze. What was this man going to do to her?

"I guess you'd be the young lady Belle called me about then. Andi, am I right?" He held the door open and gestured for her to get out of the truck.

Boy, *that* name was going to take some getting used to. She nodded cautiously but stayed in the driver's seat.

"I'm Red," he said, extending his hand for her to shake.

All the nervousness she felt just moments ago faded away and was replaced with embarrassment. She needed to quit being so jumpy around people and learn that not everyone was out to get her. Andi smiled and accepted his hand then stepped out of the truck. Once she was out, she slammed the door shut behind her and speckles of rust scattered the dirt parking lot.

"So, Belle told me you're new in town," he said, as they walked towards the bar.

"Mmm-hmm." She nodded.

"You got family that lives here?"

"No, sir," she told him.

"Well what made you want to move to Buford?"

Red unlocked the door to the bar and held it open for Andi to walk through.

"It just seems like a nice little town," she said.

"Plus, it's far away from the hustle and bustle of the city. I've had enough of loud neighbors and car alarms going off in the middle of the night. So I decided to move to the country."

Red nodded, seeming to believe her story and she let out a soft sigh of relief.

Once they were in the bar, Red started flipping on lights. Andi looked around the room and gasped. The inside of the bar did not match the outside whatsoever. The floors were a polished wood that showed their age but still looked nice. The tables and chairs were a deep stained wood and looked sturdy. There was a long bar that was set against the far right wall and it matched the stain of the other furniture perfectly. Behind it was a mirrored wall with shelves of liquor that went all the way to the ceiling.

"Wow," Andi whispered.

"Sorry? What'd you say?" Red asked, turning to look at her.

She looked in his direction and replied, "This place is really nice. I didn't expect it to look like this judging from the outside."

Red chuckled and walked behind the bar. "Yea I can see where you'd think that."

Andi followed him to the bar and sat in one of the barstools. "So, Mr. Red. Do I-?"

Red held his hand up interrupting her. "No, no, no. No mister. Just Red."

"Okay, Red. Do I get to interview for the job?" she asked cautiously.

Red took out two shot glasses and set them on the bar in front of him and Andi. "You an alcoholic?" he asked, reaching for a bottle of whiskey.

"No," she replied and gave him a confused look.

"You do any drugs?"

"No."

"You ever steal anything?"

Andi paused and thought about that one for a brief moment; the image of a bright red sports car popping up in her mind. Up until four days ago she'd never stolen anything in her entire life. It's funny how in a matter of seconds she went from running from criminals to being one herself.

"No," she lied.

"And you've never been arrested for anything right?" he asked, pouring the amber colored liquid into each shot glass.

"No, sir."

Red put the cap back on the bottle of whisky and placed it back behind the counter. He pushed one of the shot glasses toward Andi and took the other one in his hand.

"Well then you're hired," he said, tapping his shot glass to hers then downing the contents in one large gulp.

Andi smiled and attempted to follow Red's action. When the whiskey hit her throat she managed to swallow it before coughing and slamming the shot glass back down on the bar. "Thank you," she said between coughs.

Red laughed and took her shot glass, placing it in the sink to be washed. "Not a whiskey girl?"

"Oh, that burns," she said, holding her throat.

Red laughed again. "You'll get use to it eventually."

"Okay, boss," Andi said after gaining control of herself. "What would you like for me to do first?"

"We need to get ready to open here in about forty minutes," Red told her. "Norah should be here soon and I'll get her to show you how we do things around here."

"Norah?" Andi questioned.

"Yea, Norah. She's my other waitress," Red told her, followed by the sound of a truck pulling into the lot. "That'd actually be her now."

Andi watched the door and waited for Norah to enter. For some reason, she imagined a middle aged woman with a gut and bad dye job would walk in. But when the door opened she was pleasantly surprised to see an absolutely gorgeous young woman with golden blonde hair and sun kissed skin. Andi instantly felt better about her own attire when she saw Norah was wearing pretty much the same thing.

Norah smiled as she walked towards the bar. "Hey, Red!" she greeted before catching a glimpse of Andi. "Oh you've got company."

"Not company," Red said. "Employee. She's taking Laura's place and is going to help you out around here."

"Well it's about time you got me some help," Norah teased then turned her attention to Andi. "Hi, I'm Norah McKade." She extended her hand and waited for Andi to respond.

"Hi Norah, it's nice to meet you," Andi said, shaking her hand. "I'm Andi."

Norah waited for a second then asked, "Andi? Is that like Madonna or Cher?"

Andi gave her a confused look. "Sorry?"

Norah laughed softly. "I'm just asking if you have a last name."

"Oh," Andi replied with a chuckle but inwardly cringed. How could she be so stupid as to forget to come up with a last name? Without being too obvious, she glanced out the window from her peripheral vision and saw her rusty old pickup truck sitting in the parking lot. "Ford," she spouted out. "Andi Ford."

"Well, Andi Ford, it's very nice to meet you," Norah said with a smile.

"Okay, ladies, now that we've got the introductions out of the way, let's get this place ready to open," Red said, taking out a towel and wiping the bar down.

Norah placed her hand on Andi's shoulder and pulled her in the direction of the back room. "Come on, we've got to fill up the coolers. So are you new around here?"

"Um." Andi paused wondering how much she should say. "Yea I just moved here."

"That's nice. Where'd you come from?" Norah asked as she picked up a case of beer and handed it to Andi.

Andi felt her knees buckle under the weight of the beer but quickly regained control. "The east coast," she said with a grunt.

"Oh," Norah said, taking a case of beer and directing Andi back out to the bar. "Well, what brings you here then?"

Andi set the case of beer on the bar with a huff. She wondered if she'd make it through the night if she had to continue with the heavy lifting. She though waitresses just served drinks and got money. She never expected to do manual labor on top of it. "I just wanted a change of pace," she said to Norah. "I'm originally from the city, so I'm looking for a quieter place to live."

"Well, you moved to the right place then my friend," Norah said. "Nothing ever happens in Buford. So how did you hear about the job opening?"

"Oh, um, Belle Dawson, the lady that owns the diner across town, told me about it," Andi explained as she leaned against the bar.

"I thought those clothes looked familiar," Norah said with a smile as she emptied the contents of the cases into the ice chest behind the bar.

"I'm sorry?" Andi asked confused.

Norah closed the lid and turned to Andi with her empty beer case in hand. "You got those from Belle right?"

"Yea."

"They used to be mine," Norah told her. "Belle is my aunt. I gave them to her for the church charity."

Andi felt her heart stop but then remembered that Belle had told her that her niece worked at the bar too.

"They look good on you," Norah said. "I'm glad someone's getting some use out of them."

"Oh, I'm sorry," Andi said. "Belle told me that her niece worked here, but she didn't mention your name. Yea, I didn't exactly have a wardrobe for country living, so Belle offered me the hand-me-downs. Thank you for the clothes," Andi said, hoping Norah wouldn't question her any further.

"Don't mention it," Norah told her and smiled. "Come on we've got to get the chairs down off the tables before Red opens the doors for business."

With a sigh of relief, Andi followed Norah around the room and soon they had all of the chairs off of the tables.

"Girls, I'm getting ready to open the doors," Red shouted from across the room. "Norah, can you start the jukebox up with the usual?"

"Sure thing," Norah said to Red then turned to Andi. "He plays the same song every night when he opens those doors."

She walked over to the jukebox, put in a quarter and pressed button G. Hank Williams Jr. came on with his upbeat version of "All My Rowdy Friends". Red opened the doors and within minutes people started piling in the tiny bar. Andi followed Norah behind the counter and looked around the quickly filled room.

"Is it always this busy?" Andi asked Norah over the chatter and jukebox.

"Yes, ma'am," Norah replied as she pulled out a hair band and proceeded to whip her hair up in a messy bun. "You might want to put your hair up. With all these people and all the running around you're going to do you'll get too hot with it hanging down your back like that," she suggested to Andi.

"I didn't bring anything with me," Andi told her and silently berated herself for not thinking about that.

"Here," Norah said, handing a hair band to Andi. "I have an extra."

Andi pulled her hair back into a ponytail and watched as Norah grabbed up a serving tray and made her way out to the tables.

I can do this, she thought to herself.

She grabbed another serving tray from behind the bar, held her chin high and hoped that it was as easy as Norah made it look.

Chapter Five

A tiny cloud of dust kicked up around his heels as Zane McKade made his way across the dirt parking lot. The one and only beer joint in this tiny, middle of nowhere town seemed packed to capacity tonight. He could hear the muffled sound of the music blaring away, and he had a pretty good idea what the scene would look like once he opened that door.

Ranchers from all over the county would be letting loose after a long work week. Young, single women would be flaunting their stuff in their barely there tops and skin tight jeans. And of course there would also be some not so young women, who were also not so single, attempting to flaunt their stuff as well. He'd had his fair share of unsatisfied married women hit on him in the past and, although he was flattered, sleeping with a married woman never appealed to him. Deep down he was hoping to avoid that scenario tonight. He'd had one hell of a day and all he wanted was to be left alone and enjoy a few ice cold beers.

"Hey, Zane, wait up!"

Zane stopped and waited for his younger brother, Luke, to catch up. Luke with his golden blonde hair and deep blue eyes, a trademark of the McKade gene, could have almost passed for Zane's twin instead of younger brother. They had the same height and the same build; tall and athletically toned from years of hard ranch life and working with horses. Their faces shared in similarities as well with the only real difference being the shape of their jaw. Luke's had a more slender curve, giving him a boyish quality. Zane's, on the other hand, had a more defined shaped that made him look more rugged and manly.

Luke jogged towards him with one hand on his off white cowboy hat to keep it in place.

"What the heck were you doing back there?" Zane asked, his voice tinged with a hint of irritation.

Luke walked in step next to Zane as they made their way towards the bar. "I was just giving myself a final once over before we headed in."

Zane chuckled softly and rolled his eyes. "You are so vain."

Luke smiled crookedly and arrogantly. "I can't help it. When you look as good as I do it's hard not to stare at yourself."

Zane knew his younger brother was joking, but at the same time he knew there was some seriousness to his statement. Luke McKade was a charmer; what some might call a ladies' man. There wasn't a time that Zane could remember when Luke had a steady relationship. That's where they differed. Whereas Luke preferred a different woman every night, Zane would rather settle down with one woman for the rest of his life.

I almost had that.

Great. That stupid little inkling of a thought brought back a memory Zane had worked hard over the past year to forget. And, of course, now it was all he could think about.

Luke stepped ahead of Zane and reached for the door handle. "Come on big brother," he said, slapping Zane on the back. "Let's go have some fun."

The two men entered the dimly lit bar and attempted to navigate their way through the crowd.

"Damn, this place is packed," Luke commented, craning his neck to get a good view of the place. "Look there's Cody and Troy over by the pool tables."

Zane turned his head towards the back wall and found his two friends engaged in a game of eight ball.

"You want to head over there and see if we can play them off the table?" Luke asked with a grin. "We might walk home with some extra cash in our pockets."

Zane smiled in reply and nodded his head. Maybe a round or two of pool would free his mind of its wandering thoughts. "That sounds good. How about you head to the bar and get us a couple of beers? I'll meet you at the pool tables."

Luke nodded his reply and strode off towards the bar, tipping his hat towards a pretty brunette and flashing her a charming smile as he walked by.

"Holy shit!"

Zane recognized the voice coming from the pool tables and chuckled as he approached the two men.

"Do my eyes deceive me or is that Zane McKade I see walking through the crowd?" Cody said, resting the bottom of his cue on the floor.

Zane reached out and shook Cody's hand. "Yes, I'm really here."

"It's been a long time, man," Troy said when it was turn to shake Zane's hand.

"Too long," Cody added. "What've you been up to?"

Zane looked to both men before letting out a sigh and shrugging. "Oh you know, just hanging out."

They nodded at Zane's simple reply and decided not to pry any further into the statement. Both of them knew very well why their friend had been off the radar for months and, although they would have handled the situation differently, they didn't blame him one bit for his absence.

"We're almost done with this game," Cody said to Zane. "You want in on the next one?"

"Yea, that sounds good," Zane replied. "You wanna play doubles? Luke should be back in a few minutes. He just went to the bar to get us some beers."

Cody and Troy exchanged a look and then laughed.

"What's that about?" Zane asked, resting a hip on the pool table.

"There's a pretty good chance he'll get distracted once he gets to the bar," Troy said before lining his cue up for the shot. "Nine ball, side pocket."

Zane shot him a confused expression and Cody nodded his head towards the bar. "There's fresh meat. And you know if anyone can sniff that out it's your brother."

Turning his head towards the bar, Zane noticed the "fresh meat" Cody was referring too. She had her back turned away from him as she worked to fill her orders. The fact that she was thin and had dark hair was the only physical feature he could see from this angle. But hearing the way Cody and Troy talked about her, he knew she must have been an attractive woman. And if an attractive woman, especially a new woman, was anywhere near Luke he was sure to get sidetracked and forget all about the task at hand.

Zane sighed and pushed himself away from the pool table. "I'll be right back."

****

"Is this seat taken?" The man's hand connected with her rear end with a loud crack. The sudden unwelcome gesture caused her to lose her balance and all four glasses of beer she had on her tray tipped over.

Andi cursed under her breath as she laid the tray down on the empty table next to her. Although this was only her first day, it would most likely end up being her last if things kept going like this.

From behind the bar, Norah saw the accident and came to Andi's aid. "Here, I'll clean this up," she told Andi as she began to wipe up the spill with a bar rag. "You go fill your glasses back up and get them to your table."

"I'm so sorry," Andi apologized.

"Don't worry about it, sweetie," Norah said, giving Andi a reassuring smile. "It wasn't your fault."

Andi stood up, grabbed her tray with the toppled over glasses and headed back behind the bar.

"Hey, sweet thing. Where you going?" the man on the end of the bar asked to Andi.

A cold chill ran down her spine as she quickly walked past him. He was far from attractive with his bulging stomach hanging over the waistline of his pants and his teeth stained from years of tobacco use. And odd as it may sound, that's not the main reason she shied away from him. The fact of the matter was that this man frightened her; that this man reminded her of the reason she was hiding here in the first place.

"Gus, leave her alone," Norah warned.

"I'm just having fun," Gus told Norah. "No harm done." His eyes stayed on Andi as he reached for his mug of beer.

"You know, sis, the beer is actually supposed to go in a glass and not on the floor."

Norah stood up as she wadded the dish towel and tossed it behind the bar. "Very funny, Luke," she said, her voice thick with sarcasm and irritation. She brushed her hands across the front of her jeans then pushed a lock of her blonde hair away from her eyes. "It wasn't me spilling the beer. Gus here got a little too hands on with the new waitress."

"What new waitress?" Luke asked, his eyebrows coming together in confusion.

Norah nodded in Andi's direction and Luke followed her gesture with his eyes. Behind the bar had to be one of the most beautiful women Luke had ever seen. Her dark brown hair was swept back in a ponytail with a few stray strands falling around her face. The red tank top she wore clung to every luscious curve of her body, and Luke, unable to help himself, let his eyes linger on her for far longer than he had any right to.

"Who is she?" Luke asked in an astonished tone.

"Her name is Andi Ford," Norah told him. "Red hired her on this afternoon."

Andi was on her way back to the bar, having successfully delivered her tray of beer, when she noticed Norah engaged in a conversation with a cowboy; the *same* cowboy who confronted her in the diner earlier. Oh this was just perfect. She was having a hard enough time dealing with all the other jerks in this place without having to deal with him as well. But as she walked closer, she noticed that it wasn't the same man. Sure they looked alike, *a lot* alike, but it definitely wasn't the same guy.

Although a part of her was thrilled that this wasn't the same man from earlier, she couldn't help but cringe. The way he was looking at her made her instantly feel uncomfortable. Too many times tonight she had been groped or stared at, and it was starting to get under her skin a little. But the man smiled when she approached and she was taken aback by the simple gesture. He seemed so charming and she couldn't help but notice the way his blue eyes sparkled when the lights hit them just right. Andi smiled in return and dipped her head.

"Andi, this is my brother Luke," Norah said. "Luke, this is Andi."

"Nice to meet you," Andi said, extending her hand.

"The pleasure is all mine," Luke responded, but instead of shaking Andi's hand he turned it over and gently kissed the back of it.

"Oh, God," Norah said in amused disgust. "Really?"

"Can I get you a drink or interest you in a dance?" Luke asked, still holding Andi's hand.

Andi looked from Luke to Norah, who was holding her hand up to her mouth trying to hide her laugh.

"Um, I'm working right now," Andi stated and gently pulled her hand away from Luke's.

"Well, maybe some time when you're not working then," Luke suggested with a grin.

Andi didn't want to admit it, but she did feel an attraction to this handsome stranger. She smiled at Luke and decided not to respond.

"All right, loverboy," Norah said, pushing Luke aside. "Save it for another time, us girls have work to do."

Luke tipped his hat and smiled at Andi while he waited for Norah to get him his beers.

Andi gave him one last glance before returning to her nightly tasks. Maybe staying in Buford, Texas wouldn't be so bad after all.

"How about me, darlin'?" Gus said, grabbing Andi around her waist and pulling her close. "Can I interest you in doin' anything with me?"

"Let go of me!" Andi said, attempting to push her way out of Gus' grip.

"You're a feisty one!" Gus said. "Just give me one little kiss and I'll let you go." He leaned towards her and puckered his lips.

"Ew! Get off of me!" Andi yelled once more and pushed herself as far away from him as she could.

"Let her go, Gus," Norah said, stepping up and pulling on Gus' arm.

"Stay out of this, Norah," Gus warned. "This is between me and my girl."

"Come on, Gus, let go." Luke stepped up and calmly placed a hand on Gus' shoulder.

"You stay out of this too, Luke!" Gus' voice carried across the bar.

Andi struggled to free herself of Gus' grip but to no avail.

"Seriously, let go!" Luke said as he attempted to remove Gus' hold on Andi.

"Knock it off, boy!" Gus warned before letting go of Andi and delivering a solid punch to Luke's jaw.

Luke fell back to the floor, caught off guard by the action, and Norah dropped by his side. Seconds later they both watched as Zane quickly emerged from behind them, forcing himself between Andi and Gus. Andi stumbled back and fell into a table, gripping the edges so she wouldn't fall.

Luke was up on his feet and by Zane's side just as Gus was winding up for another swing. Zane ducked out of the way and hit Gus hard in the stomach, sending him back into the barstool which promptly fell to the floor. With the help of his friends Gus awkwardly stood up, stared menacingly at Zane and then turned his attention to Luke.

"What's the matter, Luke? Can't fight your own battles? Gotta have your big brother come to the rescue?" Gus taunted. The three men standing with him chuckled and waited for their move.

Luke, breathing hard, went to take a step forward but was quickly stopped when Norah stood in front of him and placed a hand on his chest.

"Enough! All of you!" she warned, looking to all of the men. "Gus, I think you and your friends have had about enough fun for one night and you should leave."

Gus looked as though he was about to say something in response to her comment when a large hand gripped his shoulder.

"You boys know the rules," Trace, the bouncer, said as he showed Gus and his friends the door. "No fighting. You get caught fighting, you leave."

Luke turned to Zane and punched his shoulder. "What the hell, man?"

"What'd you hit me for?" Zane asked, giving Luke a confused expression.

"Why'd you have to go and interrupt my rescue like that?" Luke asked with a miffed tone.

"I'm sorry," Zane told him, his voice loaded with sarcasm. "The next time I see you get knocked on the floor by a man twice your size I won't bother helping."

"Ah dammit. I guess you're right," Luke said and jokingly punched Zane's shoulder. "Thanks for the help big brother."

"Don't mention it." Zane was just about to turn behind him to check on the young woman he had helped rescue from Gus when Trace approached him.

"Sorry fellas, but I'm afraid you're gonna have to go too," Trace said.

"Why do we have to leave?" Luke asked, brushing off hat and cursing under his breath because now it was bent.

"Rules are rules," Trace told him. "I hate to do that to you guys, but if I don't kick you out as well people are gonna start to think they can just get away with whatever."

"It's fine, Trace," Zane said. "We'll go. Come on Luke." He gestured for his younger brother to follow him, and as he did he turned to get a look at the woman he'd rescued. Norah was consoling her and escorting her towards the back room, so once again Zane only got a look at her from behind. Oh but what a behind it was. Zane let his eyes gaze over her body, following the slender curve of her waist into what had to be the most perfectly round bottom he'd ever seen. Breaking his stare from the woman's incredible ass, he turned and followed Luke out the door. He smiled to himself as he walked through the parking lot towards his truck. He'd been avoiding this place for almost a year now, swearing he'd never set foot in that bar ever again. Of course now, he was swearing he'd return every night until he got to know the new waitress.

****

"Well, how was your first night?" Red asked as he sipped on a long neck bottle of beer.

Andi put her finger up to her chin and looked to the ceiling, making it look like she was thinking really hard about her answer. "I guess it was all right," she said and chuckled.

Red and Norah laughed with her for a moment before taking another sip of their beer.

"So do you think you'll stick it out?" Norah asked.

Andi nodded as she took a sip of her own beer. "Yea it really wasn't that bad."

Red took one last long sip of his beer then threw the bottle in the trash. "Okay, let's get this place cleaned up so we can get home."

They each stood up and went on to their closing duties. Red counted out the cash register, Norah and Andi wiped down the tables and placed the chairs back on the tabletops. After that, Andi swept the floors while Norah took the trash out.

"Here you go, ladies," Red said as he handed them each their pay for the night. "Drive home safely and I'll see you tomorrow."

They thanked him and exited the bar to the parking lot.

"So where are you staying?" Norah asked Andi as she placed her night's earnings into her back pocket.

"Um, nowhere right now," Andi told her. "I'm looking for a place to rent or something. But until then I was just going to get a room at the motel."

Norah stopped in her tracks. "Oh, no, no, no, we just can't have that, can we?"

"I'm sorry?" Andi asked confused.

"I can't have you stay in that dingy motel. You'll come home with me," Norah said looping her arm with Andi's.

"Wait a second," Andi protested. "You don't even know me."

"I know you well enough," Norah said.

"You're serious?" Andi asked, skeptically.

"Of course I am," Norah said. "So what do you say? Stay in a dingy motel room where the room smells like moth balls? Or come stay with me and sleep in a nice soft bed where the room smells of clean country air?"

Andi thought about it for a moment and realized that Norah's offer did sound very inviting. And Norah seemed like a genuinely nice person. So how bad could it be? "Okay you talked me into it."

Chapter Six

June 8

Today was such a crazy today. What started off as taking a break from driving turned into me taking refuge in a small country town. It seems like the perfect place to hide seeing as Vince would never expect me to live so far away from the city. I can't explain it, but there is a certain comforting feeling I have about this place. It's most likely from the friendly demeanor everyone has around here. The people are so nice and helpful, even to a complete stranger. In my short time here I have been given clothes, a job and a place to stay. As I sit here and think about everything that has happened today, I wonder if they will really ever know just how much I appreciate everything they have done. I am thankful that I'm here and for the first time in four days I feel safe.

Andi set her hairbrush on the table next to the bed, stood up and walked across the wooden floor to the window. Slowly, she pulled the curtain back to stare out at the beautiful scenery. Never before had she seen anything so breathtaking. Twinkling stars adorned the cloudless night sky, and the glow from the moon cast just enough light across the land where Andi could make out a barn and two other buildings along with fencing that seemed to have no end.

It looks so peaceful.

She let the curtain fall back and made her way towards the bed. No doubt this was *way* better than staying in a motel; and this bed was quite possibly the softest thing she had ever slept on. The soft cotton sheets felt like velvet against her skin, and the way she sank into the mattress made it feel like she was lying on a cloud. Her body was sore from all the running around she had done at the bar that night, and she was completely exhausted. Resting her head against the pillow, she closed her eyes and tried her darndest to fall asleep but with no such luck. Every time she closed her eyes she would see Sal and Tony; and that panicky, run for your life feeling would pulse through her veins making her antsy and on edge.

Andi opened her eyes and stared at the ceiling for a long moment, taking in slow deep breaths. Feeling not the least bit tired now, she decided to venture out of her room in search of a glass of water. Attempting to be as quite as she possibly could, she slowly opened the door and headed down the hallway in what she hoped was the direction of the kitchen. Her hand slid lightly along the wall, using it as a guide in this dark unfamiliar house. She froze when her foot stepped on a creaky board and waited to see if she had woken Norah. When no doors opened, she continued and soon came to an open room; what she assumed was the living area.

The curtainless windows allowed enough light so Andi could easily make her way through the room without running into any furniture. From there she passed through a large dining area and finally into the kitchen. She made her way across the slate floor to the kitchen sink and flipped the switch for the light above it. She glanced around the dimly lit room and thought it was quite charming. The off white cabinets had a rustic appearance to them and the butcher block counter top complimented them very nicely. The pale yellow paint that covered the walls was such a cheerful color and reminded her of summers at the beach with her family. Although it was a happy memory, the thought of her parents brought back other, more emotional memories as well. She pushed her thoughts aside, quietly cleared her throat and began to carefully open the cabinets in search of a glass.

"Aha! There you are," she whispered when she had found the right cabinet. Standing on her tiptoes, she reached for the glass.

The main kitchen light flicked on overhead and was followed by a man's voice asking, "What the hell are you doing?"

Andi let out a startled squeal and spun around, dropping the glass on the floor where it shattered into a thousand pieces. Scared beyond belief, she stared at the man as he lowered the baseball bat in his hand to his side.

Oh this is not happening.

"*You*?" Both Andi and Zane said at the same time. Silence filled the room as the two of them stared each other down.

"I'll ask you again," Zane said. "What the hell are you doing?"

"What am *I* doing?" Andi replied. "What are *you* doing? Jesus, you just scared the crap out of me!" she said, clutching her chest and taking in a deep breath to calm herself.

"Don't try to change the subject, *princess*," Zane said, taking a step into the kitchen and crossing his arms.

Andi's heart was beating so fast that it felt like it was going to beat right out of her chest. And she wasn't quite sure if it was from being startled or the fact that Zane was standing against the doorframe wearing only a pair of navy blue pajama bottoms. She had to give the man credit, even though he irritated her to the point that she wanted to slap him, he did look pretty darn good without his shirt on.

"I was just trying to get a glass of water," she explained, trying to keep her focus on his face and not his perfectly sculpted upper body.

"So you just break into people's houses in your underwear and steal glasses of water?" he asked in a sarcastic tone.

Andi, unaware that her nightshirt had ridden up over her bikini bottoms, began to self consciously tug at the hemline of her shirt attempting to cover herself.

"Your house?" she asked. "I thought this was Norah's house?" Confusion swam through her mind. What the heck was going on here?

They were momentarily distracted by a set of footsteps running down the hall, and then Luke came bursting into the kitchen wielding a hand gun. Andi let out another startled scream at the sight of the gun, and when Luke realized there was no danger he quickly dropped it to his side. He smiled when he caught site of Andi and lifted his empty hand to comb his hair back.

"What'd you bring a gun for?" Zane asked with a raised eyebrow to Luke.

Luke diverted his eyes from Andi and turned his attention to Zane. "I heard a woman scream," he explained and shrugged. "What'd you expect me to do?"

Two more sets of footsteps could be heard running down the hallway and seconds later Norah appeared in the kitchen along with an older woman carrying a rifle in her hand.

"For the love of God don't shoot!" Andi begged when the older woman aimed in her direction.

"Put the rifle down, Mom," Luke said reaching out and pushing the barrel of the gun towards the floor.

Linda looked to Andi with a confused expression, then turned her attention to both of her sons. "Would you care to explain yourselves, boys?"

"Mom, this is Andi," Luke quickly explained. "She's the new waitress at The Rusty Spur." Luke looked from his mother to Andi and gave her a smile.

"Okay," Linda said, dragging the word out. "Would anybody like to tell me why the new waitress at The Rusty Spur is standing in my kitchen in her underwear?"

Andi began to tug on the ends of her nightshirt again.

"So far we've established that she's getting a glass of water," Zane said with that same sarcastic tone.

Andi gave him a hard look and wondered what his problem was. As far as she was concerned, she had done no harm. She was invited to stay here and did not break in regardless of what he thought.

"All right stop it. I can explain," Norah said, stepping around her mother and brothers and walking over to Andi. "I invited her to stay here."

Andi searched each one of their faces, looking for some sort of sign that they had accepted Norah's simple explanation and that they could all just forget about this and go back to bed.

"Now what'd you go and do a stupid thing like that for?" Zane asked heatedly.

Andi, shocked by how angry Zane had become, took a step back towards the cabinets and leaned against them for support.

"Stop it, Zane. I did it because it was the right thing to do," Norah explained harshly.

"You don't even know her, Norah! She could be a murderer and yet you brought her home anyway like she was some sort of stray animal," Zane argued, using the same excuse Andi had used earlier in the day for leaving him stranded on the side of the road. He looked to Andi now and shot her a disapproving look.

"Zane, do you really think anyone that beautiful could be a murderer?" Luke asked, trying to lighten the mood.

"Shut up Luke!" Zane and Norah yelled in unison.

"All right, enough!" Linda called over top of the bickering and held her hand out to stop them from talking. "It is three o'clock in the morning and we all have to be up soon. So let's go back to bed and we can discuss this over breakfast."

"Mom," Zane started to object but was interrupted by Linda.

"I said enough. Now everyone get back to bed." Linda waited patiently as Zane and Luke slowly walked out of the room.

"We'll go to bed as soon as we get this glass cleaned up, Mom," Norah told her while reaching for the broom and dust pan.

"Good enough. Good night, girls," Linda said as she too walked out of the room.

Andi waited till she was almost positive everyone was far enough away from the kitchen before she spoke. "You didn't tell me you lived with your family."

Norah handed the dust pan to Andi and began to sweep up the tiny shards of glass that scattered the floor surrounding them. "I'm sorry. I didn't think you'd go wandering the house in the middle of the night. I was going to tell you in the morning."

Andi sighed and bent down to the floor, holding the dust pan so Norah could sweep the glass into it. "It's okay. I mean it would have been nice if they hadn't seen me in my underwear though," she said with a nervous laugh.

"Yea sorry about that," Norah replied with a chuckle.

"That guy standing beside Luke, he's the other guy from the bar tonight, isn't he? Andi asked as she let out a sigh.

"Oh, yea that's my oldest brother Zane," Norah told her.

"He doesn't like me very much," Andi bluntly stated and waited for Norah to respond.

Norah was quiet for a moment, picking up the dust pan and walking it over the trash can. She dumped the contents into the bag and placed the broom and dust pan back in the closet. "I wouldn't let it bother you. The man's got issues," Norah said as she walked back towards Andi.

"Issues?" Andi asked, waiting for Norah to explain.

"It's too long a story to tell you right now," she said, placing her hand on Andi's back and directing her to her room. "Come on, we better get back to bed. Days start early on a ranch and we don't want to be dragging our feet around all day now do we?"

"I guess not," Andi said, a little confused as to what that had to do with her. She said good night once more to Norah, walked back to her room, crawled into bed and curled up under the covers. She laid there unable to fall asleep for the longest time. Thoughts of a certain incredibly handsome blonde haired, blue eyed cowboy standing in the doorframe of the kitchen plagued her mind. She wondered what his story was and why he seemed to hate her so much. It couldn't possibly be just from the earlier events of the day. Norah had said he had issues, but what kind of issues can make a person that angry towards a complete stranger? She let out an exasperated sigh and closed her eyes.

"Stupid, sexy, cowboy."

Chapter Seven

Andi gasped and shot straight up out of bed. "What the hell is that?" she cried as she heard the unfamiliar sound once more. A light tapping sound coming from the door distracted her momentarily.

"Andi? Are you awake?" she heard Norah ask from the other side of the door.

"Yes, I'm up," Andi replied groggily.

"Can I come in?" Norah asked.

"Sure," Andi said, adjusting the covers so only the top half of her body could be seen. She'd figure this family had had enough of seeing her underwear for one lifetime.

Norah opened the door halfway and peered in the room. "Mornin'," she greeted with a smile.

Andi sighed, trying to calm her startled nerves. "Morning."

"Are you okay?" Norah asked and gave Andi a concerned look.

"Yes, I think so. I just heard this noise and it scared me right out of my sleep," Andi explained, taking in a deep breath.

"Noise? What kind of noise?" Norah couldn't remember hearing anything out of the ordinary and wondered what kind of noise could have startled Andi so.

Andi heard the unfamiliar sound once more and exclaimed, "That! What the hell is that?"

Norah gave Andi a confused look then burst into laughter. When she was able to control herself she looked to Andi to explain. "It's just our rooster. Don't tell me you've never heard a rooster crow before."

"Oh," Andi said feeling embarrassed. "What time is it?" she asked, trying to change the subject.

"It's about seven thirty," Norah told her.

Andi gave her a shocked expression. "Seven thirty? Why on earth are we up this early?" She groaned and fell back down in the bed, throwing the pillow over her head.

"We've got work to do, sleepy head." Norah walked over to the bed and removed the pillow from Andi's face.

"Work?" Andi groaned.

"Yes, ma'am. Now get up and get dressed. I'll meet you in the kitchen," Norah said as she exited the room, closing the door behind her.

Andi rolled onto her back and stared at the ceiling. "What have I gotten myself into?" she asked herself. With a sigh, she crawled out of bed and stretched. She drug her feet across the floor to the chair in the corner of the room where her duffle bag was. From there she pulled out the pair of jeans and baby blue t-shirt that she had taken from the box of clothes Belle had given her, along with her own undergarments. With her clothes in hand, she walked over to the door and was about to turn the handle when she realized that it probably wasn't the brightest idea to leave her room in just her nightshirt and underwear again. She set the rest of her clothes on the dresser next to the door, grabbed the pair of jeans and slid them on before making her way out of the room.

She was just about to walk into the bathroom when she saw Zane emerge from a room down the hall and she froze. Her eyes glanced over him from head to toe as he walked toward her, taking in how every piece of clothing he wore seemed to be made just for him. From his light gray t-shirt that hugged every part of his taut chest and abs down to his snug fit blue jeans, the man looked like a model in a magazine instead of a cowboy from Texas. She caught herself staring and quickly diverted her eyes from his all too perfect body to look at his face. Unable to control herself, she began to blush, knowing that he must have seen her checking him out.

"Good morning," she managed to say as he approached and gave him a smile.

"Mornin'," he replied with lack of emotion and a slight nod as he walked past her.

Andi watched him walk away with a confused expression. *What is his problem?* She grabbed the door handle to the bathroom, gave it a turn, and was just about to enter but stopped to give Zane one last look, trying to see just how perfect those jeans fit.

"Damn," she whispered under her breath and bit her bottom lip.

Zane stopped and turned to face her. "Did you say something?"

Andi broke her gaze and felt the heat start to flood her cheeks again. "Nope," she nervously blurted out and quickly entered the bathroom, closing and locking the door behind her.

****

Andi was nervous as she rounded the corner of the kitchen. She wasn't quite sure who she would encounter and what kind of mood they'd be in. When she stepped into the kitchen she was surprised to see only Norah and her mother moving around from the countertop to the stove and so forth.

"Good morning," she greeted as she walked towards the two women.

"Hey, Andi," Norah said as she wiped her hands on a dish towel. She walked over to her mother and placed a hand on her shoulder. "This is my mother, Linda."

"Hi Andi, it's nice to meet you," Linda said, reaching her hand across the table.

Andi shook her hand and smiled. "It's nice to meet you too. I'm sorry about last night. I didn't' realize when Norah invited me to stay over that she lived with anyone."

"It's quite all right, dear," Linda said, smiling at Andi.

Andi couldn't help but notice how uncanny the similarities between Linda and Norah were. Linda's hair was the exact same shade of blonde as Norah's, the only exception being that Linda's had streaks of white running through it and hers was shoulder length whereas Norah's hit the middle part of her back. Other than that, Linda looked like an older version of Norah. It was almost obvious as to where all three of her children had gotten their good looks from. That being said, Andi was only judging by what she had seen so far, seeing as she hadn't met their father yet.

"Can I help with anything?" Andi offered as she watched the two women continue to make breakfast.

"We're actually almost done," Linda said. "But you can set the table. The plates are in that cabinet, utensils in that drawer and I think you know where the glasses are." Linda smiled and chuckled.

Andi smiled and laughed softly, glad that they were able to find some humor in last night. Once she had all of the places set she went to the fridge and grabbed the pitcher of freshly squeezed orange juice and the container of milk. She placed each of them on the table, took a step back, and smiled at how charming it looked with the mismatched place settings.

"Andi would you be a sweetheart and call the boys in for breakfast?" Linda asked as she set a steaming hot plate of sausage on the table. Norah followed with a plate of eggs and a plate of pancakes, setting them on each end of the table as well.

"Sure," Andi said and headed towards the back door. She opened the screen door and stepped out onto the porch, letting the door swing closed behind her. It slammed shut and rattled, causing Andi to jump. She peered in through the screen of the door and quickly apologized.

"It's fine," Norah said. "We do it all the time."

Andi nodded and walked over to the porch steps. She took in a deep breath and cupped her hands around her mouth. "Luke! Zane! Breakfast!"

Andi could hear Norah and Linda giggling from inside the house.

"Did I do it wrong?" she asked confused.

"No, sweetie, you're fine," Linda said still giggling. "But they won't hear you yelling if they're in the barn. There's a bell hanging on the post there. Just give it a good hard ring and they'll hear it."

Andi nodded, gave the bell three hard rings and walked back into the house to help with anything else she could.

****

"Guess it's time for breakfast," Luke said as he led his mare out into the pasture. He unhooked the lead rope from her halter, gave her neck a few gentle pats and sent her to graze with the other horses. As he walked into the barn, he hung the rope on a hook next to all the other horse tack. "Come on, Zane, let's go eat."

"I'm coming, just let me turn the water off to the trough first." Zane entered the barn a second later, removing his work gloves and placing them in his back pocket. The last thing he felt like doing right now was sitting down at his family's table with that woman. What was Norah thinking asking her to stay the night there? She had known this woman for what, an hour or so and now they were best friends?

There was something odd about the whole situation that was putting him on edge. How did this woman go from driving a flashy sports car and wearing fancy clothes to wearing holey jeans and working in a bar? He stared across the yard at the rusty Ford parked in the driveway. Why did she give up her car for that piece of crap? Zane shook his head. This whole thing had trouble written all over it and it was leaving a bad taste in his mouth.

"So what do you think?" Luke asked, getting in step next to Zane.

"About what?" Zane asked in reply.

"About the stock market, Zane. Jeesh! What to do you think I'm talking about?" Luke said sarcastically.

Zane knew Luke was asking about Andi and really didn't feel like having a conversation about her. "What's there to think about?"

Luke rolled his eyes. "I can think of lots of things to think about. Her dark, shiny hair, her warm brown eyes, and the way her skin seems to glow."

"Okay I get it," Zane interrupted. "You think she's hot."

"And you don't?" Luke asked with a raised eyebrow.

Of course I do. Even though the woman appeared to be trouble with a capital T, Zane couldn't help but think that she was the most attractive woman he had ever seen. It was all he could do last night to keep from staring at her perfectly slender body beneath her less than concealing nightshirt. The visions of her standing in the kitchen and her toned, tanned legs haunted his mind all night long. "She's all right," Zane replied with a shrug.

They made their way up the porch steps, removed their boots by the back door and walked in the house. Luke entered the house first and removed his cowboy hat, stealing a glance at Andi and giving her one of his most charming smiles. "Mornin'," he said in his smooth southern voice.

Andi smiled. "Morning."

The screen door opened again and in walked Zane, placing his cowboy hat on the wall just as Luke had done. Andi smiled when Zane glanced at her, and he simply nodded his head then walked over to the sink. He felt the strangest fluttering sensation in his stomach and instantly became upset with himself.

Stop it right now.

They all took their seats at the table, and Andi was just about to reach for the biscuits when she noticed the four of them bow their heads and begin to pray. Caught off guard, she quickly dipped her head and followed up with an "Amen". The food was passed around to each person and plates were filled.

Linda cleared her throat and picked up her fork. "So Andi," Linda said as she poured herself a glass of juice. "Norah tells me that you're new in town."

Andi felt her heart stop. She had that all too familiar feeling that these people were going to want to know her whole life story and, to be honest, she wasn't quite sure what to say. *Well I'm on the run and hiding from my abusive ex-boyfriend,* was the explanation she should give them, but she *really* didn't want to do that.

"Yes, ma'am," Andi said after swallowing a piece of pancake.

The conversation revolved around Andi for the next few minutes. It felt like her head was swimming from all the questions being thrown at her, but then one question cleared her mind and made her heart ache.

"Do you have family back in Summerville?" Linda asked her now, reaching for her cup of coffee.

"No, ma'am," Andi said softly. "I don't have any family to speak of. My parents passed away a while ago."

"Oh, I'm sorry to hear that," Linda said, followed by Norah saying the same thing.

Luke reached his hand over and carefully laid it on top of hers, giving it a gently squeeze. "I'm sorry too."

"How'd they die?" Zane asked bluntly, not believing her story and hoping to catch her in a lie. God she was so pretty sitting there across the table from him. But the fact that he even thought that was making him madder by the second. He ignored the way his stomach flipped and waited for her to give him any signs that she was fibbing.

"Zane!" Linda berated him. "Now is not the time or place to be asking her that. Show some compassion."

"What?" Zane said. "I'm just trying to find out more about this stranger staying here."

"Stop." Linda gave him a stern look and pointed a finger to his face.

Zane let out an exasperated huff and continued with his breakfast.

"That's another thing I wanted to ask you," Linda said, now turning her attention back to Andi.

"Norah was also telling me that you were looking for a place to stay."

Andi could feel Zane's furious stare as she began to respond to Linda. She started to feel uncomfortable and wished she could just run and hide. "Yes, ma'am," she answered quietly.

"Well, we have the spare room available if you'd like to stay here until you can find a place," Linda offered. "I won't charge you rent, but you can work for the room by helping out around the ranch."

Both Andi and Zane gave Linda a shocked expression.

"Mom, you can't be serious," Zane said.

"My house my rules," she stated frankly.

The anger was clear on his face and he dropped his fork and knife on the plate. The loud *klink-klank* seemed to echo in the all too quiet room. He pushed himself away from the table with enough force that his chair fell sideways to the floor.

"Now where are you going?" Linda asked as she watched him stalk towards the door.

He grabbed his cowboy hat and shoved it onto his head. "I'm not hungry," he said without looking back. The screen door slammed shut behind him and the sound of his boots stomping across the porch boards faded when his feet hit the grass.

Andi stared after him, shocked and confused. Although Linda's offer for her to stay here was a Godsend, living under the same roof as Zane McKade was looking to be pure hell.

"Well?" Linda asked, drawing Andi's attention away from Zane's dramatic exit.

Andi took in a deep breath and let out one long sigh. She desperately needed a place to stay and why not stay here? Besides the fact that Zane appeared to hate everything about her, there were three other people here who had been nothing but helpful and friendly to her.

"Okay," she said and shook Linda's hand.

Chapter Eight

Zane cursed under his breath the whole way out to the barn.

What the hell are they thinking? Bunch of lunatics; letting a stranger just move right in. None of it makes any sense.

He continued his rant as he walked into the small room just inside the barn that housed all of their tools where he grabbed a pitch fork, a shovel, and the wheelbarrow before heading towards the horse stalls. Mumbling and cursing under his breath, Zane went to work, starting with the first stall and making his way down the line.

She's hiding something I know she is. Probably a con artist or a criminal on the run or something. Knocked off a convenience store or robbed a bank, and now she's hiding in my family's house.

His little tirade was brought to a halt when he heard a scream come from outside. He dropped his shovel and ran through the barn door, looking for the direction where the scream came from. To his left, he could see Andi running away from the chicken coop. She stopped when she was about twenty feet away and placed her hand over her heart.

"What the hell are you screaming for?" Zane yelled over to her.

Andi quickly turned her head in Zane's direction and let out an exasperated sigh. "That *thing* just tried to kill me!" she cried, pointing towards the chicken coop.

"What thing?" Zane yelled back.

"That rooster!" she said, her voice thick with aggravation. She was expecting him to roll his eyes and turn away from her, but instead he strolled across the yard in her direction. "That thing is the devil," she whined when he was six feet away from her.

Expecting him to make fun of her for being a sissy, she placed her left hand on her hip and dangled the basket for the eggs she was supposed to collect in her right. She dug the heel of her boot into the ground and waited for his smart ass remark; but none came.

Zane shocked her by walking straight up to her, looking her in the eyes and snatching the basket from her. He walked away from her before she had time to protest or ask what he was doing. A few minutes later he emerged from the chicken coop, basket in hand filled with eggs. He walked back towards her and shoved the basket into her hands.

"If you can't handle something as simple as collecting eggs then how the hell are you expecting to help out with any other chores?" he spit through his teeth before turning away and heading back towards the barn.

Andi, fuming from his rudeness and unable to help herself yelled, "You're a real jerk, you know!"

Zane spun around on his heel and headed back in her direction with a furious look on his face.

Andi, desperately wishing she had just kept her mouth shut, froze in place and waited for his retaliation. This whole scenario brought back the memory of the one time she decided to stand up to Vince, which left her with a cracked rib and a busted lip. Instinctively, she braced herself and got ready for the blows she just knew were coming.

"You got a lot of nerve calling me names on my own property," Zane said pointing a finger at her.

Andi was a little shocked and relived that all he was doing was yelling at her. She didn't enjoy being yelled at by any means, but she'd welcome it any day over being slapped in the face. "I just don't understand what your problem is and why you hate me so much," she threw back at him.

"My problem is that you are a complete stranger. My family knows nothing about you and yet here you are living under our roof," he said heatedly. "You may have the rest of them fooled, but not me."

"What are you talking about?" Andi asked and gave him an irritated look.

"I don't trust you. You're hiding something and I know it." Zane studied her face and waited for any indication that he was right.

Andi kept her cool and knew what he was up to. He was trying to get under her skin, and she hated to admit it but it was working.

Just stick it out and deal with it. Sooner or later Vince will get tired of looking for me and I'll be free to be on my way. An amusing thought popped in her mind and she held back a smirk. *Two can play at this game. If he wants to get under my skin then I'll do the same.* "Okay, you caught me."

The furious expression faded from Zane's face and was replaced with a suspicious look. "What?" he asked.

"You caught me." Andi sighed and shrugged.

"So you're fessing up that you've been lying this whole time?" he asked in disbelief.

Andi nodded. "Yes, sir. Can't hide anything from you."

"Okay, so what's your real story?" Zane asked, crossing his arms over his chest.

Andi took in a deep breath for dramatic effect and lowered her eyes to the ground. She lifted them slowly to look him in the eye, and with a straight face she started. "I'm a criminal on the run. See, I use to live in this small town where I was a waitress, working in a diner. I was bored with my life and wanted some excitement. One day I met this guy and I realized he was my ticket to a more entertaining lifestyle. So, we left town. We started out small, knocking off gas stations but eventually upped the ante and starting robbing banks."

Zane held his hand up to keep her from saying anymore. "You are such a little liar."

Andi laughed and gave Zane a smug smile. "It's the truth," she said, pleased that her story had worked.

"It's the story of Bonnie and Clyde, Andi. I'm not some stupid hillbilly," Zane said, giving her an irritated look before turning and walking back to the barn.

Andi, pleased with how well her plan work, decided keep amusing herself and followed him to the barn. "Okay, okay. How about this then? My best friend and I decided to take a weekend fishing trip but along the way we stopped at a country bar where my friend was assaulted by some drunk guy. I caught him before he could hurt her but ended up losing my temper and shot him dead. Instead of going to the cops, we decided to make a run for Mexico—"

"Stop shooting me movie plots, Andi. Or whatever your name is," Zane said, fully annoyed with her now. "It's starting to piss me off."

"Boy, you're a poor sport," she said. "Good at dishing it out but you can't take it in return." She leaned against the door frame of the barn and watched as he picked up a shovel and entered the horse stall.

"How about you leave me alone and go finish your chores? Seeing as you're supposed to be working for the room you're staying in," Zane said, not looking in her direction.

"I was only asked to collect the eggs, and seeing as you've done that for me I don't really have anything else to do until lunch time," she informed him in a matter of fact tone.

"Go bother someone else," he told her, lifting the shovel and dumping its contents into the wheelbarrow. "I'm sure my mother or Norah could find something for you to do."

"They left a little while ago to go to the store," she said. "So it looks like you're stuck with me."

He stopped shoveling and turned to look at her, causing her heart to literally skip a beat. Why did he have to be so darned good looking and irritating at the same time?

With his shovel in hand, he crossed the saw dust ground to stand in front of her. Andi felt her heart completely stop beating then pick up again at an abnormally quick rate. He was less than a foot away from her. So close that she could smell the woodsy sent of his aftershave mixed with sweat and—*Oh God*—the combination was almost intoxicating. Her breath caught in her throat as he leaned toward her and removed the basket of eggs from her hand.

With her back pressed firmly against the wall of the barn, she waited to see just what the heck he was doing. He leaned in, inches away from her face and stopped. Good lord, he was going to kiss her. But, why? And then she didn't care. She slowly started to close her eyes to welcome the kiss she just knew was coming, but stopped when she felt a hard metal object thrust into her hands.

"Good, then you can help me clean the horse stalls," Zane said with a smirk as he walked away to get another shovel.

Andi looked from the shovel to Zane in disbelief.

Zane walked past Andi and back to the horse stall, glancing in her direction before he started shoveling again. "You wanna wipe that stupid look off of your face and get to work?"

Shoveling horse manure was definitely not on her "list of things to do before I die". She could tell he was just trying to get back at her for her movie plot stories, but she'd be damned if she let him know how much it bothered her. So she followed in step behind him, keeping her mouth shut the entire time. Once they were done and the last bit of straw had been spread, Zane handed the shovels over to Andi and lifted the handles of the wheelbarrow.

"Why'd you give me the shovels?" she asked.

"So you can put them away," he explained as though he were speaking to a child, then started to walk towards the exit of the barn.

"Yea I got that smart ass," Andi said sarcastically. "I meant, why'd you give me the girl job?"

Zane set the wheelbarrow back down and turned to look at her over his shoulder. "You want to haul the manure out back?" he asked, his voice thick with amusement.

Andi lifted her chin, set the shovels against the stall door and walked over to him, shoving him aside and gripping the handles of the wheelbarrow.

"It's heavy," he warned.

"If you can do it, I can do it." She lifted the wheelbarrow and let out a soft grunt. Jeesh, he wasn't kidding. Trying not to let him see her struggle, she made her way out to the back of the barn. When she had reached the place where Zane had told her to dump it, she stopped and began to lift it in order for everything to come out. She almost had it high enough when she lost her balance and the wheelbarrow tipped over, bringing her down with it. "Whoa!"

Zane heard the commotion from inside the barn, sighed and rolled his eyes. "What has she done now?" he asked out loud to himself. He walked through the barn towards the back, stopped when he reached the doorframe and burst into laughter. There sitting in the pile of manure from the toppled over wheelbarrow was Andi.

"I'm glad you think this is funny," she said unamused. "Ew!"

"I think it's more than funny," Zane said in between laughs. "I think it's hilarious."

Andi gave him a hard look and pushed herself into a standing position. "I hate you, Zane McKade!" she spit through her teeth then stormed past him in the direction of the house.

"Yea well the feeling's mutual, princess!" he called after her.

"What was all that about?" Luke asked, giving Zane a curious look as he walked around the corner of the barn.

Zane turned to Luke still chuckling and replied, "She's just mad because she fell in a pile of horse shit."

Luke shook his head as he led the two year old colt he was working with into the pasture. "Why do you have to be so hard on her?" he asked as he unhooked the lead rope from the colt's halter and set him loose. The colt took off in a dead run and bucked in the air as he went to join the other horses.

"She's not as dainty as she seems," Zane said staring after Andi. A smile tickled the outside corner of his mouth and when he realized what he was doing, he shook his head and cleared his throat.

He turned to look at Luke with a serious expression, "I'm just being cautious, Luke. We don't know her."

Luke scoffed and walked past Zane into the barn. "You've got to get over your trust issues there big brother. Not all women are heartless liars." Zane went to protest but Luke stopped him.

"Don't even start, Zane," Luke said. "It's like you're looking for a reason to hate her. She's not a criminal, or a murderer or whatever other stupid thing you've come up with in your head. She's new in town, end of story. And if you were any kind of gentleman you'd welcome her instead of acting like a jerk."

Zane stared at his younger brother in disbelief. "When did you become so insightful?"

Luke shrugged and then smiled. "Maybe you should go talk to her and try to apologize."

Zane turned his head in the direction Andi had stormed off in. She must have disappeared into the house because she was nowhere in sight. "I guess you're right," Zane said with a sigh.

"What?" Luke said, tilting his head and cupping his hand around his ear. "I'm sorry I don't think I heard you clearly. Did you just say that I was right?"

Zane chuckled and punched Luke's shoulder on his way out of the barn. "Don't get used to hearing it." Although Luke did have a point, Zane couldn't help but feel that this woman was hiding something. "There's only one way to find out," he said quietly under his breath.

****

"Stupid jerk," Andi mumbled as she removed her work boots by the back door and kicked them to the side. She opened the screen door and stepped across the threshold onto the rug. Knowing Linda would kill her if she walked through the house in her manure covered clothes, Andi began to peel the filthy items from her body. In nothing but her sweat-soaked bra and underwear, Andi made a beeline for the laundry room. She threw her clothes in the washer and immediately started it, then high-tailed it for her bedroom.

Zane heard the door slam as soon as he entered the kitchen.

Oh boy.

Having removed his own boots by the back door, his stocking clad feet moved quietly across the hardwood floors. As he made his way down the hall, he rehearsed his apology in his mind over and over again until he found himself standing in front of her door. He took in a deep breath and let it out slowly as he knocked.

"Andi?" he said. At the faint "Come in", Zane turned the door handle and slowly pushed it open. "Andi I'm-" He froze and couldn't help the wide eyed expression that appeared on his face. Good God Almighty... She was naked.

"Zane!" Andi screamed and scrambled to pull the quilt from the bed in order to cover herself. "What the hell are you doing?"

"I-I," he stammered, unable to take his eyes off of her even though the quilt was now blocking his view.

"Spit it out, cowboy!" she said as she adjusted

the quilt around her body.

"I…knocked. You said 'come in'," he explained, now realizing that he had been staring and turned his eyes to the floor.

"I said 'don't'! Don't come in!" she corrected him. And she thought falling in a pile of horse manure was embarrassing. Dear Lord, this was ten times, no, fifty times more embarrassing than that. He was still standing there, obviously looking for the right words to say, but she just wanted him gone. "Oh my God, Zane, just go! Get out!"

Zane quickly shut the door, managing to get out, "I'm sorry." A loud thud against the now closed door followed his muffled apology and he assumed that whatever Andi decided to hurl was meant for his head. As he walked back out to the barn, he wished whatever she'd thrown had actually hit him instead of the door. A good solid blow to the head was the only thing that would erase the image of her standing there naked from his mind. Oh, who was he kidding? That memory would be burned into his brain for the rest of his life.

Chapter Nine

"Hey Andi, can I get a beer?" Luke called from across the bar.

"Sure thing," she replied with a smile. "Longneck Coor's Light, right?"

"You know me all too well." He gave her one of his charming smiles, sat down in one of the empty bar stools and leaned on the counter.

"Can I get one t-?" Zane started to ask but Andi walked away before he was able to finish. He let out an exasperated sigh and took the seat next to Luke.

"Maybe she didn't hear you," Luke said with a shrug. "It is kind of loud in here."

Andi was back just a few seconds later with Luke's beer. She popped the top and slid it across the bar towards him. "There you go, Luke."

"Thanks, sweetheart," he said and took a long sip.

"Andi, can I get one too?" Zane asked, knowing she had to have heard him that time.

Andi looked right past him to Luke. "Luke, if you need anything else you just holler, okay?"

Luke just smiled and tipped his hat as she turned away from them and headed towards the other end of the bar to wait on more customers.

"You've got to be kidding me," Zane said under his breath.

Luke let out a soft chuckle. "Boy, you really pissed her off. What's it been, three days now and she still won't talk to you?"

"Talk to me? Hell she won't even look in my direction." Zane's plan of being nice to Andi so he could get information from her was severely backfiring. After the whole horse manure incident he realized that he wasn't going to get anywhere acting the way he had been. So when lunchtime rolled around that same day he decided to try to apologize again and wave the white flag of truce, but she was nowhere to be found. He made several attempts over the next few days, but every time he came within fifteen feet of her she'd turn and hightail it in the other direction.

"Not drinking tonight, Zane?" Red asked as he approached and gave Zane a curious look.

"I was just waiting for your new waitress there to come back down to this end of the bar," Zane said, nodding toward Andi.

"You want your usual?" Red reached down into the cooler and pulled out a beer for Zane before waiting for his response.

"Sure," Zane said and stole a glance at Andi. Even though it went against everything he thought about her, he couldn't help but be taken aback by how beautiful she looked tonight. She wasn't wearing as much makeup as she had been since the first time he met her. He rather liked the more natural look instead of all that stuff caked on her face. The skin tight black shirt and blue jeans she wore left little to the imagination. Zane had to tear his eyes away from her before his imagination began to run wild. Instead he stared at the shelves of liquor bottles behind the bar and took a sip of his ice cold beer.

"Get your hands off of me!"

Recognizing the woman's voice, Luke turned around in his barstool towards the dance floor. "Ah dammit," he said catching Zane's attention.

"What?" Zane followed Luke's eyes to a table close to the dance floor where Andi was slapping away a man's hand from her bottom. "Is that Gus?"

"Looks like it," Luke replied and finished his beer in one big gulp. "That man never learns." He stood up from his barstool and started to walk over to assist Andi.

Zane downed the rest of his beer and quickly caught up with Luke. They could see Andi pointing her finger and arguing with Gus as he and his buddies continued to laugh it off as just having fun. Andi started to walk away from the table but was abruptly pulled to a halt as Gus stood up and grabbed her around the waist. What happened next stopped Zane and Luke dead in their tracks and made their jaws hit the floor. Andi spun around in Gus' arms and brought her knee up into his groin as hard as she could. The rush of air and the loud groan that followed could be heard throughout the bar. As Gus doubled over in pain, Andi brought her right arm around and connected her fist with his nose. She continued to shake her finger at him and yell as he laid on the floor holding his groin and now bloody nose.

Andi left the scene, shaking her hand and flexing her fingers. She bit her bottom lip to keep from smiling at all the hoots and hollers she was receiving. When she saw the look on Luke and Zane's faces she couldn't hide the smile anymore and chuckled. "What?"

"Where did you learn to do that?" Luke asked wide eyed.

"I got tired of these jerks groping me all the time, so your sister taught me some things to help me take care of myself," she answered. "Damn, that hurt." She shook her hand again and flexed her fingers while sucking in a breath of air.

"Here, let me see it," Zane said reaching out for her hand.

Andi snatched her hand back and gave him an evil glare. "I'm fine."

Zane took in a deep breath to calm the anger building in his body. What was it about this woman that made him mad enough to spit fire? "I'm sure you are but just let me look at it. Something tells me you've never punched anyone before and I just want to make sure you didn't break anything." He reached out and grabbed her hand before she had time to snatch it away again. It was the first time he had ever made any sort of physical contact with her. An electric current pulsed through his fingertips as he gently ran them over her knuckles searching for any signs of broken bones.

Andi was unable to distinguish whether or not the tingling sensation she felt when Zane caressed her hand was from the effects of the punch or from his gentle touch. She studied his face and realized that he genuinely seemed worried about her. It was a far cry from the Zane she had dealt with just three days ago. She was used to him trying to pick a fight with her over the littlest things, and seeing him so caring and so nice was a complete shock.

Zane turned her hand over and gave it a gentle pat. "You should put some ice on it. I don't think anything is broken but you'll probably have a bruise."

"Thanks for the diagnosis, doc," Andi said with a bit of sarcasm.

Zane laughed it off and adjusted his cowboy hat. "Anytime," he said with a smile as he tipped his hat and walked away.

Andi watched him as he left and wondered why he was all of a sudden being so nice to her. *Maybe he's finally realized that he was being a complete jerk.*

Or maybe this is all part of some evil plan he's brewing in an attempt to rat you out, her subconscious chimed in.

"I can't believe you just did that," Luke said astonished.

Andi broke her gaze from Zane and turned to look at Luke with a smile. "I honestly can't believe I did it either."

"Come on," he said and wrapped his arm around her shoulder, leading her in the direction of the bar. "I'm gonna buy you a beer. Any woman that can crack a man's nose like that deserves a nice ice cold frosty beer."

****

Later that night, Andi sat in her room and stared out the window into the night sky as she braided her hair to the side. In the short time she had been there she had grown to love everything about this place, which surprised her because she never thought she'd love anything more than the city. But the air was just so clean out here in the country and on certain days, when the breeze was blowing just right, you could smell a hint of the wildflowers that grew down by the creek. She loved every bit of this stone ranch style house and how, no matter what window you looked out, you got an amazing view of the open land and the horses grazing. Heck, she'd even grown to love the rooster. A light tapping at the door caught her attention. She quietly stood up from her chair and crossed the room to stand at the door.

"Yes?" she whispered.

"Andi, it's Zane."

She rolled her eyes. "What do you want?"

"I was wondering if we could talk," he said quietly through the closed door.

"About what?" she asked, trying to keep her voice down.

"Andi, can you please open the door?"

She let out a sigh and cracked the door enough so she could see him. "What?"

"I want to talk to you about something," Zane said. "Will you come out on the porch with me?"

"Zane, it's late. Can't it wait till the morning?"

"I promise I won't make it long. Just give me ten minutes?" he pleaded.

Andi wanted to slam the door in his face for acting the way he did the other day. But, seeing as he was so nice to her just a few short hours ago, she decided it wasn't worth waking everyone else up by being rude and obnoxious. She let out another sigh and told him to hold on. She closed the door and grabbed a robe to put on overtop her camisole, and headed back towards the door. "All right, let's go," she whispered as she pulled the ends of the belt tight around her waist.

Zane escorted her to the porch swing and instructed her to sit down.

"Is this really a sit down conversation, Zane? I mean, can't you just hurry up and get it over with so I can go to bed?"

"Please," he asked in his nicest tone and gestured once more for her to take a seat.

With a sigh, she sat down and crossed her arms over her chest. She waited patiently for him to start, which seemed to take forever. Finally he broke the silence and began.

"I wanted to apologize to you," he said staring at the floor then turning his eyes to hers.

Her heart skipped a beat at the sight of his angelic face in the moonlight. Never before had she seen anyone so unbelievably perfect. He was so handsome, and yet so rugged at the same time. She had to take a deep calming breath to regain her senses and focus on their conversation. "Okay."

"I've been a complete jerk to you," he said. "And you haven't deserved it."

"Uh-huh." Dear God she was starting to sound like an idiot answering him with only "okay's" and "uh-huh's". *Think of a better response*, she prompted herself.

"I feel like I've jumped to conclusions about you and have since realized that it was wrong to go about it like that." Zane studied her face and hoped she was buying into his apology. If he was ever going to learn the truth about her, she needed to believe that his apology was sincere.

Andi gave him a suspicious look. "Are you being serious or is this some sick joke of yours?"

Zane gave her his best shocked expression. "Of course I'm being serious. Here I am trying to apologize and you think I'm playing a joke? That's not right."

Andi threw both of her hands up to stop him from going on. "Okay, okay, I just had to make sure. If it's a truce you want then you can have it."

Zane attempted to channel Luke's charm and smiled at Andi, hoping that he could pull it off as well as Luke did. It worked. Even in the dark of the night, with just the faintest hint of the moonlight casting over them, he could see the rosy pink color flush over her cheeks. "Friends then?" he said and held out his hand.

Andi took in deep breaths and tried to control the blush that was slowly starting to creep down her neck and to her chest. She took Zane's hand and this time was positive that the tingling sensation was coming from his touch. "Friends," she agreed and shook his hand.

Chapter Ten

June 14

I had a dream last night that Vince found me. It was all too real and scared me so bad that I couldn't fall back asleep. I dreamt that I was alone in the barn at night. I was searching for the light and when I found it and turned it on he was there. It was one of those horrible dreams where you can't run or scream or even move.

He came at me in slow motion with this menacing glare and as I waited for him to attack me, feeling helpless and paralyzed, I watched as out of the darkness Zane appeared. He stood between Vince and me in a protective stance and warned Vince that if he ever touched or harmed me in any way ever again, that it would be the last thing he ever did. To my surprise Vince simply walked away and disappeared into the darkness.

Zane turned to me then and gently wrapped his arms around me, pulling me close and resting his chin on the top of my hair as I cried into his chest. His soothing words were as comforting as a lullaby, and I had never felt safer than I did in that moment. As I pulled away to thank him, we locked eyes and shared this indescribable moment together, lost in each other's gaze. And then, he kissed me.

That's when I woke up. My heart was beating so fast and my head felt like it was spinning in every direction. After I was able to regain control of my senses, I started to think about why I would dream such a thing. The only thing I can come up with is Zane's recent change of attitude toward me. For the past few days he's been nothing but a gentleman. Seeing this nicer, more charming side of him has me thinking about him all the time. With every glance he gives me, I feel my heart skip a beat. I know it's too soon to even be thinking about such things, considering the kind of relationship I just came out of. But I must admit that it is nice to think about letting myself fall for him.

Andi walked outside on the porch, shielded the sunlight from her eyes with her hand, and gazed upon the open land. From the corner of her eye she saw Norah riding on one of the horses in the long corral. Confused as to what exactly Norah was doing, Andi set out across the yard to find out. She watched as Norah started from the head of the ring, raced her horse around each of the barrels, and then urged the horse to run back to the gate. She did this several more times as Andi approached. When Norah spotted Andi standing at the corral she waved and trotted her horse over.

"Sorry I wasn't trying to disturb you," Andi apologized. "I was just watching."

"Oh it's okay. I was just finishing up anyway," Norah replied as she dismounted and slid the reins over the mares head.

"What were you doing?" Andi asked, hoping it wasn't a stupid question.

Norah slid her hand up and down the Palomino's neck and gave it a few pats. "I was just exercising Cheyenne here for the rodeo coming up next week. She's one of the best barrel racing horses in the county," Norah said with pride.

Andi had never been to a rodeo or even seen one on TV. It confused her as to why someone would race their horse around barrels like that. What was the purpose of it? She shrugged off the question and decided not to ask. "She certainly looked fast," she commented.

Norah smiled and nodded. "Well, I have to walk her over to the barn to take her saddle off and brush her down. You wanna come?"

"Sure." Andi met Norah at the gate and the two walked side by side to the barn. As they crossed the yard, Andi wondered about an observation she had made since first coming here to the ranch. She had wanted to ask Norah for a while now but had always talked herself out of it; thinking that if she started asking questions about them that they would expect to know more about her. As it was, curiosity had gotten the best of her and she couldn't hold her question back any longer. "Hey Norah, would you mind if I asked you something?"

"Not at all," Norah responded as she led her horse into the barn.

"It's kind of personal," Andi warned.

"That's okay, Andi. What do you want to ask me?"

Andi watched as Norah removed the bridle from Cheyenne's head and replaced it with a black halter, attaching the end of the lead rope hanging from the stall door to it. As Norah began to remove the saddle, Andi gathered her courage and asked her question.

"Well, it's more of an observation than a question I guess. It's just that I noticed… Well…" She paused and let out an exasperated sigh. She wasn't sure what kind of a reaction she was going to get from Norah and it was making her nervous. She took in an encouraging breath and continued. "I wanted to ask you why I haven't seen your father around here."

Norah paused as she slid the saddle and blanket from the mare's back, giving Andi a blank stare. "Um," she said softly.

Andi scrunched her eyes and held out her hand to stop Norah from explaining. "I'm sorry. It's none of my business. Just forget I asked, okay?"

"No, no, you're fine," Norah quickly said. She was silent as she walked the saddle over to the tack room and placed it with the others. When she emerged from the room, she tossed Andi a brush, then took her own and began to run it over the horse. "It's been forever since I've talked about him," Norah explained without emotion.

Andi looked at the brush in her hand then to the mare. This was the closest she had ever been to an animal this big, and she was standing at least six feet away. Carefully and slowly, she approached the horse on the opposite side from Norah. She reached her hand out and gently began to stroke the brush down the mare's back. After a few seconds, Andi reached her empty hand to the horse, gave it a tender pat and smiled.

"I actually don't even remember him," Norah continued her story, reclaiming Andi's attention.

"Did he…" Andi paused. "Die?"

Norah shook her head. "No, no, it was nothing like that. See, my mom got pregnant with Zane and shortly after they found out they got married. They were young and in love and as a wedding present my grandparents gave them one hundred acres of land so they could start their own horse ranch; that had been a dream of my mother's since she was a little girl. Two years later Luke was born and then another two years later I came along. By that time my parents had started to have problems. My father didn't want to be involved in horse ranching anymore and wanted to sell our land and move to someplace like Dallas. Mom said he told her he didn't want to be a country bumpkin for the rest of his life." Norah let out a disgusted huff. "One day my mom came home from the store and found a letter from him on the kitchen table saying that he had met someone who shared his dreams and that the two of them had taken off for a bigger and better life. He left my mother with three young children without even saying good-bye."

Andi stared at Norah with a shocked expression. "I'm so sorry, Norah," was all she could manage to say.

Norah shrugged. "Like I said, I don't remember him. I was only one when he left. Luke was only three so he doesn't really remember him either. I think Zane is the only one who really has any memories of him."

"That's so sad," Andi said quietly and continued brushing the horse with a blank stare.

Norah nodded. "It's affected him the most obviously because he has those memories. Even now, twenty-three years later, he still feels the loss more than Luke and I. It's part of the reason why he has problems trusting people." Norah walked around to Andi and held her hand out for the brush.

"Well that's understandable." Andi handed the brush over to Norah and pondered whether she should ask the question that just popped in her head. "Are there other reasons?"

"Oh, um…" Norah started, but stopped when she heard horses approaching the barn.

Andi turned to see Zane and Luke riding up to the barn on their horses. Her heartbeat went into double time as she gazed at Zane sitting tall on his jet black horse with his lasso looped around his shoulder. He smiled when he caught her staring at him and tipped his hat. Andi immediately felt embarrassed that he had caught her gawking at him and began to blush. She quickly dipped her head so he and the others wouldn't see her flaming red cheeks.

"You boys get in enough practice?" Norah asked, leading her mare out of the barn.

"Yes, ma'am. I've got a good feeling we're going to win this year," Luke said as he reached down to pat the side of his mare's neck. "Lady here comes out of that shoot quicker than a bolt of lightning. Hell, she's probably even faster than Cheyenne," Luke said with a smirk.

"Ha! Doubt that." Norah laughed.

Andi lifted her head, finally rid of the blush that had consumed her, and listened as Luke and Norah went back and forth about whose horse was faster. Zane dismounted from his own horse, looped the reins over its head and lead him into the barn where Andi stood.

"That's a really pretty horse," she said, attempting to strike up a conversation.

"Thanks," Zane replied. "You know much about horses?"

"Not really," she admitted. "What's his name?"

"I call him Cash," Zane said.

Andi gave him a puzzled looked. "You named your horse Cash?"

"Yea," he told her. "After one of my favorite singers."

She still looked confused.

"Johnny Cash," he explained. "You know, because he wore black all the time."

"Oh, okay." She still had no idea who he was referring to. "Do you want help brushing him?"

"Sure," he said as he began to unsaddle his horse.

Andi went to the tack room and grabbed the brushes she and Norah had just used. When she came back out, Luke was unsaddling his horse as well.

"You going to help me next?" Luke asked with a smile.

"Sure," Andi said and handed Zane one of the brushes. His fingertips grazed her hand as he took the brush from it, sending a warm tingling sensation up her arm and down her spine. "So what were you guys practicing for?"

"Zane and I compete in the calf roping competition," Luke explained.

Andi had no idea what calf roping was. Fearful of sounding like an idiot she decided not to ask. "Well that's nice."

"Have you ever competed in a rodeo?" Luke asked her.

"No, I can't say that I have," Andi replied.

"You really should. It's a lot of fun," Luke said. "You'd probably be good at doing barrel racing like Norah."

Andi let out a nervous laugh. "I don't know how good I'd be considering I've never ridden a horse." All of a sudden she could feel all of their eyes staring at her. "What?"

"You've really never ridden a horse?" Norah asked in disbelief.

"Really. Why?" Andi was confused as to why they had a hard time believing this.

"It's just kind of unheard of around here, that's all," Norah explained.

Luke opened his mouth to speak but was cut off by Zane. "You know Andi, if you ever wanted to learn how to ride I'd be more than happy to show you."

Luke stood there dumbfounded. Zane had just completely stolen his thunder.

"I think I'd like that," Andi said and smiled at Zane. He returned her smile and it reminded her of the dream she had last night. It was exactly how he had looked at her before he kissed her.

Silence filled the barn as they continued to brush his horse. Norah, feeling the tension that seemed to fill the room, decided now was a good time to turn her mare out to pasture and left the barn. Luke watched as Andi and Zane stole glances at one another from across the horse's back. His stomach began to twist into knots as a surge of jealousy ran through him. When he couldn't bear the sight of them any longer he stormed off to the tack room to get his own brush.

Chapter Eleven

"You ready?" Zane asked as he handed Andi the lead rope.

With a shaky hand, she took the rope and held it tight. She swallowed convulsively as she led the Buckskin mare from the pasture and towards the barn.

"Are you okay?" Zane said with concern in his voice. "You kind of look like you're going to throw up.

"I'm fine," she lied. She was nervous as hell. The thought of climbing onto the back of this large creature scared the living daylights out of her. They made their way to the barn and Zane instructed her to hook the mare up to the rope attached to the stall. Moments later he was back with the bridal, saddle, and blanket.

"Okay, I'm going to show you how to do this. The next time we have lessons I'll have you do it with my instructions. After that I'll expect you to know how to do it yourself," he said and watched as Andi's face went blank and all the color drained from it. "Are you sure you're okay?"

Andi nodded sheepishly. "What do you do first?"

She watched and paid attention to Zane's instructions as he saddled the horse. *I'm never going to remember this.*

"And that's how it's done," he said, taking a step back from the horse. "Simple. Right?"

"You did that really fast," she said.

Zane chuckled. "Years of practice m'dear. Let's lead her out to the corral and we'll get started."

He handed the reins over to Andi as they made their way out to the corral. When they reached their destination, Andi walked the horse through the opening and Zane shut the gate behind them then walked over to where Andi was waiting. He instructed her to slide the reins over the horse's head then gently took hold of Andi's arm and led her to the side of the horse.

"Okay, now what you want to do is take your left hand and grab the saddle horn, then put your left foot in the stirrup, grab hold of the back of the seat with your other hand and hoist yourself up, swinging your right leg over to the other stirrup," he instructed.

"You want me to grab hold of what and put my foot where?" she asked confused.

Zane let out a soft laugh and sighed. "Okay, this here is what we call a saddle horn," he said pointing to it. "And this thing here is the stirrup. This is where your foot goes."

"Oh, okay," she said a little embarrassed. She followed his instructions and attempted to hoist herself up with no success.

"Want some help?" he asked.

"Please," she said with an exasperated sigh.

Zane stood next to the horse and cupped his hands. "Okay, put your foot in my hands and I'll hoist you up."

Still holding onto the saddle horn, she did just that.

"Ready? One, two, three." Zane lifted his hands and Andi flung her leg over the horse's back. But the momentum from his generous help kept her in motion and instead of staying in the saddle she slipped and landed in the dirt.

Zane quickly ran around to the other side of the horse. "Holy crap, are you all right?"

"Ow," she said, pushing herself into a sitting position.

"Did you bruise your butt?" he asked, holding back a chuckle.

"Ha, ha," she replied.

"I'm sorry. I've just never seen anyone do that before, outside of the movies," he said. "Here, let me help you up."

He held out his hand and she accepted it, allowing him to pull her to a standing position. Andi brushed the dirt from her jeans and walked back around to the other side of the horse with Zane. Zane stood next to the horse again and cupped his hands like before.

"I think I'll try it without your help this time," Andi told him.

He smiled and took a step back as he watched her attempt it on her own. "Try hopping a little," he suggested.

She gave him a suspicious look.

"Seriously, try it," he encouraged.

Andi listened to his advice and was successful in her attempt this time. "Ah ha! I did it!" she exclaimed.

Zane smiled at how pleased Andi was with herself. "Okay, now grab hold of the reins. All I'm going to do is walk you around the corral a few times and then I'm going to let you try it yourself."

The excited feeling quickly faded from her body and was instantly replaced with fear. She gripped the reins with her right hand and held onto the saddle horn with her left as Zane led the mare around the corral. To her surprise there was nothing to be scared about. Zane kept the pace nice and slow and kept glancing back at her to make sure she was doing okay. After a few laps around the corral, she became more comfortable and let go of the saddle horn, resting her hand on her thigh.

"You think you're ready to try it by yourself?" he asked, pulling the horse to a stop.

Andi bit her bottom lip. "I think so."

He stepped away, walking backwards towards the center of the ring, and let her take the mare around the corral by herself.

"This is easy!" she called out to him with a smile on her face.

Zane laughed in response. "All you're doing is walking."

She brought the mare over to where he was standing and pulled her to a stop. "Okay, well show me how to do the harder stuff."

"You sure?" he asked a bit skeptically.

"If you can do it, I can do it," she told him with a smile.

"All right," he said. "Lead her over to the railing. We're going to start out walking then I'm going to urge her into a trot."

Andi followed his instructions and began to walk the mare around the corral again. She heard him click his tongue a couple of times on the roof of his mouth and was surprised when the horse began to trot. Andi quickly grabbed hold of the saddle horn again to keep her balance. It felt like she was going to bounce right out of the saddle. "Am I doing this right?" she called out to Zane.

"You look too stiff," he said. "You kind of want your body to go limp and move with the horse."

She listened and found his instructions helpful.

"That looks better," he called out to her. "You want to take her into a canter?"

"Sure," Andi said, although she was unsure what a canter was.

Zane clicked his tongue again and the mare picked up speed into a graceful jog. "You're bouncing too much," he told her.

"Well, how do I stop bouncing?" she asked, trying to pay attention and keep from falling off.

"Stay loose," he told her. "Focus on keeping rhythm with the horse."

She tried following his directions but still found it hard not to bounce all over the place.

"Andi, don't put any pressure on your feet and rock your hips with the rhythm of the horse." A sly smile spread across his face. "Try to mimic the way you move when you have sex," he suggested with a chuckle.

"What!" she exclaimed and heard his deep throaty laugh from the middle of the ring. Although she found the suggestion preposterous, she tried it and to her surprise it worked.

Zane watched as Andi followed his suggestion and was instantly glue to the way she moved with the horse. He felt his heart rate quicken and a tingling sensation came from deep down in his stomach and traveled throughout his body. His imagination began to take off and think of things that had nothing to do with horseback riding.

"How does this look?" she asked. "Am I doing it right?"

Zane swallowed hard. "Yes, you're doing it right. I'd say you're a natural." He cleared his throat and called out for the horse to slow down.

Andi reached down and pat the side of the mare's neck as she walked over to Zane. "That was fun," she said breathlessly.

"Glad you liked it," he said with a smile. "I think that's enough for one day. We can pick back up tomorrow."

As he and Andi made their way back to the barn, all he could think about was how amazing she looked riding that horse and how he desperately needed a cold shower.

****

Over the course of the next few days, Zane and Andi continued with their riding lessons. Zane stayed off to the side mostly, just watching as he let Andi do all of the commands herself. She was even able to saddle her own horse, although Zane had to assist her in tightening it. One day, as Andi was making her way out to the barn for her usual lessons, she was surprised to see Zane leading two horses from the barn.

"Why do you have Cash saddled as well as Dolly?" she asked confused.

"I thought we'd venture outside the corral today and take a ride down to the creek," he said handing over Dolly's reins to her. She went to put her foot in the stirrup and he stopped her. "I got something for you." He reached to the saddle horn and grabbed the off white cowboy hat that he had perched there. He placed it on her head and gave her an approving smile. "There, now we're ready to go riding."

Andi smiled and thanked him for the hat. "Does it look good on me?"

He chuckled softly. "It looks very nice." Zane stood next to her horse and waited till she was in the saddle before he mounted his.

As they rode out of the yard, Andi was amazed by the scenery of the open field. The deep green grass rippled with the light breeze and the pale blue sky was crystal clear. They rode in silence for the majority of the trip, occasionally chatting about the scenery or the wildlife Zane pointed out to her. After a while, she caught the faint scent of wildflowers and just knew they had to be close to their destination. They approached the trickling water and dismounted from their horses.

"Why don't you go pick a spot to sit and I'll tie the horses up," Zane suggested.

She walked over and picked a shady spot underneath of an old oak tree and waited for Zane to join her. Moments later he was by her side and sat down next to her. He removed his hat, setting it on the ground next to him, and ruffled his hair. Andi too removed her hat and ran her fingers through her thick strands, hoping she didn't have hat hair.

"Well this is nice," Zane said, resting his arms over his drawn up knees. He picked a wildflower from the patch next to him and twirled it with his fingers.

"It's really peaceful here," Andi replied.

There was a long moment of silence before either of them spoke.

"So," Zane said, not sure what to talk about.

"So," Andi replied with a smile and nodded.

"Tell me about yourself, Miss Andi Ford," he said and leaned back onto his elbow. He was hoping that all of his nice gestures lately would finally get him somewhere with getting information out of her.

Andi sighed. "What do you want to know?"

Zane had to hold back his excitement. "Everything really," he said. "Where you're from, your parents and so on."

"Those are really hard questions for me to answer, Zane. If I'm giving up answers about my past, you're going to have to answer some questions for me." She gave him a serious look and waited for his response.

"Deal," he said. "I'll even let you go first." He couldn't imagine what kind of questions she would have for him, but determined that they couldn't be that bad.

"All right," she said and turned to face him. "I want to know the reason behind you hating me so much when I first came here. I know we didn't have the greatest first meeting, but that couldn't have been the whole reason behind your dislike for me. And I know you didn't trust me at first, and I keep getting the excuse that you have trust issues. Norah explained part of the story to me but never finished."

Zane's expression went from expectant to shocked. "What did Norah tell you?"

"She told me all about how your father left when you were little and how you're the only one who remembers him. She said that was only part of the reason, so I want to know the rest." She looked at him and watched as he sighed and moved back into a sitting position.

"You better answer my questions after this," he said.

She crossed her heart and held her hand up. "I promise."

"Okay, yes I did get most of my trust issues from when my father left. The second part of the story happened about a year and a half ago. Luke and I were at The Rusty Spur having our usual night out when this tall, blonde, Texas beauty queen named Brianna Wilkinson walked in. She was just passing through town and had gotten a flat, so I offered to fix it for her. One thing led to another, we ended up going out that night, and we hit it off. She ended up staying in town, we continued to see each other, and it became serious. After we had been dating for a few months I decided that she was the one and I asked her to marry me. We had a big affair planned at the ranch for October of that year."

Zane paused and watched the ripples in the water for a long moment. "The last time I saw her was the night before our wedding. I kissed her goodnight, told her that I loved her and that I couldn't wait to be married to her. After that I left her alone because we had agreed not to see each other until the ceremony." He looked to see Andi's expression.

She looked at him intently waiting for him to go on. "What happened to her?" she asked quietly.

He let out an exasperated sigh and continued. "Well, the morning of the wedding came and she and my best man were nowhere to be found. Norah found a note on the nightstand in the room Brianna was supposed to be in explaining that she and Dean, my best friend and best man, had fallen in love and she couldn't get the courage to tell me to my face. That was the second time in my life that someone I loved left a note saying that they didn't want anything to do with me anymore."

Andi reached out her hand and laid it over his. "I'm so sorry, Zane."

He cleared his throat and looked at her hand upon his. "I guess you coming into town kind of reminded me of the whole thing. Beautiful stranger shows up and attracts my interest," he said and added a soft laugh. "I actually didn't realize how ridiculous it sounded till just now. I'm sorry for being such a jerk."

Andi looked at him and smiled.

"What?" he asked, smiling back.

"You think I'm beautiful?" she asked.

Zane felt his heart flip as he stared into her twinkling eyes. "Well, yea."

Andi stared back at him and tucked her hair behind her ear.

Zane's gaze fell to her lips for a brief moment, but then he cleared his throat and looked away. "But enough about my sob story. Let's hear yours."

Andi knew this part was coming and she quickly rehearsed her lines in her head before beginning. "All right. Well, I grew up in Pennsylvania in a town called Summerville; it's just outside of Pittsburgh. I've lived in town and the city my whole life, but I'm sure you already guessed that, huh?"

He laughed and nodded his head in agreement. "Yea, I can most definitely tell that you're a city girl. That and the fact that when I first met you, you were driving around in a Mercedes Benz."

"Oh yea," Andi said, just knowing what he was going to ask her next.

"Speaking of," he started.

Here we go.

"Why *did* you get rid of your car?" he asked.

She sighed. "Honestly? I hated that car."

"You hated your Mercedes Benz?" he said incredulously. "Don't hear many people say that."

"Is it bad that I wanted something a little simpler? That maybe I didn't want that car and the life it represented?"

Zane looked at her then, his deep blue eyes holding hers as a slow smile spread across his face. "No, that's not a bad thing. Is that part of the reason you moved here? Wanting a simpler life?" A part of him, the less believing part of him, wondered how truthful she was being with him.

"Yes," she answered honestly. "That and the fact that I didn't have a reason to stay there anymore. With my parents gone, I felt no need to stay put."

"What happened to your parents?" he asked cautiously.

"Um," she started, then paused to take in a deep breath. Her parents' death was something she never talked about. It brought back to many painful memories. But she decided that since Zane had told her of his painful past that she sort of owed it to him to be truthful with some parts of her story.

"Well, my father developed lung cancer when I turned twenty-two. He went through the treatments but never did get better. He died a year later on an early spring morning." She took in a shaky breath and looked to the ground so Zane wouldn't be able to see the tears filling her eyes.

"My mother didn't handle his death well at all. He was her whole life and the fact that he wasn't around anymore sent her into a deep depression. We started to argue all the time and it got to the point where it was hard for me to be around her. I spent most of my time with my…friends." She had to catch herself for instead of friends she was about to say boyfriend, and that would lead to the story she *never* wanted to tell him.

"One day I came home from my friend's house to get some clothes. I remember walking in and calling her name but got no answer. Her car was in the driveway so I knew she had to be there. I kept calling her name and searching for her throughout the house. And then I found her lying on the bedroom floor with an empty bottle of pills on the nightstand." Andi's voice broke as she brought her hands up to her face and began to sob into them.

Zane was taken aback by how this story was affecting her. A few moments ago he was thinking everything she told him was a lie, and now he was starting to think she'd been telling the truth after all. The thing that bothered him most right now though was seeing her so upset. "Andi, are you okay?" he asked with concern in his voice.

She nodded, wiping a tear away from her cheek with her fingertips. "It's just hard to talk about. I can't even remember the last words my mother and I shared. I don't even think I told her I loved her."

"I'm sure she knew," Zane said, reaching out his hand and placing it on her shoulder.

"I loved them both so much and it's difficult not having them around," she said as another round of tears began.

"Oh, Andi," Zane said and pulled her into his chest, wrapping his arms tightly around her and resting his head on top of hers. As she cried, he stroked the back of her hair and couldn't help but think about how nice it felt holding her in his arms.

When Andi was able to control her tears, she gently pulled away from Zane's chest and wiped her eyes. She looked at him and let out an anxious laugh. "Boy, we're a mess aren't we? Here we are supposed to be having a nice time and all we've done so far is share sob stories about our past."

Zane smiled and let out a soft chuckle as well. "Yeah, I guess you're right," he said brushing a loose strand of hair behind her ear. He paused when he realized what he was doing. For the past year or so, he had been careful around women; making sure he didn't get too close so he wouldn't get his heart broken again. But Andi seemed different from every other woman he had ever met and he was having a hard time following his own rules. Unable to help himself, he looked into her dark brown eyes and instantly became lost in them.

Andi noticed the look in his eyes and it automatically reminded her of her dream again. She wanted to know if his kiss would be as wonderful in real life as it had been in her dream. As if she had made the request out loud, Zane leaned toward her and she prepared herself for her wish to come true.

The light sound of movement through grass caught both of their attentions before the kiss could happen. Zane looked from Andi to the tree where the horses were tied and noticed Cash wasn't there. He looked around and saw the gelding twenty feet away grazing in the tall grass.

"Damn horse," he cursed under his breath as he got up and called for Cash to come back. The horse perked his head up at Zane's whistle and came trotting back to the tree.

Andi had made her way over as well and handed Zane his hat while placing her own back on her head. "We should probably head back I guess," she said with sadness in her voice due to the ruined moment.

"Guess we should. I promised Luke I'd help him with some stuff and he's probably waiting on me." Zane walked over and got Andi's horse for her and handed her the reins. He was a little ticked off that a horse of all things ruined his chance to kiss her. He climbed into his saddle and they began to ride back towards the house. It was a silent ride, as neither one of them really knew what to say. The quietness provided Zane with nothing but time to think. He had to hold back a chuckle as he thought about how funny it was that less than a week ago he was trying everything he could to get rid of this woman; and now he was thinking of everything he could do to make sure she stayed. All of his rules seemed to disappear and he found himself falling for Andi.

Chapter Twelve

Luke drove into the yard just as Zane and Andi approached the barn on horseback. He gritted his teeth at the sight of them together and cursed under his breath. Today had been bad enough as it was and seeing the pair of them together was the icing on the cake. As he slowly pulled up towards the house he watched as Zane dismounted from his horse then walked over and helped Andi down from hers, letting his hands slide up her waist and around her back once she was settled on the ground. Luke's blood began to boil when he saw the adoring look they were sharing.

He cursed under his breath and slammed the gear shift into park. Filled with anger and jealously, Luke decided he better cool himself down before exiting the truck cab and heading towards the barn where Zane and Andi were. It took him a few minutes until he was finally able to breathe normally and stop from shaking. He reached for the door handle and noticed Andi walking away from Zane and towards the house with a love struck grin on her face. Luke rolled his eyes and stepped out of his truck, sucking in a breath of air and rubbing his right thigh.

"Ouch." He limped around to the bed of the truck, grabbed his farrier tools, and headed off towards the barn.

By the time he arrived at the barn, Zane had both horses unsaddled and was giving them a quick brush. He entered the barn and noticed Zane do a double take.

"What happened to you?" Zane asked, tossing the brush towards the tack room and giving Luke a concerned look.

"Nothing," Luke mumbled without looking at Zane and brushed past him.

Zane stumbled backwards and lost the concerned look. "Okay. If you're not going to tell me what happened to you then you can at least tell me what the attitude is for."

Luke walked into the tack room without responding and began to put away his tools.

"The silent treatment is pretty childish," Zane said.

Luke still didn't respond.

"Are you mad at me because I didn't go over to Grandpa's and help you with the horses? I didn't mean to lose track of time, it just kind of happened," Zane explained.

Luke let out a sarcastic huff and shook his head. He finished putting the last tool away and hobbled back to the stalls where Zane was standing. If Zane wanted to know what his problem was then he was certainly going to let him have it.

"Yes I am mad at you. It's because of you that I ended up with a bruise the size of Texas on my thigh. If you hadn't been fooling around with that stranger you despise so much then it wouldn't have taken me all afternoon to get all of Grandpa's horses' feet trimmed, and I wouldn't have gotten kicked by that new filly he has," Luke explained heatedly.

Zane held his hands up in defeat. "All right I'm sorry. I didn't mean for you to get hurt. I'll make sure next time I hang out with Andi that I don't lose track of time."

Luke could feel his blood begin to boil again. "And that's another thing," he said, his voice increasing in volume. "Why the hell are you spending so much time with her lately?"

"Are you jealous?" Zane asked giving Luke a puzzled look.

"I'm not jealous, Zane. I'm pissed off!"

Zane let out a sigh, rolled his eyes and crossed his arms. "All right, Luke. Why are you pissed off?"

"Don't talk to me like that," Luke said with frustration and shoved Zane's shoulder.

Zane, caught off guard, stumbled backward slightly. "Talk to you like what? I'm trying to find out why you're pissed off," he retorted and shoved Luke back.

"You knew I liked her and you just swooped in and knocked me out of the picture. Big man Zane McKade stealing his brother's love interest," Luke spouted out with a sarcastic tone and shoved Zane once more.

Zane gave Luke an irritated look. "I didn't just swoop in and steal her. And how was I to know you really liked her when you hit on every woman you see? Get over it little brother," Zane said and shoved Luke back so hard he fell back into the hay bales that were stacked along the wall.

Luke recovered from the fall quickly and charged Zane, grabbing him around the waist and slamming him into the horse stall door. Zane felt the whoosh of air escape from his lungs and brought his arms around to Luke's waist, attempting to break his hold. As they wrestled, they lost their footing and fell to the floor. A cloud of dirt and dust surrounded them as they rolled around, each of them cursing at the other and attempting to get in one good punch. The two horses that were still tied to the stall doors began to prance nervously and pull at the ropes holding them in place.

"Stop being a baby, Luke!" Zane yelled and blocked Luke from hitting him.

"Stop being a jerk!" Luke yelled back. "You'd think you'd learn not to do what Dean did to you when he stole Brianna from right underneath your nose!"

Zane, shocked by the words Luke just said, stopped fighting back and gave Luke a blank stare.

Not realizing Zane had stopped, Luke brought his right hand back and around, connecting it with Zane's right eye.

"Dammit, Luke!" Zane said grabbing his eye and rolling over. "Enough already." Still holding his eye, Zane stood up and walked over to the horses to calm them down.

Luke stood up as well and began to brush the dirt and sawdust from his clothes.

"Is that really how you feel?" Zane asked, turning to Luke.

Luke nodded. "Well, yeah. But the thing that doesn't make sense to me is that you don't even like her, yet here you are spending all this alone time with her. I know you're up to something. I can see your mind working some sort of evil plan to get into her brain and make her want to leave."

Zane let out an exasperated sigh and began to brush his clothes off as well. "Look Luke, I wasn't trying to steal her away from you, okay? And you're right, I was trying to come up with a way to get her out of our lives because I didn't trust her."

"Was?" Luke asked. "So what you've given up on trying to get her to leave now?" He couldn't remember a time when he felt more confused and frustrated at the same time.

"Yes," Zane simply stated.

"Why the sudden change?" Luke asked, his voice more even and calm now.

Zane shook his head. "It's not worth arguing over anymore. I'm not going to let a woman come between us. You're my brother and my best friend and, if you want me to, I'll stay away from her from now on."

Luke's expression went from one of confusion to realization in an instant. "You like her don't you?"

"I said I'm not going to argue over it anymore, Luke." Zane walked over and unhooked both horses' lead ropes from the stalls and began to take them out to the pasture.

Luke followed behind him. "I'm not arguing, Zane, just tell me the truth. Do you like her?"

Zane opened the gate and turned both horses loose. "Yes, I like her," he confirmed without looking at Luke. Zane turned then to face his younger brother and let out a long sigh. "I haven't felt this way since Brianna."

"Really?" Luke asked in disbelief.

Zane nodded and headed back to the barn.

"Well hell, why didn't you say something?" Luke asked. "If I had known that you really had feelings for her I wouldn't have been so pissed off. I thought you were just trying to mess with her and break her heart so she'd leave and never come back."

Zane entered the barn and hung the ropes on the wall. "I didn't really know that I liked her until a few days ago. She's amazing and I find myself wanting to be with her all the time."

"You're that serious about her?" Luke asked.

Zane nodded and began to walk to the house and Luke followed.

"Well," Luke began and sighed. "I sure didn't see that coming."

They walked in silence for a few moments and Luke took in everything that had just happened. Zane had finally found someone to fill the hole the Brianna had left. And what kind of a man would he be to stand in the way of that? Yes he did have a small amount of feelings for Andi, but Zane seemed to have truly and deeply fallen for her. He let out a sigh and wrapped his arm around Zane's shoulder, giving it a gentle squeeze.

"You know, brother," Luke said. "As much as it breaks my heart to just let her go, I guess I can let you have her; but only because it's you. If it were any other man I'd stand my ground and fight if I had to," he joked.

"Then what would you call that back in the barn?" Zane asked with a chuckle.

"That was a misunderstanding between brothers," Luke replied with a grin. "You know, as much as this whole thing pissed me off, I don't think I stood a chance with her anyway."

"Why's that?" Zane asked confused.

"I've seen the way she looks at you, and I'm pretty sure everyone else has noticed it to." Luke said. "That girl has fallen for you."

Zane couldn't hold back the smile that tickled the corners of his mouth. After all these years he had finally found someone who made him happy. He looked to the house and saw Andi standing on the porch, leaning against the post. She smiled and waved, and for a moment Zane saw what his future could be like.

He envisioned a life with Andi, spending their days working side by side on a ranch of their own and spending their nights locked in each other's embrace. And maybe down the road there would even be a few kids in the picture.

Luke removed his arm from Zane's shoulder and tipped his hat toward Andi as he walked up the porch steps. She smiled as he walked past, glanced over his dusty clothes and turned her attention toward Zane.

"Why are you covered in dirt?" she asked as she brushed her hand over his shirt attempting to remove some of the dust.

"Luke and I had a misunderstanding," he replied with a smile.

Andi gave him a curious look but decided not to ask. "Well come on, dinner's on the table," she said sweetly and held her hand out for his.

He took her hand tenderly in his and intertwined their fingers as an electric current ran up his arm and down his spine. "Andi, wait a second," he said, pulling her to a stop.

"What is it Zane?" she asked, staring into his deep blue eyes.

Without saying a word, Zane leaned down and pressed his lips to Andi's. As his lips caressed hers, he wrapped his arms around her waist and pulled to her him, molding her body to his.

Andi felt her legs go numb and wrapped her arms around Zane's neck to keep from falling. His kiss was even better than in her dream. With every brush of his lips against hers she felt dizzier and soon realized that she was holding her breath. She reminded herself to breathe and as she did the woodsy scent of his aftershave sent her senses spiraling out of control.

Zane tenderly ended the kiss and slowly pulled away to look at Andi.

"What was that for?" she asked breathlessly.

He reached his hand up and gently brushed his fingertips down her cheek and along her neck. "Just wanted to know if it would feel as wonderful as I thought it would."

"And?" she asked raising an eyebrow.

"It did." He smiled crookedly and leaned down joining his lips with hers once more.

Chapter Thirteen

June 19

He kissed me. Words cannot describe just how wonderful it felt, but I'm sure going to try because I never want to forget that moment. One second we were about to walk into the house and in the next I was wrapped tightly in his embrace. The moment his arms were around me I felt my heart begin to pound uncontrollably like it was trying to escape from my chest. But when his lips met mine it stopped pounding and slowly melted, sending a warm tingly sensation throughout my entire body. I felt my legs turn to jelly and I wrapped my arms tightly around his neck for support. I swear if his arms weren't holding me up I would have collapsed right there. It was the most beautiful thing I have ever experienced. I've never known intimacy to feel so tender and sweet. But then again, I've never known anyone like Zane before either.

Andi bustled about the bar passing out drinks and taking orders. She was making her way back to the bar with her empty tray in hand when she felt a pair of arms slip around her waist from behind her. Without thinking, she quickly maneuvered out of the stranger's arms and wacked him on the arm with her tray. When she got a good look at who the stranger was, she dropped her guard and immediately began to apologize.

"Oh my gosh, Zane, I am so sorry!" She set the tray down on the table next to her and gently grabbed his arm.

Zane let out a soft chuckle. "Hey it's my own fault. I should have known better than to try to surprise you like that. At least you didn't break my nose or anything."

Andi laughed, remembering the last encounter she had with Gus where he ended up on the floor with a bloody nose. "Yes, that would have been bad."

Zane took a step towards her and wrapped an arm around her waist, drawing her close. "So are you getting a break anytime soon?" he asked in a smooth deep voice.

"Maybe," she playfully said and tilted her head back so she could look into his eyes. "What did you have in mind, cowboy?"

A mischievous grin spread across his face and he leaned in to whisper in her ear.

Andi gasped in shock and playfully slapped his shoulder. "Zane McKade, you dirty dog! I am not that kind of girl."

Zane laughed wholeheartedly and sighed. "All right then. How about a dance?"

"Now *that* I can do," she said with a smile.

Zane took her hand and led her across the dance floor to the jukebox. He pulled a quarter from his pocket, placed it in the machine, and selected a slow song.

"Nice choice," Andi complimented as Zane led her out to the middle of the dance floor.

He wrapped his right arm around her waist and let it slide to her lower back as he slowly began to turn them in a small circle. Andi rested her head against his chest and as she did Zane caught the fruity scent of her shampoo. He took in a slow deep breath and enjoyed how wonderful it felt to hold her in his arms. The song seemed to end way too soon and Zane reluctantly stopped their dance but still held her close.

"I don't want to let you go," he said so quiet that it was almost a whisper.

Andi smiled and caught her bottom lip between her teeth. "I don't want you to either."

Zane leaned down and pressed his lips against hers for one long sweet and tender kiss. The sound of someone clearing their throat caught their attention and they turned to see who it came from.

"Sorry to interrupt," Red said with a smirk. "But I could use my waitress's help for the rest of the night. It's almost closing time and after that ya'll can keep on with your smooching."

"Aw, come on Red. Can't I keep her for another minute?" Zane joked and pulled Andi even closer.

"No, sir," Red said. "You'll have her all to yourself for the next two days while ya'll are off at the rodeo."

"Are you sure you'll be okay with both me and Norah not here to help?" Andi asked to Red.

"Aw hell, I could run this place blindfolded with one hand tied behind my back. I'll be fine, don't you worry," Red said with a nod and headed back towards the bar.

"Guess I better get back to work." Andi sighed.

"All right, I guess I'll just have to wait till later for some more smooching," Zane teased and gave her a crooked smile.

She stood on her tip toes and gave him a quick peck on the lips. "I'm looking forward to it," she whispered against his lips and headed back towards the bar.

****

The late June sun hung high in the sky as Zane and Luke took care of unloading the horses from the trailer. Andi leaned against the tire and fanned herself with her hand.

"You doing all right?" Norah asked as she came around the end of the horse trailer with her Palomino and all decked out in her rodeo gear. She wore a turquoise western style shirt with red roses embroidered across the back of the shoulders, black fitted jeans, shiny black boots and a black cowboy hat.

"I'm fine," Andi lied. The midday heat was going to kill her. She had no idea how they were handling it so well seeing as all three of them were wearing long sleeves, and she was having a hard time staying cool in her sleeveless button up.

Zane came over with Cash, tied his lead rope to the horse trailer, and adjusted the saddle making sure everything was tight. Andi took in his appearance and marveled at how amazingly handsome he looked in his dark blue jeans, brown boots, white cowboy hat and western cut shirt that was the exact same shade of blue as his eyes.

"So what time is the calf roping again?" Andi asked him.

"We've got to be at the corral at twelve-thirty. So that gives us about a half hour," he told her. "Why?"

"Just asking," she groaned and wiped a bead of sweat from her forehead.

Zane gave her a concerned look and walked over to the bed of the truck. He leaned over the side and opened a cooler that contained iced down water bottles. He grabbed two bottles and headed back towards Andi, handing one over to her and keeping one for himself. "There you go and there's plenty more in the cooler."

She took a few long sips, closed the lid, and placed the bottle against her cheek. "God bless you, Zane." She sighed as the cold bottle gave her some relief from the intense heat.

He chuckled softly and took a sip from his bottle.

"Zane? Zane McKade?" a man's voice called from the end of the horse trailer.

Zane turned his head in the direction he heard his name being called and saw a tall, lean cowboy walking in his direction.

"Well I'll be damned, it is you! How you been?" the cowboy asked, reaching his hand out and shaking Zane's.

"Been doing good, Ty. What's it been? Two years since I've seen you last?" Zane replied in a friendly tone.

"At least," Ty said turning his attention to Andi. "Hello there, sweet thing. I'm Ty Murray."

"Andi Ford," Andi replied and shook Ty's hand.

"My girlfriend," Zane added and wrapped his arm around her shoulders proudly.

Girlfriend. It was the first time Zane had referred to her as that. And she had to admit, she rather liked the sound of it.

"Nice to meet you," Ty said, tipped his hat and turned to Zane. "Ya'll staying the night?"

"That's the plan," Zane said. "And we'll head back home in the morning."

"Well if ya'll ain't got plans I'm having a shindig at my place tonight. We got a band, a bonfire, barbeque and plenty of beer for everyone. Ya'll should stop by for a bit, I'm sure there'd be a lot of people who'd like to see you," Ty said.

"That's a nice offer, Ty, and I'm sure we'll end up stopping by at some point," Zane said. "Just let me talk it over with Norah and Luke first."

"Talk to us about what?" Luke asked and smiled when he noticed who Zane was talking to. "Ty! How you been?"

Ty shook Luke's hand and tipped his hat to Norah. "I was just telling old Zane here that I'm having a party at my place tonight. Told him ya'll should stop by."

"Well hell I'm in! I can't remember the last time I went to a Ty Murray party. 'Course I don't always end up remembering most of my night when I go to a Ty Murray party either," Luke said with a laugh.

"I'm in too," Norah chimed in.

"All right, well I'll see ya'll around seven then." Ty said his goodbyes and headed off towards the bleachers.

"We best be getting over to the corral before they a start without us," Luke suggested to Zane and asked Norah to pin his numbered paper on the back of his shirt.

Zane turned to Andi and handed his paper over to her. "Would you mind?"

"Not at all." She pinned the piece of paper to the back of his shirt and let her eyes wander south of his back to admire just how nice he looked in his Wranglers.

"You ready?" Luke asked as he went to stand next to Zane.

"Just a second, I've got to get my good luck kiss before I go," Zane replied with a smirk and leaned down to join his lips with Andi's.

She reached her hands around to the back of his neck and twisted her fingers in his hair. It had grown out from the first time she saw him and was now beginning to curl slightly at the ends. She loved how it looked on him and hoped he wouldn't break down and end up cutting it.

"Good luck," she said as the kiss ended. "I'll be over with Norah in just a few minutes to watch you."

"I'll be looking for you," he told her and winked.

He smiled and the sight of it made her feel weak in the knees. He began to walk away but stopped when he noticed Luke wasn't following.

With his reins in his hands, Luke walked up to Andi and tipped his hat off from his forehead, closed his eyes and leaned towards her puckering his lips.

"What are you doing?" she asked leaning away from him and giving him a suspicious look.

"I'm waiting for my good luck kiss too," he replied with his lips still puckered.

"Luke, come on stop messing around. You're going to make us late," Zane chided.

Luke didn't budge.

Andi rolled her eyes and sighed. She grabbed Luke's face, pinching his cheeks in as she turned his face to the side and gave him a small peck on the cheek. "There now go," she said with a laugh and pointed in Zane's direction.

Luke swung up into the saddle and adjusted his hat as he trotted his horse towards Zane.

Andi watched as Zane shoved Luke's shoulder and raised his hand like he was asking *"What was all that about?"*

Norah approached and looped her arm through Andi's. "Come on, let's go find some seats and cheer the boys on."

****

The yard was full of pickup trucks and horse trailers when the four of them pulled up to Ty's house. The western sky was filled with beautiful shades of purple, pink and orange as the sun began to set. Zane parked his truck in line with the others and stepped out of the vehicle, shaking his pant legs down in the process. He reached for the lever on the seat and pulled it forward so Andi could step out from the backseat. Before she could get settled on

141

the ground, Zane took her in his arms and planted one long, hot and steamy kiss on her lips.

"Have I told you how pretty you look in that dress?" he asked letting his eyes run over the simple pale yellow sun dress she was wearing.

"Thank you. You don't look half bad yourself there, cowboy." She was surprised that he had chosen to wear a black t-shirt instead of one of the western shirts he packed in his overnight bag. But then again she couldn't blame him for even though the sun was setting it still felt hotter than a bonfire in hell. Zane adjusted his white cowboy hat and took Andi's hand in his, leading her around to the front of the truck where Luke and Norah were waiting.

As they made their way around to the back of the house they could hear the band playing Tim McGraw's "Down on the Farm." Luke caught sight of a pretty little blonde wearing a white eyelet dress standing across the yard with a small group of other women.

He smiled his most charming smile when he caught her looking in his direction. She blushed, dipped her head, and looked up at him through her eyelashes.

Luke adjusted his hat and nodded in the blonde's direction. "Well, if ya'll are looking for me that's where I'll be for the rest of the night," he said before strutting across the yard.

Norah caught the sight of an old friend of hers and excused herself from Zane and Andi to go and talk to her.

"And then there were two," Zane said and wrapped his arm around Andi's waist. "What would you like to do?"

"Eat. I'm so hungry that I may end up clearing out the entire buffet table," she told him with a laugh.

Zane laughed with her and walked with her over to the buffet line. As they walked along the table they each took turns filling their plates with barbeque pork, chicken, corn bread, corn on the cob, potato salad and various other kinds of barbeque food. With their filled plates in hand they walked over to an empty picnic table and Andi took a seat. Zane set his plate down across from her and went to get them each a glass of sweet tea. Andi was just about to take a bite of her pulled pork sandwich when a tall and beautiful blonde woman approached her table.

"I'm sorry to bother you, sweetie, but is anyone else sitting here?" the lady asked in a smooth southern belle voice.

"No it's just my boyfriend and me. Help yourself." Andi said and gestured for the woman to take a seat.

"Thank you. My husband is making us plates and I told him I'd get us a seat," the lady said. "Shoo, I don't think I've ever seen Ty's place so packed before."

Andi took in the lady's appearance and wondered what a woman like that was doing at a back yard barbeque in the middle of nowhere Texas. With her perfectly curled hair and perfect makeup, down to her perfectly manicured nails and toes, she looked like she belonged on a runway in New York instead of sitting at an old picnic table with her.

"Say, I don't recall ever seeing you here before," the lady said catching Andi's attention. "You live around here?"

"I live east from here in a little town called Buford," Andi said cutting into her cornbread and spreading butter onto it.

The lady seemed to freeze at the mention of Buford but then seemed intrigued and leaned closer towards Andi. "Buford you say? You wouldn't happen to know the McKade's would you?"

Andi nodded as she took a bite of her cornbread. "Yes I do, actually," she said around a mouthful of food and swallowed. "I'm staying with them." Andi was starting to become annoyed at all the questions this stranger was asking her. Why was it any of her business anyway?

The lady's eyes popped wide open and her mouth gaped slightly. "So you know Zane then."

Andi nodded once more. "He's my boyfriend."

The two of them turned their heads as the sound of boots walking across the grass caught their attention. Zane froze in place with a cup of sweet tea in each of his hands and stared at the blonde lady.

"Hello Zane," the lady said. "It's been a long time."

Zane bit the inside of his cheek and gritted his teeth. Of all the places he'd been in the past year he'd never once imagined that he'd run into her here. "Brianna," he said with a tinge of irritation.

Andi sucked in a surprised breath and began to choke on the piece of cornbread she had just placed in her mouth. She coughed frantically until the piece of bread was clear from her throat.

"Are you okay?" Zane asked in a panic as he rushed to her side and patted her back.

"I'm fine," she coughed and wiped her eyes.

"Well," Brianna said dragging the word out. "This is quite awkward."

"Indeed," Zane agreed.

Andi wasn't sure what to say or if she should say anything at all. She just sat there and looked from Zane to Brianna, waiting to see what was going to happen.

"Look, I'm not trying to ruin anyone's night so I'll be on my way. It was good seeing you, Zane." Brianna smiled sweetly and walked over to the buffet tables toward Dean.

Zane turned to Andi and she noticed a flash of anger in his eyes. She held up her hands and told him, "I'm sorry I didn't know who she was. She didn't tell me before I told her it was okay for her to sit down."

He sighed and shook his head. "Andi, don't act like that. I'm not mad at you." He took both of her hands in his and laid them next to her sides. He leaned in and gently kissed her forehead. "I know that was probably just as awkward for you as it was for me. But let's try not to let it ruin our night, okay? You want to finish eating now?"

"Surprisingly, I'm not hungry anymore," she told him with a chuckle.

"You want to dance?" he asked in an upbeat tone. He didn't wait for her to answer. Instead he took her hand in his and quietly led them out to the grassy part of the yard that was marked off as a dance floor. They joined in with the other dancers and slowly swayed back and forth to the rhythm of the music. Andi leaned her head against his chest and listened to his heartbeat while they danced. It was more beautiful than any melody she had ever heard. The song came to an end and everyone clapped for the band. Ty took the stage and approached the microphone.

"Hey ya'll, everyone having a good time?" he said into the microphone. His voiced boomed loudly through the speakers placed throughout the property and everyone clapped and cheered. "Good, good. Has anyone seen Zane McKade?" Ty asked looking out into the crowd.

A murmur swam through the crowd and a sea of heads began to turn in every direction looking for Zane.

"Oh crap," Zane mumbled under his breath and froze.

"What's wrong?" Andi whispered leaning into him and giving him a concerned look.

"Here! He's here!" a man called out five people away from Zane and pointed in his direction.

Ty smiled and pointed to Zane. "Ah ha! Trying to hide are ya? Well not for long. Get your butt on up here and sing us a song."

Andi turned to Zane and saw that his face had lost all of his golden tan and now looked ghostly white. "Are you okay? What's he talking about singing?"

"Come on ladies and gents, give him a clap for encouragement," Ty said clapping his hands and standing back from the microphone.

"Damn it all to hell," Zane groaned and took in a deep breath.

"Are you going up there?" Andi asked.

"Can't really back out now, can I?" he said with a nervous laugh.

"Guess not," she agreed although she felt very confused.

Zane took in another deep breath and let go of Andi's hand. "I'll be right back," he said with a smile.

She watched as he made his way through the crowd and up the steps to the stage. A man greeted him at the top of the stairs and handed him a string guitar. He looped the strap over his head and shook hands with Ty before turning and talking to the rest of the band. When he approached the microphone he adjusted it to his height and greeted everyone.

"Well, for those of you who don't know me I'm Zane McKade."

The crowd cheered and whistled.

"We're gonna keep things slow. I'm gonna sing a little song by a country artist I'm sure ya'll know. It's a little number called "Must Be Doin' Somethin' Right" by Mr. Billy Currington. Here goes."

Zane stepped back from the microphone and began to strum the tune on the guitar as the rest of the band picked up with the song as well. Andi was amazed as she watched his fingers work the strings of the guitar. He looked in her direction, smiled and winked, and she felt every bone in her body melt. Zane stepped back up to the microphone and began to sing. His eyes never left hers throughout the duration of the song, and for a little fun he changed out the blue eyes lyrics to brown eyes for that personal touch. No one had ever made her feel so special in her entire life. In this one moment, with Zane on stage and keeping his beautiful blue eyes locked with hers while he sang to her, she felt like the only woman in the world. That was the kind of love she had yearned for; and she realized that she had found it in Zane.

Chapter Fourteen

Andi waited by the side of the house as Zane went to track down Luke and Norah.

"He's pretty good isn't he?"

Andi turned to see Brianna standing next to her staring at Zane as he walked away.

"Yes, he is," Andi agreed wondering why Brianna was talking to her.

"I'm sorry. We didn't get to do formal introductions earlier. I'm Brianna Wilkinson-Simpson."

Andi shook her outstretched hand. "Andi Ford."

"So, have you and Zane known each other long?" Brianna pried.

"Almost a month," she answered.

Brianna laughed under her breath and Andi gave her a confused look.

"Sorry, I was just thinking that after I knew him for only a few months we were engaged to be married," Brianna said. "Did he tell you that?"

"He did," Andi said and tapped her shoe on the grass wishing Zane would hurry back so she didn't have to sit here and talk to Brianna again.

"He's a good guy, Andi," Brianna told her. "You're a lucky woman."

Andi couldn't help herself. "If he's such a good guy then why didn't you marry him?"

Brianna gave her a shocked expression. "I was young at the time and stupid. I left because I was scared to be stuck in that small town for the rest of my life and be nothing but a rancher's wife. And when I met Dean, well, we shared the same idea of something better than country life; a house in the suburbs, nice cars, a nice cushy job for him in a corner office. I got all that but at what cost? I have a big beautiful house, a nice expensive car, and a husband who I barely see because he works all the time. That's not a marriage. That's not the kind of love I wanted. I had it all Andi, and I just let it go. If I could take it all back I would do it in a heartbeat."

Andi was surprised at what Brianna had told her. Did she really just basically admit that she was still in love with Zane and wished she had married him instead? "That was a pretty stupid mistake," Andi agreed.

"I know," Brianna said quietly. "Take care of him, Andi. Love him and hold on to him. Guys like that only come around so often."

Andi saw Brianna's eyes glisten with tears as Dean called for her from a distance. She watched as Brianna walked away and absorbed everything that just happened. Zane was back soon after with Luke and Norah.

"You ready for some camping?" he asked and reached for her hand as Luke and Norah walked past them and to the truck.

"Yea," Andi said as she looked away from Brianna and took Zane's hand.

****

The camp site was a fairly simple setup. It was a spot they picked every year when they went to the rodeo. Trees surrounded the small clearing that sat next to a small pond hidden by another set of trees. Zane and Luke took care of pitching two tents, one for the guys and one for the girls. Andi and Norah collected firewood and set up a campfire. The horses were unloaded from the trailer and tied to a line that was strung securely between two trees, allowing them to graze at will. Andi and Norah sat down on and old log next to the fire and watched as Luke moved his things from one tent to the other.

"Just what do you think you're doing?" Norah asked him.

"Switching my things with Andi's," Luke said. "I'm bunking with you tonight and Andi is staying with Zane."

Andi felt her heart drop into the pit of her stomach. Staying with Zane? Whose idea was this? Yes they had been staying under the same roof, but had never spent the night together.

Norah laughed softly when she caught sight of the look on Andi's face. "You look like a virgin on her wedding night. Why so nervous all of a sudden? You're just sharing a tent with him."

Instantly embarrassed from her reaction, Andi felt the heat flood her cheeks. She covered them with her hands, resting her elbows on her knees and attempting to hide the fact that she was blushing. The heat from the fire wasn't making it an easy task and she began to fan herself.

"Tell me again, why do we have to have a fire when it's already hot enough out here?" Andi asked, not specifically directing her question to a particular person.

"It keeps the bugs away," Luke said joining them with a beer in his hand. He let out a huge yawn and downed the rest of his beer in a few large gulps. "Well, I'm about done for one day. Think I'll be heading off to bed here in a few."

Zane emerged from his tent wearing a pair of khaki cargo shorts and a gray t-shirt. Andi felt the butterflies in her stomach begin to flutter like crazy. She rarely saw him without his usual cowboy getup. Although she found the cowboy stuff sexy, *extremely* sexy, she kind of liked this more laid back look as well.

"I'm all done in there if you want to change," he said to Andi, sitting down on the log next to her and picking up a stick. He twirled it around in his fingertips and let it spin on the tip of the flames.

"Luke!" Norah said shaking his shoulder before he passed out in the flames of the fire.

"Huh? What?" Luke exclaimed as he jumped up from the log.

"Go to bed before you end up hurting yourself," Norah suggested. "Here, I'll help you." She grabbed Luke by the arm and helped him into a standing position. "I guess I'll call it a night as well. See ya'll in the morning." She and Luke disappeared into the tent and she zipped it shut.

"Just you and me again." Zane grinned and looked to Andi. The flames from the fire highlighted every perfect feature of his face, from his strong smooth jaw to his high cheekbones.

"Guess so," she said and smiled back, trying to ignore the thoughts that proceeded to run through her mind. She stared into the flames of the fire, hoping that maybe she could burn the images from her head; but the heat radiating from the flames only reminded her of how hot his kisses made her feel. She quickly stood up and Zane gave her a surprised look.

"I'm going to go get dressed for bed," she said.

He nodded and she quickly walked over to the tent. Once she was inside, she zipped it shut behind her.

Andi rummaged through her duffle bag as she looked for her bed clothes. She groaned silently when she pulled out the pink tank top and pink plaid shorts. If she had known she'd be sharing a tent with Zane instead of Norah, she'd have packed something a little nicer; something a little sexier. With a sigh, she stepped out of her clothes and into the tank top and shorts. She grabbed her brush from her bag and roughly ran it through her hair. Lotion and body spray were the next items she pulled from her bag. After she was done with those, she decided that she'd put on a tiny bit of lip gloss and headed back out to Zane.

Zane inhaled deeply, breathing in the scent of her lotion that lingered in the air as she plopped down beside him on the log. God how he loved that smell. It was flowery but not the overpowering kind like most women wore. It was subtle and he had the strongest urge to lean in closer just to get a better whiff. He turned to look at her and smiled when she looked back.

"I don't know about you but I'm not really tired," he said, brushing a loose strand of hair from her face. "You wanna take a walk?"

"Sure," she said. "I'd like that."

"Okay. Just let me put this fire out first and then we'll go." Grabbing a bucket of water sitting next to the log, Zane lifted it to douse the flames. He then walked over to the truck and grabbed a flashlight and a quilt from the backseat. Andi waited patiently for him by the log and took Zane's hand when he approached, allowing him to lead her away from the camp site.

"Where are we going?" she asked.

"There's a quiet spot over there by the pond where we can talk and no one can hear us," he said and flashed his flashlight in the direction he was referring to. When they had reached their destination, Zane let go of her hand and spread the blanket on the ground.

"I had a really nice time today," she said as they sat down underneath a large oak tree. The moonlight danced along the ripples in the water as a warm breeze blew through the air.

"I'm glad you did. I had a nice time with you too." Zane sat down next to her at the water's edge and inched closer to her.

"I had no idea that you could play a guitar or sing like that. You have an amazing talent, Zane," she told him. "In my opinion you're so good that you should try to do it professionally."

Zane laughed softly and picked up a small stone from the ground next to him. He drew his hand back and skipped it across the water. "Nah, I don't know about all that."

"I'm not just saying it, Zane. I really believe it."

He turned his gaze from the moonlit pond to stare at her. The light bouncing off the soft ripples in the water were dancing across her face. He lifted his hand and gently brushed his fingertips across her forehead and down her cheek. As he leaned in to kiss her, he slid his hand down to her neck but was shocked beyond words when she slapped his hand. He quickly pulled back and gave her a confused look.

"Ouch! I swear these darn bugs are going to eat me alive!" Andi complained rubbing her neck.

Zane let out a sigh of relief and chuckled softly.

"Oh, I'm sorry," Andi apologized. "I didn't mean for it to seem like I didn't want you to kiss me. It's just that these bugs are horrible. Kind of makes me wish the fire was still going."

"There are other ways of keeping the bugs away." Zane gave her a mischievous smile and stood up. He pulled his t-shirt over his head and tossed it to the side.

Andi's breath caught in her throat as she let her eyes trail down from his face to his now shirtless torso. Sure she had seen him without a shirt before, but it had been a while and she had almost forgotten how perfect his body was. If she had her way he'd never wear one ever again. "What are you doing?" she whispered in shock.

"Taking a dip. Come on." He reached his hand out for hers and waited patiently for her to take it.

"I'm not getting in there." Andi shook her head disapprovingly and drew her knees up to her chest.

Zane shrugged. "Suit yourself." He stripped down to his boxers and walked slowly into the cool, still pond, stopping when the water rose above his hips. "The water's really nice, Andi. Come on and get in."

"I can't," she whispered loudly to him.

"Why not?" he asked. "Can't you swim? It's not deep right here."

"No," she whispered. "I can swim. It's just that…"

"Just what?" he asked, smiling and cocking his head to the side. He ran his hands atop the pond water, creating tiny ripples as he waited for her reply.

"I don't have a swim suit on," she explained with a shy tone to her voice.

"So what. Just come in with your bra and underwear." He shrugged. "It's the same thing."

Andi let out an exasperated sigh. "Zane," she whispered again.

"Andi," he whispered back mocking her.

She sighed once more. "I'm not wearing a bra or underwear," she said slowly.

It felt like a bolt of lightning had shot threw him, leaving his whole body tingling and sizzling. "Well that's…" he paused for a moment and swallowed hard "…unfortunate." He sat there for a minute and contemplated if he should dare suggest the next best thing. *What the hell*, he thought to himself. He reached under the water and carefully maneuvered out of his boxer shorts and tossed them to the shore.

"Now what'd you do that for?" Andi asked in a shocked tone as she glanced from his shorts, which were now crumpled in the grass, then back to him. "There," he said with a smirk. "Now I don't have a swim suit either."

Andi bit her bottom lip and felt the heat begin to flood her cheeks. The sharp pinch on her arm snapped her out of her trance and she quickly swatted at the bug. "Okay, okay. Turn around and don't peak." The light from the moon made it easy for her to see his questioning glare. "What?"

"Turn around?" Zane asked, trying to hold back a smile. "Need I remind you that I've seen you naked before, Miss Ford."

Her cheeks grew even warmer. "You just had to bring that up, didn't you?" Holding back a smile of her own, she gestured with her hand for him to turn around.

Zane grinned, closed his eyes and turned around to face the other side of the pond. He could hear the rustling of the bushes and assumed that she was laying her clothes on them. The sound of toes dipping in the water came next, then the splashing sound of someone diving in.

"Okay you can turn around now," she told him.

Zane turned to see Andi running her hands through her wet hair and wiping the water from her face. She was careful to keep everything from her chest down in the water as she made her way towards him.

"Feel better?" he asked.

She nodded. "Surprisingly, yes. No bugs and it's a little relief from the heat."

Zane gave her a crooked smile, and in that instant she was absolutely positive that he was up to no good. He held her gaze as he slowly sank into the water and began to swim in circles around her, reminding her of the way a shark stalks its prey.

"What are you up to?" she asked, attempting to sound flirtatious and sexy but not succeeding. Her voice was too breathless, too nervous, too excited.

"Up to?" Zane asked with that same mischievous smile. "I'm not up to anything. I'm just enjoying this moment and taking it in for all it's worth. It's not every day I get to take a middle of the night skinny dip with a beautiful woman."

Skinny dipping. The realization of what they were doing hit her like a ton of bricks in that moment. They were naked, in the middle of a pond, with Norah and Luke just a short walk away.

Oh God, what if someone sees us in here? she thought frantically to herself, sinking deeper into the pond till the water covered her shoulders.

She was all of a sudden consumed with an uncomfortable nervousness that made her want to forget all about skinny dipping and make a run for her clothes. Dear God, what was she thinking anyway? But then, as she stared across the glimmering water into Zane's blue eyes, the nervousness that had crept into the pit of her stomach quickly washed away with the adrenaline that now pulsed through her.

Zane stopped his circling and sank lower into the water, swimming in her direction. Her heart began to race and her breath quickened. He stopped a few feet away from her and reached his hand out across the top of the water for hers. Andi gently laid her hand in his and allowed him to pull her close, but the action was quicker than what she expected. She gasped in shock and immediately stiffened the moment her body collided with Zane's firm chest. All the nervousness she felt moments ago came back in a rush but for a completely different reason. She didn't mean to be frightened, and yet she was. Vince had been the only other man she'd been intimate with and, needless to say, he wasn't really a giving kind of man. He was a selfish lover, taking what he wanted, when he wanted it, and sometimes with or without her consent.

But Zane's not Vince, she told herself.

Feeling Andi tense, Zane loosened his grip slightly. "Did I hurt you?" he asked, his voice low and full of concern.

She shook her head as she looked down, diverting her eyes and quietly said, "No. You didn't hurt me."

"Did I scare you?"

She shook her head no again and turned her face slightly away from him.

"Hey," he said, gently taking her chin and forcing her face back to his. "Don't go all quiet on me, Andi. Something's bothering you. Am I doing something wrong here? Do you want me to stop?"

Once more she shook her head no and she briefly closed her eyes as Zane's fingers caressed her cheek.

"Then tell me what's going on in that beautiful

little head of yours." He smiled and waited patiently for her to answer.

Lord help her. She wanted to tell him exactly what was bothering her, but she just couldn't force the words through her lips. "It's just..." She paused taking in a deep breath and let it out slowly. "It's just been a while for me. I guess I'm just a little nervous, that's all."

Zane looked at her with such understanding and adoration that it almost made her want to cry. His fingers stroked her cheek and down the slender curve of her neck. "Close your eyes," he whispered and smiled crookedly at her confused expression. "Please, Andi. I'm not going to do anything weird or hurt you. Now, close your eyes."

Slowly her eyes fluttered shut and she was consumed in darkness with nothing but the sound of the frogs and the crickets and the water rippling around their bodies. Zane moved his hand to tangle his fingers in the damp, thick locks at the back of her neck as he slowly pulled her closer to him. His lips brushed against hers with careful, fleeting movements. Once. Twice. And on the third he parted his lips slightly, dipping his tongue out to trace her bottom lip. He moved both of his hands then, cupping her jaw with his thumbs resting in the hollow point beneath her ears.

When Zane moved in to kiss her again, Andi parted her lips and welcomed him most eagerly. His touch was soft, tender, and oh so thorough. Her head was buzzing from the slow, torturous kisses and that intoxicating feeling began to travel throughout the rest of her body, making her limbs numb and her knees begin to shake.

She pulled herself closer to him, attempting to plaster her body to his. Zane broke the kiss, moving his hands to her waist and feathering kisses along her jaw and down her neck. One hand slid up her taut stomach, grazed her ribcage and settled on her breast, teasing the hardened tip with the pad of his thumb.

"Oh, Zane." Andi moaned and tilted her head back as Zane continued to torture her with his warm lips against her throat and his work-roughed hands against her breast.

He toyed, he teased and the more he did the more the aching need to have him inside of her grew. His hand moved from her breast then, and she was just about to protest when she felt his hand glide along the curve of her hip and settle there, his thumb tracing lazy circles on her heated skin.

"Andi," he said, his voice low and husky.

"Hmm," she replied, the sound coming out more of a content moan rather than an actual "yes I'm listening" sound.

"You can open your eyes now."

Had she been keeping them shut the entire time? She let out a soft laugh and opened her eyes, blinking a few times until her eyes adjusted to the darkness of the night sky. After a few brief moments she lifted her eyes and found herself lost in Zane's familiar blue gaze. Every bit of desire and lust that she was feeling was reflected in his own eyes.

He cocked his head to the side and a sly smile spread across his face. "So are you still feeling nervous?" The hand on her hip moved painfully slow to the more sensitive skin of her inner thigh, inching closer and closer to her sweet spot, then retreating and making that agonizing journey back up her thigh.

"Yes," she sighed because, God, she wanted him to keep going. But then she quickly remembered his question and said, "I mean no."

Zane smiled and kissed the corner of her mouth, along her jaw and lightly grazed his teeth on her earlobe. "Well, which is it? Yes or no?" His voice was low and raspy and just the sound of it as it hit her ear made her stomach coil with anticipation.

"No, I'm not nervous anymore." How she even got the words out was beyond her. They came out so soft and rushed together that she was surprised he even understood her. Her heart was beating so fast and she desperately tried to keep her breathing calm and even, but was failing miserably.

"What do you want me to do, Andi?" he asked against the hollow of her neck, sucking gently on the tender spot between her neck and shoulder.

She shuddered.

He did it again.

Oh dear God. She couldn't think straight. With his hot mouth on her skin, and the hard length of his arousal pressing against her belly, and the way his fingers continued to tease her relentlessly—she was about to explode, and he hadn't even really done anything yet.

"Answer me, Andi. Tell me what you want."

She gasped as he sucked on that tender spot of

her neck and reached between her legs, cupping her femininity in his large, calloused hand.

"Oh my God, Zane," she breathed. "*You*. I want you."

A low growl came from deep down in Zane's chest as he crushed his lips to hers. His hands found their way to the back of her thighs and with one swift motion he lifted her to him. Andi moaned and wrapped her legs tightly around his waist as she let him carry her through the shallow end of the water to the shoreline.

Zane's lips never left hers as he gently laid her down at the shore with her back against the soft blanket. Her hands were in his hair and on the back of his neck as he continued to kiss her longer, deeper. His hands made their way back to her breasts and she arched against him, pressing herself harder into his hands. Letting out a low groan, Zane moved his lips down her neck and to her breast, trailing hot and wet open mouth kisses along her skin.

Andi let out a low moan and clutched onto Zane, making a disappointing little sound when his mouth left her breast. He continued to taste her skin but his kisses weren't taking him back to her mouth. His tongue swept along the contours of her stomach, her hip, her outer thigh and her inner thigh. A shudder rippled through Andi as she realized what he was doing and the fact registered in her mind that Vince had never taken the time to do any of this stuff. Pleasing her had been the last thing on his mind. Immediate satisfaction on his part was all that mattered to him. All thoughts of

Vince and what he didn't do left her memory the moment she felt Zane part her legs and his hot breath against her sensitive skin.

"Oh my God!" Andi cried out when Zane's tongue began to explore her feminine folds. Her back arched and she gripped the blanket in both hands as she tried to hold back her cries of pleasure. God knows that last thing she needed right now was Luke or Norah coming to ruin this. A rush of heat washed over her as a tingling sensation began to build where Zane was so thoroughly claiming her with his mouth. She whimpered softly and bit her bottom lip as her breathing became more choppy and uneven.

He pulled away from her, pressing his lips against her inner thigh and massaging his fingers against her skin. "Andi, we're all alone out here," he said against her heated skin. "I can tell you're holding back. Just let go. No one's going to hear you. *Let go.*"

A loud cry escaped from her lips as he dove back in, his tongue sliding against her and making her legs begin to shake. Her fingers wound into his hair as she felt that tingling sensation build again with such intensity, taking her higher and higher until finally she spiraled out of control. Her back arched off the blanket as she rode out the waves of her orgasm, loving how every part of her body felt as though they were hit with an electric current.

Andi lay there breathing hard as she came back down to earth. Okay… So Vince had *never* made her do that before. It was kind of sad in a way that in all their time together and all of their time spent in the sheets that she never had an orgasm. But if she was going to be honest with herself, she was glad Vince never did that for her. She was so unbelievably happy that Zane was the man to take her to that point of no return—that one minute he could make her feel like she was going to die and the next never feel more alive.

She leaned up slightly, resting on her elbows and looked up at him. He was now kneeling and slowly running his hands up and down her thighs. "Wow," she breathed because, really, what else was there to say?

Zane chuckled softly. "I'm glad you liked it." He moved then, bracing his hands against the blanket on either side of her head and slightly holding his body over hers. Leaning towards her, he pressed his lips against hers. The kiss started off soft and slow then morphed into need and want.

Andi ran her hands along the strong muscles of his back and felt them flex with every move of his toned body as he rested his body lightly on top of hers. Her hand slid around his waist, reaching between their writhing bodies and taking hold of him. Slow, teasing strokes were followed by Zane taking in a sharp breath of air through his teeth.

"What's wrong?" Andi asked, all of a sudden worried that she did something she wasn't supposed to or that she had somehow hurt him.

"Nothing's wrong, Andi." He kissed her and leaned on his elbow to gently stroke her face. "It's just been a while for me too, and if you keep doing that…"

"Oh," she said and caught her bottom lip between her teeth as she stroked him once more.

Closing his eyes, Zane took in a shaky breath and moved her hand away from him, pinning her wrist just above her head. He stared at her, looking as though he wanted to say something, and she searched his eyes for the unspoken words. She was just about to ask him what he was thinking when he leaned down and joined his lips with hers.

The kiss was tender but filled with urgency as he slid his hand away from her wrist, down her arm, along the slender curve of her waist and settled on her hip. He pulled away then, much to Andi's dismay, and rested himself on his knees as he reached for his cargo shorts in search of his wallet. She watched him pull out the square, silver package and then toss his wallet off to the side with his shorts. The foil crinkled slightly as he ripped it open, and even though he was moving at a fairly quick pace it just wasn't quick enough. She sat up, running her hands over his torso and then helping him cover himself. She looked into his eyes briefly and then leaned in to press her lips to his taut chest, darting her tongue out to taste him.

The next thing she knew her back was against the blanket again as Zane pressed his body onto hers. His hand moved slowly down her hip as he stared into her eyes. "Now?" he whispered and held onto her gaze as he waited for her answer.

Andi nodded her head and traced his jaw with her index finger, then moved her hand to the back of his neck to pull him down for a kiss. She felt his body weight shift and his arousal press against her, slowly at first and then with one quick thrust of his hips he was inside her.

"Oh my God," she breathed as he groaned against her ear and began to move, setting a rhythm that was both slow and steady. Although what he was doing was having fabulous effects on her body it still wasn't enough. She wanted more, but instead of telling him she decided to show him by flexing her hips to meet him thrust for thrust.

"Jesus, Andi," Zane said, leaning his forehead against hers. "If you keep that up I'm not going to…"

She kissed him then, because although she wanted this experience to last forever she also wanted to feel that glorious sensation shoot through her body again. She gripped his hips with her hands, urging him to go faster but with no success. As long as he was the one on top it appeared as though he was going to call all the shots.

Kissing him harder, she pressed her hand against his chest and gave him a gentle nudge. The look on his face was one of pure confusion and Andi took advantage of that moment to push him over and onto his back, rolling with him and keeping their bodies connected.

"My turn," she said in a low seductive voice. She moved on top of him, rocking her hips as her hands ran over his sculpted torso. Zane leaned his head back and let out a low groan as her movements increased. His large, calloused hands gripped her hips and attempted to slow her down, but having him hold her down like that only increased her need for release. That now familiar tingling sensation began to build in her core, and she started to move against him faster and harder.

"Oh, Zane. Yes. Yes! *Yes!*" She threw her head back and stilled her movements as her body buzzed and tingled from her toes to her fingertips.

Just as she was coming down from her sexual high she felt Zane's grip on her tighten and his hips thrust into hers one final time as a long groan escaped from his lips. Another shot of electricity swam through her body and her limbs began to tremble.

Unable to hold herself up any longer, Andi collapsed against him. They were both breathing hard and as she lay there with her head against his skin she could hear his heart beating rapidly.

"Good Lord," Zane breathed. "That was…"

She lifted her face to look at him, resting her chin on his chest. "Don't leave me hanging there, Zane." She gave him a smile—a dreamy *that was the best sex of my life* smile. "That was what?"

"Freakin' amazing," he told her as he turned his head to look at her. "*You* were freakin' amazing." A sly, teasing smile spread across his face as he added, "It looks like those horseback riding lessons are starting to pay off."

She sucked in a breath of air and swatted his chest playfully. "Stop it." They laughed together as they lay there with their bodies still intertwined. She rested her head against him again and took a deep, settling breath. "That was really something, Zane. You made me feel things that I've never felt before. I feel like I should thank you or something, but it feels silly to say it." She let out a soft laugh and met his eyes.

"I could think of other ways you could thank me." He smiled and waggled his eyebrows.

"You're a mess," she told him as she returned his smile and shook her head.

"And you're beautiful." Taking her chin between his forefinger and thumb, he tilted her face to gift her with a sweet, slow, lingering kiss.

And that's when she realized that she was falling in love with Zane McKade.

Chapter Fifteen

"Well hells bells look what the wind blew in," Belle called from behind the counter.

Andi smiled and waved. "Ha ha, I know." She crossed the tiny diner and took a seat at the counter.

"I was beginin' to think you dropped off the face of the earth." Belle reached behind her and grabbed an empty coffee mug and set it in front of Andi. She then took up the coffee pot sitting on the warming plate and filled the mug with the steaming hot liquid.

"Thanks, Belle," Andi said as she spooned sugar and cream into her coffee.

Belle placed the coffee pot back on the warmer and turned back to Andi, resting a hand on her hip. "Well, whatcha been up to kiddo? I ain't seen nor heard anythin' from you in weeks. You found a place to stay I assume," Belle said with a wink.

Andi took a sip of her coffee and placed it back on the counter with a nod. "Yes, ma'am, I did."

"Well that's good," Belle said. "How's it workin' out over at Red's?"

"Everything is great," Andi told her.

"I'll say," Belle said. "You look like a completely different person than the girl who walked in here a month ago."

"How so?" Andi asked raising an eyebrow.

"I'm not sure how to explain it," Belle said. "But you've got this glow that wasn't there before."

The bell rang over the door and Zane entered the diner.

"Oh my, well this is a day full of surprises. How's my favorite nephew doin'?" Belle asked as she came around the end of the bar to greet Zane with a hug.

Zane laughed and wrapped his arms around his aunt. "Don't let Luke hear you say that."

"To what do I owe the pleasure of this visit?" Belle asked stepping back to take a good look at Zane. "My gosh you look different than the last time I saw you."

"I was just taking a ride out." He paused and leaned towards Belle to whisper, "I got a hot date."

A huge grin spread across Belle's face and she gave Zane a gentle slap on the shoulder. "I knew it, I knew you had met a girl. Well who is she? I wanna know all about her."

"Okay, okay. How about you pour me a cup of coffee and I'll tell you." He walked over and took the barstool next to Andi.

"I can't believe this. I haven't seen you this happy in a long time. She must be a special girl." Belle placed a mug in front of him and filled it with coffee.

"Oh she is," he said with a smirk and gave a sideways glance to Andi.

Belle turned around to place the coffee pot back on the warmer, talking to Zane the whole time about how she knew this day would come and he'd find love again. When she spun back to face him, he had his arm wrapped proudly around Andi and drew her close to his side.

"Well," Belle said in shock. "I… How…?"

"I ended up saving her life her first night at Red's and she instantly fell for me." He winked and Andi playfully shoved his shoulder.

"I don't know about the whole instantly falling for you part. I seem to remember a week or so of evil attempts to get me out of your house," Andi teased.

The shocked look never left Belle's face. "Wait, this is where you are staying?"

"After I saved her life," Zane said and dodged another shove from Andi, "Norah invited her to stay at our place. We butted heads for about a week, but she came around when she realized she couldn't resist my charms."

Andi smiled and covered his mouth with her hand. "What he's trying to say is that he finally started being nice to me and I realized that he wasn't born a jerk and he is actually a very decent man."

Zane pulled her hand from his mouth and tenderly kissed the back of it before pulling it down to his lap and intertwining her fingers with his.

"Well, I'm speechless." Belle exhaled and looked from Andi to Zane.

"Aren't you happy for me, Aunt Belle?" Zane asked giving Belle a bewildered look.

"Of course I'm happy," she said. "You two make a beautiful couple."

Zane's face lit up into a brilliant smile and he pulled Andi even closer to him. "Thanks." He leaned over and gave Andi a gentle peck on the cheek. "I'm happy, too," he said adoringly.

Andi looked into Zane's eyes and in that moment Belle could feel the love that the two of them shared for each other, even if they didn't realize it was love just yet.

"Well, ya'll want somethin' to eat? I can whip somethin' up real quick," Belle asked.

"No thanks, Aunt Belle," Zane said. "We're actually on our way to grab a bite to eat in Wilhelmina County. I just wanted to stop by and show off my new girlfriend."

"Well, let me get another hug before you go." Belle rounded the corner and reached her arms out to Zane. "I'm very happy for you. And don't let it take you a month before you come and see me again," she said wagging her finger at him.

He chuckled softly and agreed before reaching for Andi's hand.

"Why don't you go ahead out to the truck and I'll be right there?" Andi suggested.

"All right, but don't be long." He smiled and adjusted his hat as he made his way out to the parking lot.

Andi turned her attention to Belle and gave her a pleading look. "Are you mad?"

Belle sighed and shook her head. "No, darlin', I'm not mad. Just shocked is all."

"I'm glad you're not mad. He's a wonderful man. I didn't know men could be so gentle and caring." Andi's eyes began to fill with tears.

"Oh, sweetie, don't you dare start tearin' up on me." Belle wrapped her arms around Andi and gave her a heartwarming hug.

"Thank you for everything, Belle. I can't tell

you how it means so much to me that you would take a chance on a complete stranger and help me out the way you did." Andi leaned away and swiped a tear from her cheek with her fingertips.

"You are more than welcome, sweetie," Belle told her.

"I don't know how I'll ever repay you," Andi said.

Belled smiled and laid a hand on Andi's shoulder. "Well, when you and Zane have a baby girl you could always name her after me."

A shocked laugh escaped from Andi's lips. "Oh my, I don't know about all that. Considering we've only just started dating, babies are the last thing on my mind right now."

"All in due time, m'dear," Belle said with a smile. "I've seen the way he looks at you and I can only think of one other time I've seen him with that look on his face. You know what they say... First comes love, then comes marriage, then comes the baby carriage."

Andi smiled in response and let her mind wander to a dream world where she and Zane were married with a ranch of their own and little blonde hair, blue eyed kids running around in the yard. "All right you have a deal."

****

"Mmm, what smells so good?" Andi asked as she entered the kitchen and sniffed.

"I'm testing out new pie recipes for the fair," Linda said. She leaned down to take a piping hot pie from the oven and placed it on the counter. "I think maybe I'll win this year."

"You win every year," Norah said with a laugh as she followed behind Andi.

"Not every year. I lost once," Linda said with a grin.

"Can anyone enter?" Andi asked.

"Oh sure, you just make a pie and enter it in the contest the day of the fair," Linda informed her.

"And when is the fair?" Andi asked.

"Next Monday. It's our town's July Fourth celebration," Norah told her. "It's normally a lot of fun. There's a band, amazing food, and vendors set up where you can buy homemade items."

"That does sound nice," Andi said. "So if I wanted to enter the contest all I would have to do it make a pie and take it up there?"

"Mmm-hmm," Linda nodded. "What kind of pie you planning on making?"

"Well, I don't really know," Andi said. "I've never made one before."

"I feel a cooking lesson coming on," Norah said with a chuckle.

Andi turned to Linda with a hopeful look on her face. "Oh would you please?" she asked clasping her hands in front of her.

"Let me get this straight. You want me to help the competition?" Linda raised an eyebrow to Andi and placed a hand on her hip.

"Please?" Andi begged.

A smile spread across Linda's face. "Oh all right. But only because you make my son so happy."

"Oh, thank you!" Andi said with excitement. "When do we start?"

"Right now," Linda told her. "Put that apron on over there and grab the flour."

The smell of freshly baked pies filled the air as Zane and Luke rode past the house on horseback.

"Smells like Mom is baking pies," Luke said taking in a deep breath. "And I know the perfect person to be taste tester."

"Me?" Zane teased as he began to unsaddle the new mare he was training.

"Uh, I was thinking more along the lines of me," Luke jokingly retorted with a huff. He began to unsaddle his own horse and noticed Zane had picked up speed. "What's the rush there, big brother?"

Zane quickly closed the stall door and began to walk briskly out of the barn. "I'm beating you to the house so I can have all the pie to myself."

"You sneaky bastard," Luke called out over Zane's laughter.

Moments later Zane entered the house and felt his heart flutter when he saw Andi standing at the counter wearing a red apron with flour smudged on her cheek. Her hair was pulled back into a messy bun and the poor thing looked frazzled.

"What's going on here?" he asked rounding the corner of the island and kissing her forehead. He brought his hand to her face and gently swiped his thumb across her cheek to remove the flour.

"Your mom is teaching me how to bake," she told him with a hint of irritation in her voice.

"You sound upset," he said with concern. "Is she a bad teacher?"

"No no, it's nothing like that," Andi told him

with a sigh. "She's done a great job. I just suck at
this, that's all."

He could see the disappointment on her face
and he wrapped his arm around her waist. "It can't
be that bad, sweetheart. Why don't you let me
decide if you suck at it. Which one is your pie?"

Andi dipped her head in embarrassment and
pointed to a dark brown disaster sitting on the back
counter. Zane walked over, sniffed the pie, and held
back the urge to cringe.

"This smells great," he lied. Reluctantly he
pulled out a knife and cut a generous piece. With
his plate in hand he sat down at the table and slowly
broke a piece off with his fork. He gave Andi a
reassuring smile before placing the pie in his mouth.
He froze and forced himself to chew and swallow.
"Mmmm," he said and gave her his best *this is
delicious* face.

The sad look slowly faded away from her face.
"You really like it?"

Zane stood up and walked over to the fridge.
"Sure do." He reached in and grabbed the carton of
milk and took a swig from it. He closed the door
and turned back to Andi, wrapping his arms around
her and pulling her close. "Best cherry pie I've ever
had," he said and kissed her on the lips.

She pulled back and gave him a smirk. "It's
apple."

Luke came bounding through the back door and
hung his hat on the wall. "Where is it? You better
not have eaten it all."

"Calm down, look I already cut you a piece,"
Zane said pointing to his burnt piece of pie sitting

on the table.

"Wow, thanks Zane. You know you're not half bad sometimes." Luke sat down and stared at the piece of pie. "Mom made this?" he asked, turning to Zane with a raised eyebrow.

Zane simply nodded and tried his best to hold back the smile that threatened to escape.

Luke shrugged and scooped a forkful in his mouth. His eyes popped wide open and he grabbed a napkin from the table and proceeded to quickly spit the piece of pie in it. "Whoa. Mom is losing her touch." He coughed.

Andi's shoulders slumped as she sighed and Zane hugged her tighter. "You'll get better, it just takes some practice." He chuckled and kissed the top of her hair.

****

Over the course of the next few days Andi continued to practice making pies. She burnt three more to the point where they were completely inedible but the fourth one came out just right.

"Wow, this isn't half bad," Zane said as he scooped another forkful in his mouth.

"Are you sure you're not lying to me?" Andi asked doubtfully.

"No, really," he said. "You did great."

"Well, thanks," she told him with a smile. "I'm glad you enjoyed it."

Zane pushed the empty plate away from him and slid his chair back from the table. "C'mere," he said gesturing for her to sit on his lap.

Andi removed the apron and laid it across the kitchen island. She walked over to where Zane was seated and allowed him to pull her down into his lap.

"Yes, sir, can I help you?"

"I don't know, can you?" He cupped his hand to the side of her neck and pulled her face to his. What started out as a slow and loving kiss quickly turned into a moment of pure passion. Zane moved his lips from hers to her jaw and down the side of her neck, leaving her skin feeling as though it were on fire.

"You are ornery," she whispered seductively as he slid the strap of her tank top down her shoulder and continued with his scorching kisses.

"Oh you haven't seen ornery," he said with a mischievous smile. With one swift motion, Zane stood up lifting Andi with him and pressed her body against the refrigerator door. Andi wrapped her legs tightly around his waist and dug her hands into the back of his hair.

They were so lost in the moment that they almost didn't hear the footsteps walking across the porch and the muffled voices right outside the door.

"Oh my gosh, Zane, there's someone at the door!" Andi whispered in surprise.

Zane quickly set her down on the floor and took his seat at the table. He was in no position to be standing anywhere right now. No sir, he'd sit right there all afternoon if that's what it took. And judging by just how much Andi turned him on it may very well take that long for him to collect himself.

Andi quickly moved behind the kitchen island and began to search for anything to keep her trembling hands busy. She brought her fingertips to her face and nervously tapped them against her mouth as she looked around the room. Her lips were still stinging hot from their brief moment of desire. She licked them, trying to stop them from burning and tasted a hint of cinnamon and sugar that must have transferred from Zane's lips to hers. Andi took in a shaky breath and attempted to calm her raging hormones. The screen door opened and she quickly grabbed a dish towel and began to wipe the already clean counter.

Luke entered the house carrying two brown paper bags filled with groceries, followed by Norah and Linda.

"Hey guys, what are you up to?" Luke asked setting the bags on the counter.

Andi shook her head and shrugged. She didn't dare attempt to speak for fear of saying something ridiculous.

"We were just having some pie," Zane said and cleared his throat.

Norah and Linda took turns setting their bags on the counter as well.

"Do you need help putting this away, Mom?" Norah asked.

"No, sweetie, I'm fine," Linda told her. "You go ahead and get ready for work."

"Okay, thanks." Norah stopped as she caught a glance of the pie sitting on the table and turned to Andi. "Did you make this?"

Andi nodded.

"It looks really good. I think you may have finally gotten the hang of it." Norah turned her attention to Linda and added, "Looks like you may have some competition this year, Mom." Norah smiled and winked at Andi as she left the room.

"Well, I've got some stuff to do in the barn so I guess I'll be heading out there now. Zane you wanna come help me?" Luke asked with his hand on the back door.

"Um, sure," Zane said hesitantly. "Give me a few minutes and I'll be right there."

Linda watched Luke walk across the yard to the barn from the kitchen window, then slowly turned to face Andi and Zane. "Okay you two, what's going on?"

They each gave Linda their best innocent looks.

"Don't you dare look at me like that," she said pointing her finger at them. "You may consider me old and naïve but I'm no fool. I can tell just by looking at you that you were up to no good. This room is hotter than three hells and I know darn well that my oven didn't cause all that. I'll tell you this once and only once, not in my house. I know you are grown adults and are going to do what adults do, but take it somewhere else. Hell Zane, you have a house of your own, take it there." Linda gave them each a serious look and headed back out to the car to get the last two bags. When she was sure they weren't looking she shook her head and chuckled softly to herself.

Andi shot Zane a confused look from across the room. "What does she mean, a house of your own?"

Zane sighed and stared down at his boots. "I kind of own my own house. It's not much but it works for me."

"Okay," Andi said still confused. "If you have your own house then why have you been living here?"

Zane hesitated for a moment. "Well, I've been staying here so I could be close to you. I kind of like having you around all the time." He smiled and Andi was taken aback by how boyishly cute he was being right now.

"Well that seems like a good reason," she said toying with the dish towel in her hands. "So do I get to see this house of yours or do you only show your serious girlfriends?" she teased.

Zane stood up from the table and walked over to Andi. "Of course you can see it. And just so you know, there have been no other serious girlfriends, with the exception of one, but she never saw it. And you mean a whole hell of a lot more to me than she ever did." He leaned in and gently kissed the tip of her nose. "You're about as serious as they get."

How the hell did you ever land a guy like this? her subconscious asked.

I'm not too sure of that myself. But what I do know is that I am madly and deeply in love with him, she answered to herself.

Andi stood on her tip toes and pressed her lips against Zane's.

"Ahem!" Linda cleared her throat.

Zane and Andi quickly stepped away from each other and went their separate ways.

"Crazy kids," Linda chuckled to herself and began to put the groceries away.

Chapter Sixteen

The warm summer night air blew through the windows as Zane drove his truck down the long dark road. Andi leaned against his shoulder and yawned as she curled into his side.

"Don't go falling asleep on me now, we're almost there," he chuckled.

"I'm sorry. I'm just exhausted," she said. "The bar was packed tonight and I felt like I was running around like a chicken with my head cut off the entire time. How much farther?"

"About another five minutes," he said and gave her shoulder a gentle squeeze with the arm he had wrapped around her.

Moments later Zane pulled his truck off the paved road and into a stone filled driveway. The gravel crackled under the tires as he slowly pulled towards the brick rancher. He parked his truck just outside the back door and turned the ignition off.

"Well, here we are. Home sweet home." He opened the driver's side door and stepped out, holding his hand out to help Andi out as well.

Andi let her eyes wander over the simple lines of the house and its surroundings. Even though it was dark outside, the light shining from the pole light near the barn made it easy for her to see the details of the home. The yard was full of green grass, and there was a simple flower bed surrounding the house filled with red mulch and white azalea bushes. The house itself was made of a stunning faded red brick with black shutters flanking each window. There was a back porch that ran down the length of the house with two rockers sitting on the far end along with a porch swing.

"This is beautiful," she said in amazement.

"Thanks. Here let me show you around the inside." He took her hand in his and led her up the steps and into the back of the house. They entered through the laundry room, taking off their shoes in the process and proceeded to enter a small eat in kitchen. Zane flipped on the light bringing the room to life. Andi left his side and let her hands run over the smooth texture of the deep brown countertops. She admired how well they matched the natural colored maple cabinets and tan tile floors.

"This is quite charming," she said to Zane.

"Glad you like it," he replied with a smile. He walked over to the opening between the kitchen and the den and turned on the lamp sitting on the side table. The dimly lit room looked very cozy with the matching sofa and loveseat along with the small brick fireplace in the corner of the room. The walls were painted a warm brown that had just a hint of orange to it and the dark stained wood floors accented them perfectly.

"There are two small bedrooms and a bathroom down that way," Zane said pointing down the hallway on the other side of the den. "And there's a small room down this way that I use for my office along with my bedroom and bathroom." He nodded his head down the hallway they were standing closest too.

"I think I'd like to see your room," she said with a smile and walked past him down the hallway. The doors were open making it easy for her to distinguish the rooms. Andi made her way into the bedroom with Zane following closely behind her. She felt along the wall and found the light switch, turning it on. The walls were a calming bluish gray color and there was a large king size bed sitting against the far wall adorned with a patchwork quilt. Two night tables flanked each side of the bed with matching lamps. A tall chest sat on one wall and a dresser on the other. In the corner next to the dresser was a small wooden chair that looked like it had belonged to a kitchen dining set at one point, and directly next to that sat a string guitar leaning against the wall.

"That's a pretty big bed for just one person," Andi said with a grin. She walked across the room and ran her hand down the quilt of the bed, then pushed on the mattress. "Wow this feels like a cloud." She turned around to find Zane standing inches away from her. He removed his hat and flung it to the corner of the room before stepping towards her and wrapping his arms around her waist. Andi felt the back of her legs hit the edge of the bed as Zane leaned down and pressed his lips against hers. Unable to help herself, Andi yawned mid kiss.

"Are my kisses boring you already?" he joked, stroking her hair from her forehead with his fingertips.

"I'm so sorry," she said embarrassed. "Here you are being so sweet and romantic and I'm ruining it." She yawned again. "Darn it."

Zane chuckled softly. "It's okay. Let's get some sleep. You've had a long night and deserve some rest."

"Thanks," she replied and looked down at her clothes. "Um, I don't have anything to wear to bed and I really don't want to hop in your bed with these smoky clothes on."

"I've gotcha covered," Zane replied and walked over to the closet. He grabbed one of his button up shirts and handed it over to her. "The bathroom is right through that door. Take your time."

Andi entered the bathroom and flipped on the light. The walls were painted the same exact color as the bedroom and the floors were a beautiful gray slate. She walked over to the counter and set the shirt Zane had given her to wear next to the sink. She peeled out of her smoky clothes, leaving only her underwear on, and folded the rest of them up. She set the clothes on the toilet lid and opened the linen closet in search of a washcloth. She took one from the shelf and ran it under warm water from the sink, then proceeded to run it across her body to remove the smell of smoke and beer from her skin. Once she was refreshed, she slipped into the shirt Zane had provided and rolled the sleeves up a few times to free her hands. She took one last look in the mirror and ran her fingers through her hair before turning off the light and heading back out to the bedroom.

Zane was standing on the other side of the bed wearing a pair of navy blue cotton pajama bottoms. The main light was now off and the only light was coming from one of the lamps. He was just turning down the quilt when he noticed Andi emerge from the bathroom wearing his favorite baby blue shirt. His heart completely stopped beating and he felt his knees buckle beneath him. "Wow," he said quietly. "Just... Wow."

Andi smile and dipped her head, tucking her hair behind her ear as she did. As she made her way across the room, she caught sight of the guitar sitting in the corner. She stopped and turned around to pick it up.

"What are you doing?" Zane asked as she walked over and handed it to him.

"Here," she said. "Play me something before we go to sleep."

"What do you want me to play?" he asked.

"Anything," she told him as she climbed into his bed. "I just want to hear your beautiful voice and have it fresh on my mind so I can dream about it all night long."

Zane smiled and sat on the edge of the bed. He adjusted the guitar as Andi sprawled across the head of the bed, resting her elbow on the pillow and her head in her hand. Zane let his eyes trace the perfect outline of her body, starting from her toes, up her silky smooth legs, over her hips, across her stomach and chest to her angelic face. He took a deep breath and tested the strings of the guitar, making sure they were in tune. He then began to strum the melody of Josh Gracin's "Stay With Me" and sang every lyric while staring into her eyes. Every once in a while he'd give her one of his crooked smiles and she could feel her body melt. When the song was over she leaned up on her elbow and brought her other hand around to applaud him; he smiled and thanked her.

Leaning the guitar against the foot of the bed, Zane froze when he felt Andi's hand slide around his waist and up to the smooth plains of his chest. Her soft, full lips pressed against his shoulder and made a trail down his bicep.

"I thought you were tired," he asked, turning his head slightly to look at her as he brought his hands up to cover hers.

"I'm not that tired anymore."

She looked up at him through thick lashes and the heat in her gorgeous brown eyes seemed to redirect all of his blood flow, sending it all to one particular part of his body. Angling his torso to face her, he pulled her close, loving the way her breasts felt against his chest—soft against hard. Her hands moved to his shoulders as she crawled on top of him and straddled his lap. A tiny moan escaped her lips as Zane feathered kisses down her throat.

"I love it when you make that sound," he mumbled against her skin.

"Mmm," she said. "Well, I promise to keep making them if you keep kissing me there."

"Is that so?" His hands slid up her smooth thighs and under the soft cotton of her panties to cup her rear as he kissed her, long and slow. Keeping his hand between the cotton and her heated flesh, he let his fingers follow the seam of her panties. "What if I decided to kiss you here instead?" He reached between her legs then, feeling her slick, wet, heat.

She sucked in a breath of air and sighed his

name as she exhaled slowly.

"I like the sound of that, too," he said, his voice low and husky. Moving both of his hands to the backs of her thighs, he gripped them tightly as he stood up from the bed with her legs wrapped around his mid-section. He spun them around, his knees hitting the edge of the mattress as he gently laid her down and crawled over her while she scooted towards the center of the bed. Instead of resting his body on top of hers, he laid down next to her, keeping as much of his body connected to hers as he possibly could. When she reached over for him and attempted to climb on top, he carefully pushed her back down on the comforter and silenced her protest with his fingers to her lips.

"Shhh," he said. "Let me love you slow, Andi." His fingers left her lips, leaving a feather light trail down her throat, across her collarbone and the swell of her partially exposed breast. Resting his weight on his other elbow, Zane began to unsnap the pearl buttons one at a time. When the last button was undone he took his time peeling the fabric away to expose her breasts and stomach.

"Beautiful," he whispered huskily and reached for her breast, teasing the hardened tip.

He heard her moaning his name as his mouth sought out the other breast, savoring the taste of her skin. She squirmed beneath his touch and his hand left her breast, gliding ever so slowly down her trembling stomach and dipping beneath the waistline of her panties.

"Oh my God, Zane," she breathed when his fingers searched and found entrance to her feminine core.

He continued to please her using only his fingers as he kissed his way up to her mouth, loving how she was responding so eagerly to just his touch. Feeling her body begin to tremble, Zane increased his movements. Her hands wound in his hair as his mouth found her breast again. When her breathing escalated and she alternated between saying his name and "Oh my God", Zane stroked his thumb over the sensitive skin of her core sending her over the edge. He lifted his head as he watch her come undone and, God, what a beautiful sight she was with her back arched and her head thrown back in sheer ecstasy.

When her body stilled he kissed her, then sat up on his knees, pulling her with him to a sitting position. He leisurely removed the shirt from her, letting his hands skim down her shoulders and arms. Tossing the shirt to the footboard, he laid her back down then crawled over her, hooking his thumbs in the waistband of her panties. He dragged them slowly down her thighs and legs, watching her skin bead up from the gentle caress of his skin against hers.

Lifting her foot, he removed the thin cotton and tossed them off to the side, placing a kiss on her ankle as he ran his hand up and down her leg. He stood then, letting his eyes linger on her naked body, taking in every curve as he removed his pants and kicked them away. Reaching for the nightstand, Zane opened the top drawer and pulled out protection. He was just about to rip it open and cover himself when he felt Andi's hand cover his.

"Let me," she said. "Please." She was now sitting on the edge of the mattress with her legs dangling on either side of his. Taking the wrapper from him, she opened it then slowly took her time covering him. Her hands moved then, sliding over and up his thighs and around to the firm muscles of his butt.

The sensation of her hands on his skin sent a thrill of anticipation up his spine, but that's not what did him in. He let out a shaky breath then looked down to see Andi staring up at him. And the lust swimming in her eyes set off a spark of desire that shot straight through to his core. No longer did he want to be inside of her, he *needed* to be inside of her.

"Andi," he breathed. "Lay back."

Something in her mood shifted, ever so slightly, but he couldn't read it.

"Please," he requested in a low soft-spoken voice.

That sexy *I want you now* look was back in her eyes, and as she slid back to the center of the bed Zane crawled over her, covering her body with his. He kissed her, taking his time although his brain was urging him to speed things up. His hands roamed her body, hitting all the parts he knew would make her moan and even discovering some new places in the process. It was such a turn-on having her squirm beneath him like that and he wanted to continue exploring her body, but his own body had other ideas—other needs.

He pushed himself up then, hovering over her as he positioned himself between her legs. His hand skimmed down her thigh, and when he reached the crook of her knee he wrapped her leg around his waist as he slid into her with one, long, slow stroke.

"Oh, Zane." Andi sighed, tilting her head back as she ran her hands up and down his back, moving her hips to match his.

It felt ridiculously good on his end, having her warmth surround him like that. And as much as he wanted to thrust his hips faster and harder he stuck to his word, keeping things nice and slow. Their lips met for a kiss, and then another, and another. When he felt her fingers dig into his shoulders, he kissed his way along her jaw and down her neck, hearing her escalated breathing brush against his ear. Her hands moved to his face, cupping his jaw as she pulled him to look at her.

"You're killing me," she breathed. "I need more. Please, Zane, give me more."

And all his restraint went out the window. Crushing his lips to hers, he picked up the pace, gripping her hip with his large, calloused hand and giving this woman exactly what she craved. He could tell she was close to her orgasm as her limbs seemed to tighten around him—her legs clenched around his waist and her fingers knotted in his hair. She moaned into his mouth as he continued to kiss her, thrusting his hips even more now that he felt his own climax approaching. The moment her body began to spasm around his he was history. A low, gravelly groan escaped his lips as Andi, too, cried out and dug her fingers tighter into his hair. He slowed his movements then, wanting to prolong both of their pleasure for just a little bit. And then he collapsed on top of her—not fully though, so he wouldn't crush her beneath his weight.

They were both breathing hard as they lay there not moving for what seemed like an hour but were really only minutes. A shudder rippled through Andi and Zane lifted his face to look at her. She had the look of a woman who had just experienced sheer bliss—dreamy eyes, flushed cheeks, kiss-swollen lips. Zane felt his heart swell at just the sight of her, and yeah maybe it was cheesy to say how he felt about her right now after having just made love, but he didn't want to hold out any longer. Taking in a few deep breaths to calm the rapid beating in his chest, he brought his fingers up to her face to stroke away the damp tendrils that clung to her forehead.

"I love you," he said in a soft-spoken voice.

Her eyes widened and for a moment he was scared he'd messed up. But then she smiled and caught her bottom lip between her teeth as she pulled him down for a kiss.

"I love you, too."

****

The warm sun bursting through the window the next morning woke her. Andi stretched and reached for Zane, only to find an empty space. She opened her eyes, sat up, and adjusted the bed sheet to cover her naked body. The smell of bacon wafted down the hall and she breathed in the delicious aroma. She grabbed her button up night shirt from the foot of the bed and slid it on as she walked out of the room and down the hall to the kitchen. Zane was standing at the stove in his pajama bottoms and a white tank undershirt. A second later he turned off the stove and spun around with the skillet of bacon in one hand and a set of tongs in the other. He caught sight of Andi leaning against the door frame and smiled.

"Hey," he said sweetly.

"Hey," she replied with a smile.

He set the bacon onto a serving plate and put the pan in the sink. "Have a seat," he said and gestured for her to sit down. "I wasn't sure how hungry you'd be so I just kind of made a little bit of everything."

Andi looked over the plates of eggs, bacon, sausage, ham steak, pancakes and biscuits. "This looks great, thank you."

She began to fill her plate, taking a little bit of each while Zane poured each of them a cup of coffee. He sat down with her, took a sip of his coffee and began to fill his own plate. They ate in silence for the most part, speaking every so often about what they needed to do over the course of the day. When the meal was done, Zane stood up and began to collect the plates.

"Uh-uh," Andi said snatching the plates from his hand. "You cooked, so I'll clean." She gave him a quick kiss and walked the dishes over to the sink before starting to clear off the table.

"All right well I guess I'll go get a shower then and get ready," he said shoving his hands into the pockets of his pajama bottoms. He watched Andi bustle about the kitchen, putting the extra food in containers and storing them in the fridge. She then moved back to the sink and began to fill it with warm soapy water to wash the dishes. His eyes trailed up her long slender legs and a sly smile spread across his face. He quietly walked up behind her and wrapped his arms under hers and around her mid-section. He rested his chin on her shoulder and whispered in a husky voice, "How about you wait on the dishes and join me in the shower?" He kissed her neck all the way up to her jaw and gently grazed his teeth on her earlobe.

Andi's eyes rolled in the back of her head and she bit her bottom lip as a series of shivers traveled up and down her spine. She turned to face him and giggled. "Haven't you had enough?"

"Oh, I can never get enough." Zane kissed her with such intensity and such heat that the room was sure to catch on fire. Without breaking the kiss, he gently lifted her and carried her off to the shower.

****

The day of the Fourth of July celebration had arrived along with the scorching July heat. Zane and Andi walked hand in hand through the fair and Andi proudly displayed her third prize ribbon for the pie contest that she had pinned to the left side of her dress.

"I can't believe I actually came in third," she marveled as she stared at the ribbon.

"I think you should have gotten better than third," Zane said and touched the ribbon.

"Thanks but I'm just glad I won something. I came a long way from that first pie I made," she said with a laugh.

"Oh, I know," Zane said jokingly and shivered.

She playfully slapped his chest and he laughed.

"Are you hungry? I can go grab us a bite to eat if you want," Zane suggested.

"That sounds great," she said. "Can you get me a cheeseburger with everything on it?"

"Yes, ma'am," he told her. "Why don't you go find a shady tree to sit under and I'll come find you once I have the food." He kissed her forehead and headed off towards the food stations.

Andi walked through the crowded fair towards the line of trees with a huge smile on her face. Life was good. She was the happiest she had ever been and had found the love of a wonderful man. Zane was about as perfect as they come and she was lucky that she had him all to herself.

As she made her way towards the trees she let her eyes scan over the crowd of people. Couples walking hand in hand sharing adoring looks. Moms and dads holding the hands of their children. And another sight that brought her to a complete halt. Her breath caught in her throat and her heart began to pound to the point where that was all she could hear. Her hands began to shake as the adrenaline rushed throughout her body and she started to panic. Quickly she darted her eyes around looking for Zane, but he was nowhere to be found. Andi turned her attention back towards the two men who stuck out like a sore thumb in this crowd of simple country folk. She ran and hid behind the dunking booth that was currently unoccupied.

"Oh dear God," she whispered to herself in a shaky voice. "How did they find me?"

Approaching footsteps on the grass caused her to go into a full on panic and she covered her mouth hoping to prevent herself from screaming.

"Andi?" Zane called out.

"Zane?" she whispered and peeked around from behind the dunking booth.

"Hey," he said adoringly. "What are you doing down there?" He chuckled at how silly she looked then realized that something was seriously wrong. "Baby, what's wrong?" he asked in a panic, dropping the food on the ground and rushing to her side. "You look like you've seen a ghost. What happened?"

He helped her on her feet and she let her eyes scan the crowd once more, looking for any signs of Sal or Tony, but they were nowhere in sight. Had she just imagined it all?

Zane brushed her hair away from her face and cupped her cheeks with his hands. "Sweetie, talk to me," he pleaded.

"I'm fine," she lied, "I'm fine." She took in a deep calming breath and quickly came up with some sort of excuse as to why she was so upset. "I'm sorry. I just got walking around here and I noticed all of these families together and it just reminded me of my parents."

"Oh Andi," Zane whispered and pulled her close to his chest. "Are you going to be okay? Do you want me to take you home?" He stroked the back of her hair with gentle rhythmic motions.

"No I'll be fine, really," she told him. "Let's stay and watch the fireworks. Then we can go home and curl up under the sheets and you can hold me all night long."

"Sounds like a plan," he said and tenderly

kissed her forehead.

****

"Andi," Zane whispered and gently shook her shoulder. "Andi!"

Andi screamed and shot upright in the bed. Tears streamed down her face and she began to hyperventilate.

"Andi, Andi! It's okay. It's okay. Shhh. It was just a dream." Zane's strong arms enveloped around her and she collapsed against his chest.

It was all too real. Sal and Tony had found her at the fair and were able to kidnap her. They bound her legs and wrists and took her to an old warehouse somewhere with poor lighting and dripping pipes. She sat alone, tied to a chair for hours in this cold and dark room. Her heart began to race when the door opened and Vince walked in. He looked just like she remembered: slicked back jet black hair, perfectly tailored suit and expensive shoes. He crossed the room slowly and before she could say anything he backhanded her across the face, tipping her chair over in the process. Her head collided with the concrete floor and she screamed in pain. He reached down, unbound her arms and legs from the chair, and hauled her to her feet.

"Please, Vince, don't do this!" she cried.

Anger flashed in his eyes and he smacked her hard across the face once more sending her to the floor again. She covered her face and began to curl into a ball when he swung his leg around and connected his foot with her ribs. Andi began to gasp for air and cried in pain from the broken bones. Just then, in the distance, she heard a soft familiar voice calling her name.

"Zane," she choked out.

Vince brought his foot around once more and that's when Andi snapped out of the dream, screaming and flailing around as to protect herself.

"Baby, are you okay?" Zane asked with such concern in his voice that it made her want to cry even harder.

"Yes, I'm okay," she said in a ragged breath and wiped her eyes with her fingertips.

"You wanna talk about it?" he breathed into her hair as he rested his chin on the top of her head.

"No, not right now. Please, let's just go back to sleep." She curled into his arms and pressed her body as close to him and she physically could.

Zane laid back down with Andi in his arms and gently ran his hand up and down her arm. "Andi, can I ask you something?"

"Hmmm?" she responded, taking in another shaky breath and blowing it out slowly.

"Who's Vince?"

She froze at the sound of his name. "Who?"

"Vince," Zane repeated. "You were screaming and you cried 'Please, Vince, don't do this' then you called out my name and you woke up."

Andi looked around the dark room and wondered how to explain. She wasn't up for having this conversation right now and quite frankly she never wanted to have it. "I don't know where that name came from, honestly," she lied. "Probably just someone my subconscious made up or something." She wrapped his arms around her tighter and buried her face into his chest.

Zane looked down to Andi and continued to rub her arm until she fell asleep. Never in his life had he seen someone get that upset over a dream. He wondered if Andi was being truthful about this Vince character. *No, she wouldn't lie, would she?* Zane shrugged off the thought and attempted to go back to sleep.

Chapter Seventeen

"Hi, Mom," Zane said as he walked through the back door.

"Hey there, darlin'," Linda replied and looked around Zane. "Where's Andi?"

"Oh, I left her in bed. Poor thing had a terrible nightmare last night that woke both of us up." Zane sighed, removed his hat and sat down at the table.

"Must have been some dream. Coffee?" she asked.

Zane nodded and Linda walked over to the cabinet and grabbed a mug. She placed it in front of him and poured the coffee into it. He took a careful sip and leaned back in the chair.

"She didn't even want to talk about it," Zane told his mother. "She was just sitting there crying and there was nothing I could do."

"She cried?" Linda asked in surprise.

"Yea." Zane nodded.

"Well, maybe she'll want to tell you about it today," Linda said trying to make him feel better.

"Maybe." Zane trailed off and stared at the cup of coffee in front of him.

"So, what are your plans for the day?" Linda asked, taking a seat at the table with him.

"Hmm? Oh, um, well I just stopped by to get a few things for Andi and then I was going to take them back to my house," he said. "I've got to work with that mare today at some point. Once Andi's awake I'll see if she feels up to coming back out here with me."

"You know, son," Linda started but paused to take a sip of her coffee. "I don't know why she just doesn't take all of her stuff to your house anyway. Ya'll are practically living together already. It's just a matter of her putting what little amount of stuff she has with yours."

Zane thought about it for a minute and replied, "You don't think that's moving too fast?"

Linda snorted.

"I know, I know," Zane said shaking his head. "It's just that, I made that mistake once and I sure as hell don't want to do it again."

Linda reached over and placed her hand on Zane's. "She's not Brianna son. Andi's a good girl, I can tell. She's a perfect match for you."

"You can tell all that from just knowing her for a month?" Zane asked with a chuckle.

"Can't you?" Linda raised an eyebrow to Zane and stood up from the table. She placed her coffee mug in the sink and began to wash the dishes.

Zane contemplated it for a moment and finished the last of his coffee. He did love the girl and his mom was telling the truth when she said that Andi practically did live with him already. He walked over and placed his mug in the sudsy water and kissed his mom on the cheek.

"Thanks, Mom."

"You're welcome, sweetie."

Zane walked out of the kitchen and down the hall to the room where Andi had been staying. With a slight spring to his step he entered the room and walked over to the dresser. He opened the drawers, itching just to take everything and pack it for her, but he'd let her do that if she decided that staying with him was what she wanted to do.

From the dresser he grabbed a pair of jeans, a fitted light pink t-shirt, socks, clean underwear, and a bra. He saw the empty duffle bag sitting on a chair by the window and he set the clothes down on the bed and went to retrieve it. He quickly grabbed it and as he did a thin journal style book fell to the ground along with a card of some sort. Zane looked in the bag to see if anything else was in it and when he found it was truly empty this time he bent down to pick up the book and the card. He paused mid reach when he noticed that the card was a driver's license with Andi's picture on it. But it wasn't Andi's name. Confused and instantly infuriated Zane picked it up and read the rest of the license.

"Kellan Marie Anderson. 101 Canal Street Apartment 12, Hoboken, New Jersey, 07030," he read aloud.

Zane let his eyes run over the person in the picture. This was not his Andi. This woman had too much makeup on and wore ridiculously huge earrings. Confusion swam through his mind but was quickly replaced with anger and the feeling of betrayal. She'd lied to him. She had actually *lied* about *everything*. Wanting to get to the bottom of whatever game she was playing, Zane shoved the license in his pocket and threw the clothes and notebook in the duffle bag before heading for the door.

Linda turned her head from her position at the

sink where she was washing dishes when she heard Zane's hurried footsteps come down the hallway. "Zane?" she asked, automatically confused as to his sudden mood shift. "What's the matter?"

"Nothing," he mumbled as he quickly walked through the room and out the back door, letting the screen slam shut behind him.

****

When Andi awoke that morning she was confused as to why she was alone. She groggily crawled out of bed and walked throughout the house calling for Zane. When she reached the kitchen she found a folded note lying on the table with a daisy on top of it. She smiled, picked up the flower and lifted it to her nose, taking in the simple yet wonderful scent. She then opened the letter.

Andi,

You looked so peaceful that 1 didn't want to wake you. I've gone to my mom's house to get you some clothes for the day. I'll be back soon.

Love,

Zane

Letting out a contented sigh as she folded the letter back up, she placed it on the table and walked over to the coffee pot, pouring herself a cup in the empty mug sitting next to it. She had just taken her first sip when she heard Zane's truck pull onto the gravel of the driveway. Zane walked in the house moments later carrying the duffle bag over his shoulder. When he caught sight of Andi standing against the counter with her coffee cup in hand and wearing his faded gray t-shirt he stopped and stared at her. So many emotions were running through him at that moment; anger, disappointment, betrayal.

"Hey, sexy," she said and placed the coffee cup on the counter. She crossed the room to where he stood and wrapped her arms around him, standing on her tip toes and pressing her lips to his.

Zane kissed her back but the action was almost robotic, like he was being forced to do it.

Andi noticed and pulled back to look at him. "What's wrong?"

Zane attempted to control his anger. "Who's Vince, Andi?"

She cringed inwardly at the name. Why oh why did she have to talk in her sleep? "I thought I explained last night that I don't know."

"Yes," Zane said taking in a deep breath. "Yes you did."

"Okay then. If I don't know then there's no reason to try to explain. I'm going to go take a shower. I'll be back in a few and then we can get started on our day." She turned and began to walk out of the room.

"You forgot your clothes," Zane said then added, "Kellan."

Andi froze and felt her heart drop to the pit of her stomach and shatter into a million pieces. Tears quickly filled her eyes and she turned to look at Zane. "What did you call me?"

"Kellan Marie Anderson." He took his time pronouncing each word as he walked closer to her.

"Oh God," she whispered. She tried to read his face but it was emotionless.

He pulled the license from his pocket and held it between his fore and middle finger as he showed it to her.

"Zane I—"

"You what, Andi?"

"I can explain."

"Well I'd say it's about time."

"Please don't be like that," she cried her voice becoming shaky.

"Don't be like what? Dammit, Andi, why'd you lie to me?"

"I had to, Zane. Please." The tears began to stream down her face and she pleadingly gripped his upper arms.

He shook off her hold and took a step back. "You know what," he said, staring at her with hurt filled eyes. "I can't do this right now." Without another word Zane turned and headed for the back door.

"Zane, wait!" Andi called, chasing after him. "Please just let me explain."

Zane stopped at the back door and gave her a look that quickly had her backing away from him. "I don't want to listen to anything you have to say right now. You *lied,* Andi! About everything! I've done this before and I'm not about to make that same mistake again."

"What do you mean?" she somehow managed to ask around the lump in her throat.

He didn't respond. He just turned and walked out the door, leaving her standing alone in the house.

Andi watched him pull away from the house,

then felt her knees give out and she sank to the floor. "What have I done?"

****

Luke climbed the ladder to the hayloft and called out for Zane. He'd been away from the house when his mother called and told him of her concern for his older brother. Apparently Zane had shut down and shut everyone out, and Luke could only think of one other time that this had happened. When he reached the top of the steps he found Zane moving from one side of the loft to the other, rearranging the already neatly stacked bales of hay.

"Hey there, big brother," Luke said, stepping onto the hay covered floor.

"Go away, Luke," Zane warned, not bothering to look in Luke's direction.

Rolling the sleeves of his shirt up to his elbows, Luke crossed the floor to assist his brother. "Well, see I can't really do that. Mom called me and said you were having some sort of fit and wanted me to get to the bottom of it," Luke told Zane. "If you don't want to tell me now that's fine. I'll just help you move these bales in the meantime."

"I don't need your help." Zane brushed past him and picked up another bale of hay.

Something was seriously up. Luke remembered how torn and hurt Zane had been when Brianna left, but this was at least ten times worse than that scenario. Had Andi left him? She didn't seem like the kind of person that would do such a thing. Then again, Brianna didn't seem to be the type either.

"Okay then. If you don't want my help then just tell me what's going on." Luke stared at Zane and watched as his shoulders slumped just the slightest bit.

Zane took in a deep breath and let his head fall back. He brought his hand to his face and wiped the sweat from his forehead and eyes as he exhaled roughly. "She lied to me."

"What?" Luke asked, not hearing Zane's muffled words.

"She lied to me!" Zane spat out, spinning around to face his younger brother.

"Lied to you?" Luke questioned. "About what?"

"About everything! Where she's from, her past, and even her name." Zane sat down on one of the hay bales and rested his face in his hands.

Luke crossed the hayloft floor and sat down next to Zane. "How do you know all this?"

Zane sat up and ran a hand through his hair, explaining to Luke the events from that morning when he found her license.

"Well, did you ask her about it?" Luke asked.

Zane shot him a disbelieving look. "Of course I did."

"Okay then," Luke said. "What did she have to say?"

"She didn't say anything," Zane said, his voice thick with frustration as he stood up and crossed the room.

"Did you give her a chance?" Luke asked, knowing his brother all too well.

"Yes. No." Zane sighed heavily. "Not really," he said quietly. "I didn't really give her time to say anything. I just got madder and more hurt from looking at her standing there in the kitchen wearing my shirt and looking all sleep disheveled. I freaking care so much about her and the fact that she just out right lied to me, lied to all of us, makes this betrayal even worse."

Luke stood and walked over to his brother, resting a reassuring hand on his shoulder. "It may seem like a betrayal right now but, honestly Zane, maybe she had a reason for all of this. I know it stings and it hurts for someone you care so much about to hide stuff from you, but you need to find out why she lied to you in the first place. Put your mind at ease, bro. Go talk to her."

Zane took in slow deep breaths. Luke was right. Maybe there was a logical explanation for all of this but he was still too mad to even be around her right now. "I need to cool off," Zane told Luke. "I can't go talk to her while I'm like this. I'm just going to finish what I'm going here and then I'll go back home." He grabbed another bale of hay and gave Luke a curious look when he too picked up a bale. Luke gave Zane a small smile and Zane nodded his acceptance in return as the two of them continued working in the loft for the next hour.

****

When Zane pulled in the driveway of his home he automatically noticed that Andi's truck was nowhere in sight. An unsettling feeling crept into his stomach but then he realized the time and knew she'd be at work by now. The day had seemed to get away from him, seeing as he had been doing everything he could to calm down enough before he talked to her. But having it take all day was not something he had planned or anticipated. He pulled to a stop and parked his truck next to the back porch. The sun had begun to set, casting an orange glow across the land as Zane exited the truck and made his way for the house. The back door hinges creaked and almost seemed to echo in the all too quiet house. Passing through the kitchen and living area, Zane made his way to his room for a shower and a fresh set of clothes. A few minutes later, Zane emerged from his room dressed in a crisp long sleeve shirt, blue jeans and boots. His hair was still damp from his shower and a few droplets of water clung to the ends. Walking through the now dark house, Zane entered the kitchen and flicked on the light. Immediately his eyes went to the table centered in the room and saw the folded note sitting on top of the thin book he recognized as the one from her duffle bag. Taking in a deep breath and letting it out slowly, Zane crossed the room and lifted the note.

Zane,

I don't know what else to say besides 'I'm sorry'. I never meant for you to find out like this. I know you probably don't want to see me or even talk to me right now. But if you still care for me and would like an explanation for why I did what I did then please read the journal I left underneath this note. It will tell you everything, even when I can't. I love you, more than anything, and I hope you still feel the same. If after you read my journal you decide you want to see me, well, you know where to find me. Please don't give up on us because I was stupid and kept things from you.

Love,
Andi

Zane laid the note back on the table and hesitantly lifted the journal, flipping it open towards the middle and began reading.

June 19

He kissed me. Words cannot describe just how wonderful it felt, but I'm sure going to try because I never want to forget that moment.

Zane finished reading the page and snorted sarcastically. He flipped through the rest of the pages, moving backward. It was obvious from her written words that she truly did have feelings for him. But what he couldn't get over is why she was lying about who she was. He got to the page where she described a dream she had about Vince coming to the ranch and confronting her in the barn. The name seemed to pop out from the page and Zane read each line carefully, hoping to shed some light on the subject. From there he flipped to the beginning of the journal, to the first entry that was from two years ago, and began to read.

May 2

I've never been one for writing, but due to the most recent events in my life I feel the need to put my thoughts down on paper. At twenty-two years of age I've lost both of my parents within a matter of months; my father having died from his long battle with cancer, and my mother, well, she couldn't bear to live without him and committed suicide just a few short weeks ago. I didn't even get to say good-bye. I feel lost and as I sit here writing down these words I can feel my heart breaking all over again. You'd think with all of this happening that I could turn to the man I love for support, but I feel like he's slowly slipping away from me as well. Vince has changed and I can't quite put my finger on what it is exactly, but I can see it in his eyes. What if he's grown tired of me? What if he decides that he no longer wants to be with me? As I sit here with those thoughts running through my mind I can feel myself dying inside. So much loss in such a short amount of time, just thinking about it makes me go numb. I can't let him leave me, I won't. He's all I have left in this world and I would die if I didn't have him.

So she was telling the truth about her parents. But why had she lied to him about this Vince guy? Zane took in a deep breath and turned the page, then realized why she had chosen to not speak about her ex.

September 27

Vince hit me tonight. God, how did I not see it coming? His attitude towards me has completely changed—he's colder, more possessive. Apparently I'm no longer his girlfriend but now his property. I have nowhere to go, and no one to turn to for help.

As I sit here in my bed, hurt and in pain because of the man I supposedly love, I can't help but wonder about how I ended up in this situation. There was no reason for him to overreact like he did. All I did was quietly suggest that he wait till we were alone, back in the privacy of our home for him to touch me the way he was instead of the middle of the club that we were in. And the look in his eyes as he glared at me sent a chill of fear down my spine. He'd always looked at me with such love and affection and this new look, this more sinister look, truly frightened me. He grabbed me, more forcefully than he'd ever done, and told me through his teeth that I was not to tell him what to do ever again, that my opinion and feelings didn't matter. Out of fear and completely in shock, I didn't speak. Tears filled my eyes but with all the strength I could manage I held them back. But when we arrived home tonight, my strength was nowhere to be found.

First he yelled at me, telling me how I made a fool of him in front of his friends. And when I went to protest, to tell him that they couldn't have possibly heard me, he struck me. The palm of his hand cracked across the side of my face with enough force that it sent me flying backward into the wall. I was completely shocked and caught off guard, and when he walked towards me I flinched. A new surge of anger flashed across his face and this time he yelled at me for being frightened of him. It all happened so fast and was over in a matter of minutes. And now, as a fresh round of tears well in my eyes I am reminded more and more of what he did to me. Every ragged breath I take hurts so much—I guess that probably means by ribs are bruised. My lip is split and it burns as I try to desperately to hold back my tears. What am I to do? I am broken, physically and mentally. How am I to pretend not to be scared when every second that passes I am terrified that he is going to burst through my door and hurt me again?

Zane's eyes widened in disbelief and his heart sank to the pit of his stomach as he felt his knees start to buckle. He quickly sat down in the chair and reluctantly continued reading.

November 16

I am in hell. Life no longer matters to me, well, this life anyway. This life where I am kept prisoner by the man I once loved, and there is no escape in sight. Nothing I do is good enough for him. And I continue to pay for my "stupidity" as he ever so gently puts it. I wonder, why does he keep me around if I'm not good enough for him anymore? Why put me through this misery day in and day out? I laugh now when I think about how just a few months ago I swore I would die without him. And now, I wish I were dead just so I didn't have to be around him. I know one of these days he's going to hurt me so bad that it's going to kill me. That thought should scare me, but with the way I'm feeling right now I welcome it with open arms.

He swallowed back the lump that began to rise in his throat as he continued to flip the pages and came across the page of her escape. Zane sighed, leaned his back and closed the book, not able to read another word. Everything seemed to make perfect sense now. He was still upset that she had been lying to him the whole time, but at least now he understood why. The severe anger he felt towards her earlier was now directed towards this abusive ex-boyfriend of hers. How anyone could lay a harmful hand on her was beyond him.

"I swear, if I ever get my hands on this guy he's going to know exactly how it feels to get the shit kicked out of him."

****

Zane entered the bar and shook hands with a few friends as he made his way through the crowd. His eyes immediately searched for Andi and found her as she bustled about from table to table delivering drink orders. The twinge of pain he felt in his heart had him forcing his way through the wall of people just so he could get to her. She turned, not seeing him coming, and headed back towards the bar with her empty tray in hand.

"Andi."

Her heart jumped into her throat when she recognized the deep, masculine voice, and she froze.

Zane reached out and gripped her shoulders, forcing her in his direction so he could look down upon her. Her eyes were wide with wonder and fear, and the fact that she looked so scared right now was absolutely breaking his heart. Without another word, Zane wrapped his arms around her middle and pulled her close, crushing his lips against hers.

Shocked but relieved, Andi dropped her tray to the floor and gripped the back of his shirt, attempting to pull herself as close to him as possible.

Amongst the hoots and whistles they received someone yelled for them to get a room which broke them apart, leaving them breathless and staring into each other's eyes.

"Is there somewhere, you know, private where we can talk?" Zane asked.

Andi nodded and took him by the hand leading him to the back room. She shot Norah a look on her way and motioned that she'd be back in a few minutes.

When they entered the back room, Zane pulled her close once more and kissed her; tenderly and almost reverent. When the kiss ended he held her tightly to his chest and whispered, "I'm so sorry, Andi."

She pulled back slightly to look up at him. "You're sorry? For what?"

"For overreacting the way I did," Zane explained. "I should have let you tell me everything before I decided to blow up and leave like that."

"It's okay, Zane," she said but he cut her off.

"No, it's not okay." He reached his hand to her face and gently stroked her cheek.

"I'm so sorry I didn't tell you sooner, Zane. When I stole that car and escaped from Vince's friends I just drove, not knowing exactly where I was heading. When I stopped for a break at Belle's diner I had no idea that I'd end up staying here for any amount of time. And I had no idea that I'd be falling in love." She took in a ragged breath and waited for Zane's response.

The look of deep concern and sadness spread across his face and he held her tighter as fresh tears began to fall down her cheeks. "Why didn't you just tell me?" he whispered as she cried into his shirt.

"I just couldn't, Zane. I tried so very hard to leave that life behind me and I couldn't bring you into this mess." She pulled back slightly to look at him. "You don't know what kind of people they are."

Zane carefully lifted his hand to her face and cupped her cheek. He swiped his thumb across a falling tear and she slowly brought her hand up to lay over his. "How can you expect me to protect you if I don't know what's going on?"

"I never thought it would come down to that," she said. "I thought I was safe here in this little off the map town and then yesterday at the fair I thought I saw Sal and Tony and—"

"Wait. What?" Zane interrupted with a shocked tone.

Andi just stared at him as another round of tears began to fill her eyes.

"They were here?" Zane asked with urgency to his voice.

Andi shook her head. "I'm not sure. I thought I saw them so I hid and then you found me and I didn't see them anymore."

"Andi, you've got to tell me these things. What would've happened if they were there and actually found you? How would I have had any idea of what could have happened to you?"

"I'm sorry, I'm sorry," she cried, scrunching

her eyes closed and resting her face in her hand.

"Andi, it's okay. Just no more lies all right. Look at me." Zane carefully lifted her chin with his thumb and forefinger so he could see her face. "Nothing but the truth from now on, okay?"

She nodded and breathed a sigh of relief. "So you're not mad at me anymore?"

"No," he said adoringly and kissed the tip of her nose. "I'm livid that that ex of yours had the nerve to touch you like that though. I swear, Andi, if I ever get my hands on that son of a—"

She lifted her fingers to his mouth, silencing him as pressed her fingers to his lips. "Let's not worry about that right now."

"I hope you know this means I'm never letting you out of my sight," Zane said when she pulled her hand away.

"That is absolutely fine with me." She smiled up at him and then rested her head against his chest.

"So does that mean you're okay with moving in with me?"

Her eyes widened and a slow smile spread across her face as she looked back at him. "Yes," she said softly, and closed her eyes as Zane kissed her.

****

"Okay, so let me get this straight," Luke said as he leaned his elbows on the table and folded his hands. "You're really from New Jersey and you're on the run from your abusive ex-boyfriend and his crazy friends?"

"That's right," Andi said as she held Zane's hand underneath the table.

"And your name is really Kellan?" Norah asked bewildered.

"Mmm-hmm." Andi nodded.

"Do we have to start calling you that?" Luke asked.

"No." Andi laughed.

"Good 'cause I like Andi better." Luke sat back in his chair and took a sip of his sweet tea before placing it back on the table.

"And your parents really are deceased?" Norah asked.

"Yes, that story was true but their names are really Charles and Jacqueline," Andi explained.

"Well," Linda said with a sigh. "That sure is a lot of information to share over dinner."

Andi turned her attention to Zane's mother and gave her an understanding look. "I know and I'm so sorry that I lied to you, all of you. But I hope you can see why I did."

Zane gave Andi's hand a gentle reassuring squeeze. "I'm sure you all can understand that this is a delicate situation we are dealing with here. So that means that none of this leaves this house."

"Of course, son. We completely understand," Linda said compassionately.

"Well, wait a second. Does Aunt Belle know all of this?" Norah asked.

"She knows I'm hiding from someone," Andi said. "The day I showed up in her diner I had a black eye, so I think she has a pretty good idea of what I'm hiding from."

Zane removed his hand from hers and wrapped it around her shoulders, drawing her close to his side and kissed her forehead. Every time he heard about this guy Vince giving her a bruised eye or a cracked rib it made his blood boil.

"So what do you want us to do?" Luke asked.

"Nothing," Zane said. "Just keep an eye out for anything suspicious. If you see anyone who doesn't look like they belong around here just let me know."

"What are you planning on doing if someone does show up?" Norah asked with a hint of alarm in her voice.

"I'm not sure," Zane told her. "But I'll be damned if I ever let that sorry bastard get his hands on her again."

Chapter Eighteen

Andi sighed and snuggled closer to Zane. "I'm so comfortable I don't want to get up," she groaned.

Zane chuckled softly and reached over the arm of the sofa for the remote to turn the volume on the TV down. "You don't have to leave if you don't want to."

"No, I have to. Norah's not working tonight. I can't leave Red hanging like that, even if he swears he can run the place blind folded with one hand tied behind his back," she joked.

"All right, well I guess I better get up too and put on a fresh shirt." He sighed as he stood up from the sofa and held his hand out for hers.

"You don't have to come with me, Zane. I'll be perfectly fine at the bar. There are plenty of people there and plus we haven't seen any signs of Sal or Tony in the past two weeks. I'm starting to think I just imagined them."

Zane helped her from the sofa and looped an arm around her waist as they walked towards the bedroom. "Is it that bad that I don't want to let you out of my sight?"

"No, it's understandable," she said. "I just feel like you worry all the time now. It concerns me."

"Your safety does concern me," he said and leaned down to kiss her. "Now go get dressed and I'll be ready and waiting for you when you're done." He gave her a gentle nudge towards the bathroom and tapped her on the bottom as she walked away.

Andi entered the bathroom with a huge grin on her face. The past two weeks had been completely wonderful now that everything was out in the open. She no longer carried the weight of all the lies on her shoulders and her relationship with Zane was better than ever. She grabbed her brush from the drawer in the vanity and ran it through her hair. She then pulled her long locks to the side and braided them loosely, securing them with a hair band. After that she quickly changed out of her lounge clothes and into a pair of faded boot cut jeans, her red tank top, and scuffed up boots. She finished off with a dash of perfume and headed back out to the bedroom.

Zane was standing with his back towards her, fiddling with something in his hands. He had changed out of his navy blue t-shirt and replaced it with a crisp white western cut shirt.

"I'm all ready," Andi said as she crossed the room toward him.

Zane quickly turned around to face her and held one of his hands behind his back.

Andi eyed him suspiciously. "What are you up to?"

Zane stared into her eyes and took a deep breath. "You know I love you, right?"

"Of course." Andi laughed. "And I love you."

"Since I've met you, things have been different. Good different not bad different. I mean, my life was pretty boring until you came along and then my world turned upside down. Upside down in a good way, though, not a bad way." Zane let out an exasperated sigh and stopped his rambling. "Oh dammit, I've screwed this all up."

Andi looked at him confused. "What are you trying to say, Zane? Don't beat around the bush, just spit it out."

Zane took in another deep breath and slowly bent down on one knee. Andi's eyes grew big and she covered her mouth with her right hand. With his free hand, Zane took her left hand in his.

"Andi, will you marry me?"

Her eyes filled with tears and an adoring smile spread across her face. "Yes, Zane, I will," she whispered.

Zane's face lit up with excitement and he pulled the ring box out from behind his back. He let go of her hand long enough to open the box and pull out the one carat brilliant cut diamond set on a white gold band. She gasped as he slipped it on the ring finger of her left hand, then quickly dropped to her knees, wrapped her arms around his neck and passionately kissed him.

****

Norah walked into the bar all decked out for her date. Her hair was loosely curled and she wore a black tank top with sequins around the neckline, dark boot cut blue jeans, and a pair of black high heels. She crossed the bar to Andi and set her wristlet on the countertop.

"All right, what was so important that I had to hurry down here before I go out on my date?" she asked to Andi.

"What are you talking about?" Andi asked as

she popped the top off of a long neck beer and handed it over to the waiting customer.

"Zane called the house and said that Luke and I needed to come down here to see you," Norah explained. "So what's up?"

Andi smiled when she realized what Zane had done. She took her left hand and slowly slid it across her forehead pretending to tuck a stray piece of hair behind her ear. The diamond sparkled and caught Norah's attention right away.

"Oh my God!" Norah cried and reached for Andi's hand.

"I know," Andi replied with a huge smile.

Norah came around the end of the bar and wrapped her arms around Andi, pulling her close and hugging her tightly. "You're getting married!"

Andi laughed and patted Norah's back.

"To my brother!" Norah continued.

"I know." Andi laughed as Norah hugged her tighter.

"Oh, we're going to be sisters!" Norah said. "I've always wanted a sister!"

Andi laughed again and slowly pulled away from Norah. "I take it you're okay with it then."

"Okay with what?" Luke said taking a seat at the bar. "Zane said I needed to see you about something."

"Zane and Andi are getting married!" Norah exclaimed and clasped her hands together in front of her.

"Well I'll be damned," Luke said and shot Andi a crooked grin. "So when are you due?"

Both Andi and Norah shot Luke a confused

look.

"Huh?" Andi asked.

"When's the baby due? If it's a boy I think ya'll should call him Luke after his good-lookin' uncle," Luke teased and adjusted the collar of his shirt.

"I'm not pregnant," Andi said. "And why does everyone around here insist that I name my children after them?"

Norah rolled her eyes and reached across the bar to shove Luke's shoulder. "What's the matter with you?" she chided.

"What? I was just kidding," he said. "Seriously, congratulations Andi."

"Thank you," she told him and smiled.

Zane snuck over and took the barstool next to Luke. "Have you all met my fiancé?" he asked and gestured to Andi with a big grin on his face.

"Yes we have. Oh I'm so happy for you, Zane!" Norah said excitedly as she went back around the bar to give Zane a hug. "Thanks for picking someone who I can actually get along with. Andi is great and I'm looking forward to having her as a sister-in-law," she whispered in his ear before she let go.

Zane smiled and nodded to Norah as she stepped away from him.

"Good job, old man," Luke said slapping a hand on Zane's shoulder and shaking Zane's hand with his other.

Zane thanked him then turned to Andi. Their eyes locked and they shared a meaningful glance across the bar.

"Well, sis, how about a beer?" Luke said.

"I'm not working tonight, dear brother," Norah came back.

"Actually I was talking to my new sis," Luke said. "What'ya say Andi?"

Andi reached down behind the bar into the cooler filled with longneck bottles of beer, popped the top and handed it over to Luke.

"Thanks. Now if ya'll will excuse me, there is a pretty little brunette sitting all alone in that corner over there looking mighty lonely." Luke grabbed his beer, adjusted his hat, and headed off to the corner of the bar.

"I have to be heading out too," Norah said. "Don't want to keep my date waiting too long."

"Have fun," Andi said.

"Thanks and congratulations again you two," Norah said to Andi and Zane and she walked away.

"Well that wasn't so bad," Andi said leaning on the counter.

"I told you they'd be happy about it," Zane said as he leaned on the bar. "And in the morning we'll take a drive over to mom's house and tell her the big news."

"Sounds like a plan," Andi smiled.

Zane met her halfway and gave her a tender kiss on the lips.

"All right you two, you're scaring the customers away," Red said walking towards them and shooing Zane back across the bar. "People don't want to be seeing all that smoochin' all the time."

"We've got a good reason to be smoochin'

though Red," Zane said and lifted Andi's hand so he could see her ring.

"Well I'll be a son of a gun," Red said quietly. "Congratulations." He reached over and gave Andi a gentle hug, then shook hands with Zane. A man at the other end of the bar called for Red so he excused himself and walked away.

"Hey, can I get some service down here?" another man called.

"Guess I'll let you get back to work," Zane said and leaned back on the barstool so he could have a good look at Andi as she walked away.

Around one o'clock in the morning Luke came stumbling back towards the bar. He leaned into Zane as he fell into the barstool next to him.

"You all right there, Luke?" Zane asked holding back a laugh.

Luke hiccupped and swayed back and forth in the barstool. "I believe I am shit-faced," Luke stated frankly.

Zane chuckled loudly. "I believe you are. You going to need a ride home?"

"No I'm just waiting on that little brunette to pull her car around and we're going back to her place," Luke explained slurring his words.

"You mean that little brunette who left an hour ago with that big burly cowboy she was dancing with?" Andi asked as she wiped down the counter.

"She did?" Luke asked wide eyed.

Andi bit her bottom lip to refrain from laughing.

"Well damn. I guess I'll just sit here and wait for her to get back." Luke reached across the counter and took the towel out of Andi's hand. He balled it up into a make shift pillow and plopped his head down on it before Andi could object.

"Luke what are you doing?" Zane asked shaking Luke's shoulder.

"I'm just gonna rest my eyes for a bit till my woman comes back to get me," Luke told him.

Andi gave Zane a look and rolled her eyes. "Take him home, Zane. He doesn't need to sleep on the bar."

"He'll be fine. He'll just sleep until you get off and then we'll drop him off before we go home. I'm not going to leave you here all alone," Zane objected.

"I'm not alone. Red's here. Please, take your brother home so he can save what dignity he has left," she said with a laugh. When Zane didn't budge she added, "Please, Zane, do it for me."

Zane let out an exasperated sigh and stood up from the barstool. "Oh, all right. I'll be back here in about an hour to get you, okay?" He leaned across the counter and gave her a quick peck on the cheek. "Luke!" Zane yelled and Luke jumped from the barstool sending it flying backwards to the floor. "Come on ya lush, let's get you home." Zane grabbed Luke's arm and pulled him to a standing position. When Luke was finally upright he leaned against Zane for support and the two of them began to walk towards the door.

"Bye, sweetie. I love you," Andi called after Zane.

"Love you too," Luke called as he tripped his way out of the bar.

Zane looked over his shoulder and gave Andi a heartwarming smile. He mouthed the words "Love you" and then he disappeared out the door.

****

"Well, I think that's the last of them. Why don't we go ahead and start closing up," Red suggested to Andi around quarter to two.

"Sounds good to me. I'm beat for one night." Andi walked over and locked the door, turning the neon open sign off in the process as well. She then walked around to each table and cleared off all of the bottles, glasses, and pitchers. Red took care of bagging up all of the trash and told Andi that he was going to run it out back to the dumpster and that he'd be back in a few.

She walked behind the bar and stretched her arms over her head, letting out a huge sigh as she picked up the broom from the corner. Walking back out to the dance floor, she reached in her pocket and placed a quarter in the jukebox. "Cowboy Take Me Away" by the Dixie Chicks came through the speakers and Andi hummed the tune as she began to sweep the dirty floor. She was so into the song that she didn't even hear the footsteps across the wooden floor. Andi jumped and dropped the broom when she felt the masculine arms slide around her waist from behind her. She was startled, only for a moment, and she playfully slapped at the hands that were lying across her stomach.

"Don't you remember what happened last time you did that?" she teased.

The hands slid down to her hips and forcefully pulled her backwards.

"Whoa," she said attempting to keep her balance.

Cool lips touched her neck and the hands slid from her hips to her ribs and slowly across her breast.

"Babe, don't do that here," she chided and attempted to free herself of his strong hands. His grip only tightened the more she tried to free herself. "Whoa, Zane, take it easy," she said starting to become annoyed. He'd never acted like this before and she didn't understand why he was being rough with her now. "Ouch, babe, that hurts."

The lips left her neck for only a moment and Andi could feel the warm breath of a whisper blow across the tip of her earlobe as she heard, "Who's Zane?"

Her whole body went numb all at once. Her feet felt as though they had been nailed to the floor. The sound of this voice had completely paralyzed her. As the panic began to set in, she felt her heart rate go from zero to sixty in a matter of seconds. She took in uneven breaths as her eyes darted around the room and quickly filled with tears. The man removed his hands from her body and slowly walked around to face her. He took his thumb and ran it across the corners of his mouth, then placed his arms by his side. Gently tugging at the ends of his sleeves, he pulled them down so they could peek out from his suit jacket.

"Vince," Andi whispered hoarsely.

"You look surprised to see me," he replied. "You had me worried, doll." He slowly closed the distance between them. "When I came home and saw you weren't there it made me nervous. I saw the safe was emptied out and I thought someone had robbed me and kidnapped you."

He was standing inches away from her now and Andi stiffened. Vince slowly brought his hand up to her face and she flinched as he gently stroked his finger tips along her cheek. Resting his hand on the side of her neck, he took in a deep breath and let it out slowly.

"But then I noticed your closet and saw the items missing from there and your dresser," he told her.

Andi stared at him wide eyed, unable to believe that he was actually standing right in front of her. "How did you find me?"

"You stole a pretty recognizable car, Kellan. Plus they put tracking devices in them now. It wasn't too hard to bribe the cops at the local precinct to have them find it for me."

Fear clenched in her chest and made it hard for her to breathe.

"I gotta give it you," Vince said. "It was a pretty smart move on your part trading it down for that piece of crap pickup truck. "

"How did you know—?"

"How did I know that you got rid of the Benz?" Vince interrupted. "Well, they traced the car to your friend's house. What's his name? Willy? Well Willy didn't seem to remember how he acquired such a nice car, so we refreshed his memory."

A shocked gasp escaped from Andi's lips. "Oh no, what did you do?"

Vince stared at her with a menacing look and

an eerie smile spread across his face. "Let's just say we had to beat it out of him." He stared at Andi with violent eyes and before she could say anything he quickly removed his hand from the side of her neck and back handed her across the face.

The force from the blow sent her flying to the floor and she smacked into a chair on the way down. Andi gripped the side of her face and began to cry hysterically. She scrambled to her feet and began to run towards the back door to find Red.

"There's no use running, Kellan!" Vince called out as he stalked after her.

Andi rounded the corner to go through the back room and abruptly stopped when Sal and Tony appeared from the shadows.

"No!" she cried as her knees gave out and she collapsed to the floor.

"Pick her up and take her to the car," Vince ordered.

Sal and Tony did as they were told and roughly hauled Andi to her feet. She struggled and fought her way against them, but they were too strong and soon she was being carried out of the bar with Sal gripping her arms to her waist and Tony gripping his arms around her legs. Vince followed behind them and waited by the black Mercedes Benz as they threw Andi into the back seat. Vince took the seat next to her, Sal took the passenger seat and Tony the driver's.

"Where to boss?" Tony asked as he started the engine.

"Just head north for now," Vince said as he caught site of the diamond ring on Andi's left hand.

"Well what do we have here?" He reached for her hand and she backed into the door as much as she possibly could. Vince grabbed Andi's hand and yanked the ringer from her finger.

"No, please don't!" she cried and took in a ragged breath.

"You won't be needing this," Vince said menacingly as he pressed the button on the door for the window to roll down. He laid his hand out the window and dropped the ring into the dirt as the car sped out of the parking lot and down the long dark road.

Chapter Nineteen

Zane pulled into the parking lot of The Rusty Spur at twelve minutes past two. He let out a huge yawn as he crawled out of the truck and walked towards the building. All he could think about was collapsing in bed with Andi by his side and sleeping in until early afternoon the next day. He didn't understand why, but as he walked through the dirt parking lot a deep unsettling feeling hovered in the pit of his stomach. He tried to shake it off but as he approached the door he found it cracked opened. *Red always makes sure this is closed and locked right at two,* he thought to himself. Zane slowly pushed the door open and let his eyes scan the dim lit room.

"Andi?" he called out. He took a careful step in and began to walk slowly through the room. "Andi?" he called once more. The unsettling feeling was slowly starting to turn into panic. Zane continued walking through the room and noticed one of the chairs toppled over on the floor. His heart began to race as he alternately began to call for Andi and Red. He rushed to the backroom and found the door leading outside hanging wide open. He ran through the opening and skid to a stop, spinning around in a circle, trying to see any traces of them. Zane leaned over, resting his hands on his knees and attempted to control his breathing. As he stood up he heard a muffled sound coming from behind the dumpster. Taking each step slowly, he rounded the metal container and gasped at the sight before him.

"Oh God, Red." Zane quickly bent down and reached for the older man. "What happened?" He reached in his back pocket and pulled out a clean handkerchief and applied it to the gash above Red's right eye, which was swollen and quickly turning a deep purple.

"Zane?" Red asked hoarsely.

"Yea, Red, it's me," Zane said.

"Wha—, What happened?" With the one eye he could see out of, Red stared up at Zane with a glazed expression.

"I don't know," Zane said with a sigh. "I was hoping you could tell me. Do you know who did this to you?"

Red tried to get up but let out a yelp and grabbed his ribs as he fell back to the ground. He breathed in short, painful pants as Zane advised him to sit still.

"Red, where's Andi?" Zane asked with a sense of urgency.

"She—" Red stopped and gasped for air. "She was inside."

Zane looked back to the door. Maybe she was hiding or maybe she was hurt just as bad as Red. The adrenaline began to pulse through his veins and his hands began to shake.

"Stay still okay. I'm going to go call an ambulance and try to find Andi. I'll be back soon. Here, can you hold this to your head?" Zane carefully took Red's hand and brought it up to the handkerchief. Seconds later he was on his feet and running back into the bar. "Andi? Come on, baby, answer me," Zane pleaded. He quickly ran over to the phone behind the counter and dialed 911. The operator's voice came through the receiver and Zane quickly explained the situation and listened to the instructions he was given before hanging up and continuing his search for Andi.

No corner was left unsearched. Zane came to a stop and leaned against the wall for support. "I shouldn't have left her," he mumbled to himself. When he lifted his head from the wall, he stared out the open entrance of the building into the parking lot. A sudden burst of hope gave him the energy to run across the room. Zane called for Andi again when he reached the empty parking lot. His eyes scanned the scenery hoping for a glimpse of anything that would lead him to her.

A small flicker of light caught his attention and he slowly walked towards the tiny object. Zane sank to his knees as the numbness started in his feet and quickly swam through the rest of his body. He picked up the engagement ring and held it between his forefinger and thumb as his eyes followed the trail of skid marks leaving the parking lot. The lump in his throat made it hard for him to swallow and his vision blurred as an overwhelming feeling of guilt weighed heavy on his heart.

****

The lights from the police cruisers flashed across the front of the building as two paramedics wheeled Red to the ambulance on a stretcher. Zane stood off to the side giving his statement to one of the officers as the others searched the area for clues or evidence. A set of headlights could be seen speeding down the road and the vehicle quickly entered the parking lot, sliding to a stop. Norah jumped out a second later and ran towards Zane.

"Oh my God, Zane, what happened?" she asked with wide eyes. "Is that Red? What's going on?"

Zane turned to the officer before answering Norah. "Do you have everything you need?"

"Yes I think I do. If I have any more questions or if we find anything I'll be sure to call you immediately." The officer tucked his pen into his shirt pocket and closed his notepad as he walked back to his car.

"Zane talk to me. What happened here?" Norah asked frantically. "Where's Andi?"

He could sense the panic in her voice and gently took her shoulder and led her to a more private spot, away from all the activity.

"I think he found her, Norah. I'm positive it was him," Zane told her with a shaky voice.

"She's gone?" Norah asked in surprise.

Zane nodded. "I knew that I shouldn't have left. I didn't have a good feeling about it but I did it anyway. Dammit!"

"Why did you leave?" Norah brought her hand up and gently began to rub it up and down Zane upper arm, attempting to console him.

"Luke was drunk and couldn't drive," Zane explained. "I wanted to let him sleep it off on the bar but Andi said it wasn't right and asked me to take him home."

Norah could sense that Zane was angry with

Luke for the whole thing. "You can't blame Luke for this. He had nothing to do with it. Things happen, Zane. It's no one's fault."

"That's easy enough to say, Norah," Zane said. "But if I hadn't taken him home I would have been here. I could have protected her, I could have done something, I could have-,"

"You could have ended up like Red," she interrupted. "I'm sure this was not a one man operation, Zane."

Zane rested his head in his hand and took in a deep breath. "What if I've lost her for good, Norah?"

"You won't, we'll find her," Norah said, attempting to sound positive. "The police are involved and I'm sure they'll find a trail here soon."

Zane snorted. "Yea, a lot of good they are. They told me that they can't do anything about it with it dark outside, that it would have to wait till the morning."

"They're right, Zane. It's too dark to see anything right now. When the sun's up they'll be able to uncover all kinds of new stuff. Just have faith." Norah patted his shoulder and gave him a reassuring smile. "There's not much more we can do tonight. Come on, I'll take you back to the house and you can get some rest. You look absolutely exhausted." She looped her arm under his and brought her hand up to rest on his shoulder.

Zane followed in silence and took the passenger seat in Norah's truck. Sleep was the last thing on his mind right now, and even though he was truly beat he knew that he wouldn't be able to rest till Andi was safe and in his arms.

****

"Wake up," Vince said as he pulled on Andi's arm.

Andi groggily opened her red swollen eyes and assessed her surroundings. "Where are we?"

"Get out," Vince ordered. He yanked her from the car and held her close as they walked towards the tall building. "Go get us a room," he said and directed Tony towards the check in desk.

"Good afternoon, sir, and welcome to the Nashville Hilton," the young man at the counter warmly greeted.

Nashville! Holy hell, how was Zane ever going to find her in Nashville?

"Oh I'm sorry, sir, but check in isn't till three o'clock. If you'd like you are more than welcome to enjoy one of our fine restaurants until then," the young man said to Tony.

Andi let her eyes scan the room. The clock on the wall said it was half past twelve. She bit her bottom lip and attempted to hold back the tears that threatened to slip down her cheeks at any moment. As far as she knew, Vince had a ten hour head start on Zane. She turned her attention back towards Tony and the young man at the counter and saw Tony lean in and slide something across the shiny wood surface. The young man carefully looked around him and accepted the generous bribe.

"I think we can accommodate you," the young man said. "I have the presidential suite available on the top floor."

Tony nodded and waited for the card key. They

made their way to the elevator and as they waited
Vince let his eyes run over Andi from head to toe.

"You look like a hillbilly," he sneered.

Andi bit the inside of her cheek and dared not
make a comment.

The doors opened and the four of them were
about to enter but Vince held his hand out and
stopped Sal before he could step in. "Go find her
some decent clothes to wear. I'm not walking
around with her looking like this."

"What am I supposed to get, boss?" Sal asked
confused.

"Everything," Vince said sharply. "Now stop
asking me stupid questions and just do what I told
you to!"

The doors closed and Vince pulled Andi
towards the back of the elevator with him. The ride
up to the top floor was uninterrupted and quiet.
When the doors opened, they stepped out into a
private lobby with mahogany paneled walls, a round
table in the center of the room with a huge
arrangement of fresh flowers, and directly around
the table was the entrance to the suite. Tony stepped
ahead of them and used the card key to unlock the
door. He turned the handle and held it open for
Vince and Andi as they walked through into the
elaborate room. With his hand still gripping her
upper arm, Vince pulled Andi through the suite and
towards the master bedroom.

"Get in there and don't make a sound." He
flung her into the room sending her straight towards
the foot of the bed. The doors closed behind her and
she quickly ran over and grabbed the handle. She

twisted and turned but to no avail.

"Vince, you let me out right now! You can't keep me in here!" Andi banged her fist on the door and kicked at it with the toe of her boot.

Three sharp pounds came from the other side of the door. "I said shut up!"

Andi spun around and leaned against the door. She had no idea what Vince's plans for her were, and she didn't intend to find out. The phone on the night table caught her attention and she quickly crossed the room. She grabbed the receiver and with rapid motions she dialed the familiar number on the keypad.

"Come on, come on, pick up," she whispered to herself. Andi let out an exasperated sigh when Zane's voicemail kicked in. With her heart pounding with worry that she'd be caught any second, she anxiously waited for the message to stop so she could leave as much information as she could. The beep finally sounded and Andi began with her frantic message. "Zane, it's me. Vince has kidnapped me and taken me to-." Her message was cut short as Vince leaned around her and pressed the button on the phone, ending the call.

"Let's not be stupid, all right." His voice was cool and calm. It sent shivers down her spine and frightened her more than when he was yelling at her. "Now, you're going to go in that bathroom, get cleaned up, do your hair and put some make up on. Then you're going to get dressed and join me out in the main room for drinks. We have dinner reservations at six thirty, so don't delay."

"That's six hours from now, Vince. It's not

going to take me that long to get ready for dinner," she smarted off.

"I'm tired of looking at you in those rags you call clothes," he said with a bit of an edge to his tone. "Now do as you're told." He turned and began to walk out of the room but stopped when Andi continued to talk.

"You can't keep me locked up forever, Vince. Sooner or later someone will find me and come to my rescue. You're not going to win this one."

He turned on his heel and crossed the room to her in three strides. He raised his hand to strike her face and she flinched. "That's what I thought," he said bringing his hand down and slowly running his fingers down the side of her cheek. "I never knew you had this much spunk. You've never talked back to me before, and I've got to be honest," he paused and leaned in, "it kind of turns me on."

Andi tensed and stiffened as Vince's face came towards her. She pinched her mouth shut as he ran his tongue over her lips then forced them apart to kiss her fiercely. She leaned away from him and spit directly in his face.

Vince let go of her and pulled out a fancy white handkerchief from the inside pocket of his coat. He dabbed it on his face, then stared her down as he replaced it back in his pocket. "Don't do that again," he warned. "And go get ready."

When the door to the bedroom closed Andi brought her hand up and began to wipe her mouth to the point where it began to feel raw. Her mouth was left with the taste of stale cigarettes and she quickly began to feel the bile tickle the back of her throat.

She ran to the bathroom and hovered over the toilet. When the spasms were done, she fell back against the Jacuzzi tub and curled her knees up to her chest. "Dear God, please let Zane find me. Please," she whispered. The tears she had been holding back began to fall down her cheeks and she buried her face into her drawn up knees.

****

Zane sat on the back porch steps at his mother's house and stared out into the endless pale blue sky. He heard the screen door open and boots shuffle across the wood boards and stop next to him. Luke groaned as he sat down and adjusted his hat to shield his eyes from the blinding sun.

"So how mad at me are you?" Luke asked.

Zane shook his head and let out an exasperated sigh. "I'm not mad at you anymore."

Luke nodded his head and squinted his eyes. Light and hangovers never mixed well. "I really am sorry. I never meant for this to happen."

Zane turned to Luke with an understanding face. "I know. No one did."

"Have you heard anything from the police yet?" Luke asked with concern.

Zane simply shook his head no and stared back towards the scenery.

Luke placed a reassuring hand on Zane's shoulder. "I'm sure something will turn up soon."

Just then Norah came running out to the porch. Both Zane and Luke shifted to look at her with perplexed expressions on their faces. "Your phone," she said breathless holding the flip phone out towards Zane.

He took it from her and still gave her the same perplexed look.

"It rang and I didn't get to it in time. There's a voicemail," she quickly spouted out.

Zane's eyes widened as he fumbled with the keys on the phone. "It's Andi!" he exclaimed. The surprised look on his face quickly dissolved to one of disappointment.

"What?" Luke asked.

"It cut off," Zane said as he shut the phone and squeezed it in his palm. "Dammit!"

"Well, what was the number?" Norah asked.

Hope filled his body once more as Zane flipped the phone back open and scrolled to his missed call log. "I can't tell what area code this is," he said.

"Here let me see," Norah said and took the phone from his hand. She quickly ran to the computer in the office and turned the monitor on. With a few strokes of the keys and a couple of mouse clicks later she was running back out to Zane and Luke. "Nashville," she stated.

"As in Tennessee?" Luke asked.

"What's going on?" Linda asked as she joined them on the porch.

"Andi called Zane," Norah quickly said.

"She did?" Linda asked in surprise. "How? Where?"

"She's in Nashville, Tennessee. Her message was cut off but we looked the number up on the computer," Norah continued.

Zane was off his feet and into the house in a matter of seconds. He came bursting out the door a minute later and ran to his truck.

"What are you doing?" the three of them ask in unison as they ran after him.

"Going after her." With a determined look on his face he placed the key in the ignition and gave it a sharp turn. The truck roared to life as he revved the engine.

"Zane, sweetie, you can't just go after her," his mother said placing a hand on his arm through the open window. "You don't know what kind of people you are dealing with, son. Let's go call the police and let them take care of it."

"I'm not waiting around anymore, Mom. I've felt nothing but useless for the past few hours and now I've got the chance to do something about it. You can call the police and let them know what's going on, but I'm not sitting here any longer." He placed his foot on the break and shifted the truck into gear.

His mother nodded and took a step back from the truck. He was just about to pull away when Luke ran around the front of the truck and entered the passenger side.

"What are you doing?" Zane asked.

"Going with you," Luke explained as he fastened his seatbelt.

"Luke, no," Zane protested.

"Look, Zane, I feel bad enough that all of this happened. Let me do this please. Plus, you've always had my back in a fight, now it's my turn to return the favor. Now drive."

Zane gave his brother an appreciative smile, then turned his attention back towards his mother and Norah.

"Norah, where did the call come from?" Zane asked.

"It was registered to one of the Hilton hotels," she said.

"Text me the address, okay?" Zane instructed. "We'll call you as soon as we can."

"Be safe," Norah and Linda cried.

Zane lifted his foot off the brake and pressed hard down on the gas pedal. The truck fishtailed out of the driveway, leaving a cloud of dust behind him. *I'm coming, Andi. Just hold on, I'm coming.*

Chapter Twenty

Andi stared at her reflection in the mirror and grimaced. With a sigh, she picked up the large powder brush and swept it across her cheekbone, cleaning up the fall out of eye shadow that fell there when she applied the dark shade to her lid. She applied a few coats of mascara then added lip gloss to finish the look.

Andi rewrapped the bath towel around her more securely, then headed out to the bedroom to change into the dress Vince had ordered her to wear. She sucked in a shocked breath of air as she picked up the barely there underwear Sal had purchased.

"Are you kidding me?" she said out loud to herself in disbelief.

She rolled her eyes and dropped the towel to the floor. After she was as comfortable as she could possibly get in the black lace thong and matching bra, she slid into the skin tight sheath black spaghetti strap dress. She then sat on the edge of the bed and slipped into the strappy stiletto heels. As she stood up from the bed and began to walk she couldn't help but feel wobbly and off balance. Funny how just a little over a month ago she could practically run in these things and now she was so used to her boots and tennis shoes that she found herself barely able to even walk in them.

"Now that's more like it," Vince approved as

Andi walked out into the main living area. He met her halfway and looped his arm around her waist. "Here, join me for a drink before dinner."

"I'm not thirsty," she objected.

Vince moved to the bar and poured each of them a serving of scotch. With a glass in each hand he walked back towards her and held hers out.

She glanced at the glass then shifted her eyes to stare out the window, ignoring him completely.

Vince brought the glass up to her face and bumped it hard against her chin.

Andi quickly brought her eyes back to him with a stunned expression.

"Drink," he ordered.

The rage slowly began to build in her body as she snatched the glass from his hand and downed the contents with one large gulp.

"Thata girl." Vince smiled at her and gave her a once over. "You know, if you keep this up we may just end up skipping dinner all together." He had moved closer towards her, so close that she could feel his breath on her neck.

Andi swallowed convulsively as she tasted the hint of vomit on the back of her throat. His hand slid up and down the side of her body as his breath continued to brush across her neck.

"Vince, I'm actually quite hungry. Why don't we go to dinner and then we can worry about that sort of thing later." She was trying to buy herself as much time as she could and right now she'd say anything just to get his hands off of her.

"All right, later it is then," he agreed with a mischievous smile. He took her glass from her hand

and placed it back on the bar along with his own. "Let's go," he said as he wrapped an arm around her waist and ushered her towards the door but stopped when they heard knocks coming from the other side. Vince motioned for Tony to answer it.

"Yes? Who is it?" Tony asked through the door, resting his hand on his side arm as he leaned in to listen.

"Nashville Police Department."

That's all Andi managed to hear before Vince hauled her back, further into the room.

"What have you done?" he hissed, pushing her shoulder.

"I swear I didn't do anything," she stammered as she quickly backed away from him. She only stopped moving away when her back hit the wall and she realized she had nowhere to run.

Vince was on her then, crowding her against the wall and bracing his hands on either side of her head. "Then why are the police here?"

Her heart felt like it was going to leap out of her chest. Zane had gotten her message, but she wasn't about to tell Vince that. She opened her mouth to tell him she didn't know when he cut her off.

"Just shut up," he said and glared at her. "Don't try anything stupid. You know what I can do to you, Kellen. And don't think I'll stop there. You say anything to them and I'll not only hurt you, I'll find your little boyfriend, too." He leaned in and breathed against her cheek. "And I'll make you watch as he pays for your actions."

Andi whimpered and forced herself to hold it

together. She closed her eyes tightly to fight back
the tears that threatened to escape. The last thing
she wanted was for Vince and his friends to hurt
Zane and his family, so she nodded and took in a
deep breath.

"Smart move," Vince said and stepped away
from her, letting her move away from the wall.

Just then the door opened widely and two
police officers stepped in the room, glancing around
and taking in their surroundings. Their eyes stopped
on Andi and Vince and slowly made their way
towards them.

"We apologize for the intrusion, sir, but we had
a phone call about a kidnapping and are here to
investigate," the younger officer explained.

"A kidnapping?" Vince said, acting confused
and gripped Andi's side in a warning that she better
play along. "Surely you're mistaken, officer."

"Be that as it may, sir," the other officer said.
"We were informed that a young woman that fits
the description of your lady friend here was being
held against her will." The officer turned his
attention to Andi. "Ma'am, is there anything you'd
like to tell us?"

"No, officer," she said. "This man is my
boyfriend and I'm not being held here against my
will."

"Are you absolutely positive?" the younger
officer asked.

Andi simply nodded, not wanting to verbalize
the lie again.

"Well then, sorry for the intrusion once more
folks. You all have a good night."

Tony saw the officers to the door and closed it firmly behind them.

"Good girl," Vince whispered against her ear and Andi shuddered.

The hope she had felt mere moments ago was now gone and she was left with the overpowering feeling of doom.

****

The hostess seated them immediately at a corner table. The linens were a crisp white and the crystal stemware gleamed in the dim lighting. She handed each of them a menu before excusing herself and walking away from the table. Andi held the menu up and pretended to glance over it as she let her eyes do a quick scan of the room. Of course Vince had to pick the table farthest away from the exit with as many obstacles as possible. There was no easy escape. The waiter was at the table moments later. He introduced himself as he poured each of them a glass of water.

"Bring us a bottle of your finest red wine," Vince said before waving the waiter away.

"Very well, sir," the waiter responded. Andi looked up at him and noticed he was doing his best to hold his tongue. She hated the way Vince treated people in the service industry. The waiter looked to her just then and she gave him an apologetic look. He excused himself so they could continue to look over the menu and to retrieve their bottle of wine.

Andi turned her attention back towards the menu and looked over the entrées. Vince laid his menu down as the waiter approached with their wine and poured them each a glass.

"Have you had a chance to decide what you would like for dinner?" the waiter asked.

Andi glanced over the menu once more and was just about to speak when Vince jumped in before her.

"We'll start off with the oysters on the half shell for our appetizer. And for the main course I'll have the New York Strip cooked rare with the russet potato gratin and a Ceasar salad."

Andi began to speak again and was immediately cut off once more by Vince.

"And she'll have the Truffle Honey Glazed Duck Breast with julienne bok choy and a Ceasar salad as well."

Andi stared at him and her mouth fell open with shock.

"Very well, sir," the waiter said taking their menus and walking away from the table.

"Um, I can order my own food," Andi said with irritation.

"Nonsense," Vince said and waved a hand towards her as he took a sip of his wine.

"I don't even like duck, Vince."

"Yes you do." He adjusted his napkin on his lap.

"No I don't," she argued.

"Yes, you do." He spoke each word slowly and menacingly.

Andi pinched her lips and sat back in her chair. She snatched the glass of wine from the table and took a sip. *Oh what I wouldn't do for a nice ice cold beer right now*, she thought. The waiter returned ten minutes later with their appetizer and didn't linger long at the table.

"Have some," Vince said placing an oyster on Andi's plate.

"I don't want any," she said wrinkling her nose.

"Have some," he ordered and pushed her plate towards her.

She sighed and picked up the oyster and quickly tossed it back as though she were taking a shot of liquor. She involuntarily shivered and placed the shell back on the plate. Her eyes wandered around the room again, taking in her surroundings. The clock on the wall said it was past six-thirty. God how she wished Zane was on his way now to rescue her. The phone call to the police obviously hadn't gone as planned. Still she couldn't help but wish that any minute now a swat team would come bursting into the fancy restaurant and save her from this horrible dream that had all of a sudden become a reality.

As she looked around the room she noticed all kinds of different people seated at the tables. There were people there on business, couples there for a romantic night out, and couples there who were cheating on their spouses or significant others. She could tell the difference in the couples by their body language. The couples who were not cheating were not distracted by anything. It was as though they were the only ones in the room. Now as for the ones cheating, well they were distracted by everything. It was probably due to the fact that they were so on edge and afraid of being caught. There was one man who kept checking his cell phone every few minutes. He'd pick it up, check his text messages, and then place it back on the table.

A sudden burst of hope shot through her at that moment. She removed her napkin from her lap and placed it on the table as she pushed her chair out to stand up.

"And where do you think you're going," Vince asked as he reached for her.

"I'm just going to the bathroom, Vince. Calm down."

"Uh-uh," he said and pointed towards the chair for her to sit.

"Seriously? I'm not going to do anything, Vince. There's too many people and it's not like I can get out of here easily anyway."

He gave her a hard look then glanced to his left and snapped his fingers. Tony made his way through the crowd of tables and Andi sighed.

"Go with her and wait right outside the room," Vince ordered.

Tony nodded and walked next to Andi as they made their way towards the restrooms. With her eye on the man's cell phone sitting at the edge of the table she glanced at Tony and saw the he wasn't paying any attention to her. They reached the table and Andi pretended to lose her balance and stumbled, landing into the table.

"Hey watch it!" the man yelled quickly grabbing his glass of wine.

His lady friend wasn't so quick to grab hers and it toppled over sending the crimson colored liquid all over the pristine table cloth.

"I'm so sorry!" Andi quickly apologized.

Tony grabbed her roughly by the arm and drug

her away from the scene as a couple of waiters ran over to mend the situation.

"Hurry up," Tony said and pushed her towards the restroom door. "And don't try anything stupid. I'll be right here waiting for you to come out."

Andi walked calmly and coolly to the restroom. Once she was inside she hurried to a stall and locked the door behind her. "I can't believe that worked!" she whispered in excitement as she pulled the stolen cell phone from her clutch. Her fingers trembled as she dialed Zane's number and waited anxiously for him to pick up.

"Hello?" She heard Zane's voice after only one ring.

"Zane!" she whispered as the tears began to fill her eyes. She tried to control herself because she was damn sure that Sal had not purchased her waterproof mascara during his shopping trip.

"Andi!" Zane exclaimed. "Oh my God you're okay! You are okay aren't you?"

"Yes I'm fine," she said with a shaky voice.

"Where are you? Did you get away from them?" Zane asked with urgency.

"I'm still in Nashville, and no I haven't been able to get away. I don't have much time so listen. I'm in the Hilton hotel and Vince has us in the presidential suite on the top floor. We're at the restaurant downstairs right now. I told Vince I needed to go to the bathroom and I stole this phone that I'm on." She was ecstatic to hear his voice, but at the same time it only made her more depressed that she wasn't with him.

"We're on our way, sweetie. I'm only a couple

of hours away and then I'll be there," Zane reassured her when heard the sadness in her voice.

"We?" she asked, taking in a ragged breath.

"Luke's with me. We'll be there soon. Just try to stay calm and act like you don't know anything. Don't let him know that we're coming," Zane said. "We'll get you out of there and then I'm never letting you out of my sight again."

Despite the fact that she desperately wanted to break down and cry, she couldn't help but crack a smile. "That's okay by me."

"Just hang tight. I'm on my way. You should probably get back to him before he suspects something," Zane reluctantly suggested.

"You're probably right," she said. "I'm surprised they haven't come bursting in here to make sure I'm still in the room."

"I love you, Andi." Zane's voice was tender and sweet as he spoke those three magical words.

Unable to control it, a tear slipped from her cheek and she buried her face in her hand. "I love you too."

****

"What's the matter with you?" Vince asked harshly when Andi returned to the table.

"What do you mean?" she asked, placing her napkin on her lap.

"I mean you look like shit," Vince sneered. "Have you been crying?"

Andi picked up the spoon lying on the table and looked at her reflection. "No, not really. I don't feel well and I got sick in the bathroom."

He gave her s suspicious look. "Well, eat your

dinner and you'll feel better."

Andi looked down at the duck breast on her plate and held her hand over her mouth. She faked a gag and then began to wave her hand like a fan towards her face.

"What's wrong now?" Vince asked through gritted teeth.

"I can't eat this. I'm going to be sick again. I think I just need to go lie down for a bit. Can I please just go back to the room?" Andi hoped her lie would work.

Vince wiped his mouth with his napkin and tossed it on the table. He snapped his fingers and Tony came from across the room once more. "Take her back to the room and lock her in the bedroom. I'm going to finish my meal in peace and then I'm going over to the bar for a drink or two. I'll be up shortly. Keep your eye on her."

Tony gave Vince a simple nod of understanding then escorted Andi out of the room.

"I'm telling you, one of your waiters stole my phone!" Andi heard the man at the table yell to the manager.

She automatically felt bad that someone was going to lose their job over her actions, but she wasn't about to give up the fact that she was the one who took it and who still had it tucked away in her bra. They made their way to the room and Andi was once again locked in the master suite. She kicked out of the stilettos and ran into the bathroom, locking the door behind her. She dialed Zane's number once more and waited.

"Andi? What's wrong?" Zane's voice came

through the receiver in a panic.

"Nothing, I'm fine," she told him. "I'm back in our room now. I told Vince I didn't feel well and that I needed to lay down for a bit. He had Tony bring me up here and he is staying downstairs for a while. I'm all alone and as far as I know Tony is the only one guarding the door."

"Good job. Have you seen any signs of the police yet?" he asked.

"Yes," she told him hesitantly. "But Vince made me lie and tell them I wasn't being held prisoner."

"Dammit," he said. "He didn't hurt you did he?"

"No," she lied, not wanting to worry Zane more than he already was. "How far away are you, Zane?"

"I'm getting there as fast I can," he explained sweetly. "It'll probably be close to ten but it may be sooner if I don't get pulled over for speeding."

Andi sighed when she saw the clock radio on the nightstand said seven forty-five.

"Andi?" Zane asked cautiously.

"Yes?" she replied.

"I promise, I'll be there soon," he said. "Just try to think of good things in the mean time."

"I'm trying to, Zane, but it's hard."

"I know, but just close your eyes and imagine that I'm there with you," he said sweetly. "Think about what you want our future to be like. Think about our wedding day and saying 'I do'."

She instinctively looked at her naked ring finger on her left hand when he mentioned the wedding. "Zane, there's something I need to tell you about that."

"You are still marrying me aren't you?" he teased attempting to lighten the mood a little. He hated hearing the sadness in her voice and hated it even more that he wasn't there with her.

"Yes I am, it's just that-"

"Shoo, you had me worried," he said and forced a chuckle.

Andi forced a light laugh back and glanced around the room. "I probably shouldn't stay on this phone for too long, someone might hear me."

"All right," he said. "I'll be there soon. I promise."

The phone went dead and Andi hung her head and sighed. "Not soon enough." She paced the bathroom looking for a good hiding spot for the phone. "Drawers are too obvious, the shower is just ridiculous," she mumbled to herself as she continued to look everywhere. She glanced at the toilet and ran over to remove the lid of the tank. She then rummaged through the drawers of the vanity and pulled out the unused shower cap. Working quickly, she wrapped the phone in the shower cap and stuck the phone in the tank of the toilet. She left just enough of the shower cap hanging over the edge of the lip of the back so that when she placed the lid back on it held the shower cap firmly in place, thus keeping the cell phone hidden and dry. "Eat your heart out MacGyver," she mumbled with a smirk.

Andi made her way back out to the bedroom. *Two and a half more hours till Zane is here,* she thought to herself. She walked around the room and over to the window, pulling back the curtains to see if it would open. No luck. What was she planning on doing anyway? Scaling the building like Spiderman until she made it to a balcony or something? Andi laughed to herself when that thought popped in her mind. She sat down on the bed and tried to let herself only think of happy thoughts like Zane suggested. Leaning her head back against the pillow, she closed her eyes and saw him. He was standing in the barn with Cash, brushing him down after his ride. He looked over to her and gave her one of his heart melting crooked smiles.

The vision changed then to a different setting. She was in the backyard of the ranch, standing at the end of a make-shift aisle. Hay bales were set in the place of chairs and tied to the end of each row was a beautiful bouquet of sunflowers with yellow ribbon flowing in the breeze. The sensation of someone looping their arm through hers caught her attention and she looked to see who it was. Red was standing next to her with an approving smile on his face. She smiled in return and the two of them slowly made their way down the aisle. She noticed Belle and Linda sitting on the front hay bale. They smiled and waved as Andi and Red walked closer.

She then let her eyes turn back towards the front of the set up and saw Norah standing off to the left wearing a knee length strapless canary yellow dress and holding a small bouquet of sunflowers. She had the brightest smile on her face and Andi watched as Norah lifted a tissue to her face to dab her eyes. Andi then looked over to her right and saw Luke standing there wearing a western cut tuxedo, complete with shiny black boots and a new black cowboy hat. He smiled and placed his hand on the man's shoulder that he was standing next to. He leaned in and whispered something then looked back to Andi with a smile. Her eyes moved slightly to the left and she saw him. Her breath caught in her throat and tears of joy began to fill her eyes.

Zane, she sighed inwardly.

Even though he was wearing the same exact thing as Luke, he was more handsome than any other man she had ever laid eyes on. He smiled at her as she came towards him and he stepped away from the preacher, only for a moment to shake hands with Red and then lead her back to the make-shift altar with him. They each took turns reciting the vows that people have spoken since the beginning of time. And when the preacher announced them man and wife, Zane stepped towards her, removing his hat and firmly wrapping his arms around her waist. Among the hoots, whistles and applause, Zane kissed his new bride. Never in her whole life had she felt more special, more loved, or happier, than she had in the moment.

Andi shifted to a more comfortable position on the bed and let out a shaky sigh. As much as she wanted to believe that Zane would arrive soon and rescue her from this hell, she couldn't help but wonder what would happen if he didn't get there in time? Or worse, what would happen if he did get there but something bad happened to him as he tried to save her? Tears filled her eyes as the unwanted thoughts passed behind her heavy eyelids. Unable to keep a handle on her emotions, Andi cried herself to sleep.

Chapter Twenty-One

It was the most realistic dream she had ever had. His lips trailed steaming hot kisses all the way from her jaw to her breast. His hands left no part of her body untouched. He was giving her everything she wanted, but it still wasn't enough.

"More," she whispered seductively.

Oh if only all dreams felt this real. She could feel the heat pulsing from their bodies. She could feel the weight of his body pressed against hers. She could smell the strong stench of scotch on his breath. Andi's eyes popped wide open and she gasped.

"Vince, what the hell are you doing?"

"What does it look like?" he responded and moved in to kiss her.

Andi quickly turned her head and Vince's lips brushed across her cheek.

"Get off!" she cried and shoved hard against his chest. To her surprise Vince rolled off of her to the other side of the bed.

Andi took five large steps away from the bed and gave Vince a hard look. "That is *not* okay!" she yelled pointing at him.

Vince threw his legs off the other side of the bed and stood up. He ran a hand through his hair to smooth it back in place as he looked to Andi. "Oh I think it is." He slowly began to walk towards her and she in turn took backward steps away from him.

"This isn't how this works, Vince. You can't just force yourself on me whenever you feel like it. And you can't force me to be with you either."

Vince let out an eerie sort of laugh and smiled. "I think I can do whatever I want. Or have you forgotten? Things are going to go back to the way they used to be. You are coming back to New Jersey with me and we're going to act like all of this never happened. You belong to me, Kellan, or have you forgotten that as well?" He cocked his head to the side and stopped his approach.

"No, I don't." Andi felt her back hit the wall and she took in a nervous breath when she realized she was cornered.

"Let's think about this now, shall we?" he asked with a perplexed look on his face. "We've been together for what, a little over two years? And in that time I have bought you jewelry, clothes, a car, designer shoes, paid for your hair, makeup, manicures, pedicures, tanning sessions. In addition to that I gave you a place to live. I've provided everything for you, and you've given nothing back. So therefore, I own you."

"I never asked for any of that, Vince," Andi stated heatedly. "You willingly did all of that for me in the beginning and at the time just my love for you alone was enough to repay you. But then all of it became more for show than anything else and you changed, Vince. You became this mean and hateful person and I began to despise you for it. I *never* deserved to be treated and beaten like that! I'm not going back to that, *ever*."

Vince spun around on his heel and walked over

to the nightstand. He yanked open the drawer and pulled out a handgun. He cocked it back and aimed it towards her with a vicious look in his eye.

Andi's heart stopped beating and she pressed herself harder up against the wall for support. "Vince, I—"

"You what?" he asked, his voice loud and frightening. "You want to retract your statement?"

"I'm sorry," she quickly said. "Look just put the gun down, please."

"Oh now you want to play nice," he said.

"Vince, please, just put the gun down."

"It's going to take a lot more convincing than that," he said menacingly.

Andi took in a deep breath and closed her eyes. She needed to get out of here and fast. But first she needed to get that gun out of his hands. "All right," she said in a slow and even voice.

"All right what?" Vince asked.

"I'll convince you. I'll do whatever you want." She moved from the wall and slowly walked towards him.

"What are you doing?" he asked, keeping the gun pointed at her.

"Giving in. There's no use fighting anymore, Vince. And it appears that no one is coming to my rescue. So why don't you put that gun down and we'll start where we left off." She stood next to the bed and reached for the zipper on the side of her dress.

The hard look on Vince's face faded away as he understood what Andi meant. He carefully laid the gun down on the dresser by the door and closed the distance between them in a matter of seconds. His hands were rough as he yanked her towards him, his lips feverishly traced every part of her exposed skin. Andi positioned herself and waited for the right moment. In the midst of his rough kisses and groping, Andi placed her hands on Vince's shoulders, took a quick step backwards and brought her knee up hard into his groin.

Vince's face turned red and he let out a loud groan as he cupped his hands over his damaged manhood and collapsed to the floor. Andi took a step back and watched with a pleased smile on her face as Vince gasped for air. She went to run past him but was brought up short and fell to the floor as Vince grabbed a hold of her ankle.

"You bitch!" he choked.

"Get off of me!" she yelled and brought her knee up to her chest then straightened it out with a jerk, connecting her foot with Vince's nose.

He yelled once more and released his hold of her ankle. She scrambled to her feet and grabbed the gun on the dresser. With his gun in her possession, Andi opened the doors and ran through them, swiftly closing them behind her and locking him in just the way he had done to her. She ran through the suite towards the only way in and out of that place and stopped when she realized that Sal and Tony were probably standing on the other side.

"Damn it," she cursed under her breath. She stood there for a minute and contemplated how she was going to get out of this. A loud bang coming from the bedroom made her decision for her. She burst open the door and found Sal standing there keeping watch. She aimed the gun and cocked it back as he threw his hands up and gave her a shocked expression. "Up against the wall," she demanded. When he didn't move she threw in, "Now!"

Sal did as he was told and backed against the wall so Andi could get by. She kept the gun pointed at him the whole way to the elevator and never relaxed her arm till she was in and the doors were closed. Her body began to shake from the mix of shock and adrenaline as she watched the numbers above the door decrease. Andi looked down to the gun still clenched in her hand and realized that she couldn't very well run through the lobby with it.

"There's gotta be a plant or trashcan or something that I can dump it in," she said out loud to herself. *I've got to act normal, like nothing is wrong*, she thought.

She then remembered that her dress was hanging open, so she quickly set the gun on the floor of the elevator and zipped her dress back up. She ran her hands through her hair to make it look presentable and sighed with frustration when she realized that she wasn't wearing any shoes. "Oh well, nothing I can do about that now." She quickly picked the gun back up as the elevator dinged and the doors opened to the ground floor. Keeping her hands tucked behind her and keeping the gun out of view from the waiting passengers, she hurried out the doors towards the lobby. She discarded the gun in the pot of a ficus tree as she made her way into the lobby.

With her head held high and her eyes scanning

the room she calmly and slowly made her way through the large open room towards the exit. Andi stopped in her tracks and her heart did a double skip as she watched Zane burst through the doors and look around in every direction before locking his gaze on her. With a look of relief on his face he ran towards her and scooped her into his arms. Andi buried her face into his chest and cried uncontrollably as she held onto to him for dear life.

Zane pulled back slightly and brought his hands to her face. He gently swept the hair away from her forehead as he asked, "Are you okay? Are you hurt?"

Andi tried to speak but the words just wouldn't come. So she simply nodded that she was all right and looked to him with tear filled eyes.

Zane cupped her cheeks in his hands and affectionately brought his lips to hers. She gripped the back of his shirt with her hands and held him as close as she possibly could during the duration of the kiss.

"How did you get away?" Zane asked wiping a tear from her cheek.

"I," she started but was interrupted when she heard a familiar voice yell from behind her.

"There she is! Get her!" Vince hobbled out into the lobby with blood streaking down his face and onto his once crisp white shirt.

Sal and Tony moved swiftly through the lobby towards Andi and Zane.

"We gotta move, come on!" Zane yelled and grabbed Andi's hand. They ran out of the building and jumped into the truck where Luke was waiting with the engine running. "Go! Go! Drive!" Zane yelled as Sal and Tony came running out of the building.

Luke quickly shifted the truck into gear and peeled out of the parking lot. Gun shots filled the air around them and they all ducked instinctively.

"Holy shit! They're shooting at us!" Luke yelled as he pushed the truck to seventy miles an hour.

Andi screamed and Zane leaned over her, covering her body in a protective way with his.

Minutes later, a black Mercedes Benz came up on them out of nowhere. Another three gunshots sounded through the air and missed the truck by inches.

"Jesus, these guys aren't going to give up," Luke said in disbelief.

Zane quickly pulled out his cell phone and dialed 911. He explained the situation to the operator and waited for her instructions. "No this is not a joke!" Zane argued into the phone. He gave the operator their whereabouts and hung up the phone. Luke sped through the unfamiliar streets, weaving back and forth in an attempt to doge the bullets.

Andi screamed once more as one of the bullets hit the passenger side mirror and shattered it to pieces. The faint sound of sirens could be heard in the distance and grew louder in a matter of minutes.

"Well it's about damn time!" Luke exclaimed. "I'm not sure how much longer I can keep them off of us. It's too damn dark out and I'm not sure where I'm going."

"You're doing fine, Luke. Just keep it up," Zane yelled over all the commotion.

The police cruisers came up quick on the black sedan and a voice came over the bull horn instructing them to pull over. Another gunshot sounded from the Benz and hit the front tire of one of the cruisers sending it veering off the road.

"Now they're shooting at the police?" Luke yelled. "Who are these guys?"

Luke stared into the rearview mirror to see what was happening.

"Luke," Zane said quietly staring out at the road before them. "Luke!" he yelled to get his attention.

"What? Oh shit!" Luke cursed and slammed on the brakes, causing the truck to spin a full three-sixty before slamming to a stop. The blockade of police cruisers blocking the street was something straight out of a movie. All three of them turned their heads at the screeching sound of tires on the asphalt. The Benz slid to a stop twenty yards away from them and they each held their breath as they waited to see what was going to happen next.

"You are surrounded," a voiced boomed through the bull horn. "Slowly roll down your windows and toss out your weapons."

Anticipation and anxiety filled the air as Andi, Zane and Luke waited to see if they would follow the instructions.

"Look," Andi said in amazement as the dark tinted windows of the sedan rolled down and three hand guns were tossed to the ground.

"Well damn, I didn't expect them to give up

that easily," Luke said as he watched Sal, Tony and Vince raise their empty hands out the windows.

"That's about the smartest thing they've done. They know that they can't take down this many cops," Zane said.

Sal, Tony and Vince were yanked from the Benz, handcuffed and taken into custody. After they were each placed in the back of the cruisers, Luke, Zane and Andi stepped out of the truck. Zane kept his arm firmly wrapped around the distraught and frightened Andi as a couple of officers made their way over to them.

"We're going to need to know what happened here," the young officer stated. "If you'll follow me we'll get a statement from each of you."

****

"And then I managed to escape from the room and all of this happened," Andi explained with a shiver.

"Okay, I think we have everything we need. I have your information and will be in contact with you should we need anything else," the young officer said.

"Thank you, officer," Andi said quietly.

"Yes, thank you," Zane said and gave Andi's shoulder a gentle squeeze.

"Not a problem." The officer turned his attention back to Andi and said, "You're a very lucky woman, Miss Anderson. Not many women go through that kind of situation and live to talk about it." He smiled and nodded as he walked away.

"Officer Mitchell," Andi called after him.

"Yes, Miss Anderson?"

"What's going to happen to them?" she asked nodding her head towards the cruisers that contained Sal, Tony and Vince.

"Oh I'd say that according to all of these offenses they've racked up that they'll be behind bars till they're old and gray, maybe longer." The officer nodded once more and walked back towards his car.

Andi looked to Zane and let out a contented sigh followed by a smile.

"Some day, huh?" Zane asked with a crooked smile.

"I'll say. Shoo!" Luke came up to stand next to him and placed his thumbs in the pockets of his jeans.

"That was some pretty good driving there, Luke," Zane complimented.

Luke shrugged and smiled. "I chalk it up to all those Dukes of Hazzard re-runs."

They all three laughed in unison and watched as the cruisers with Sal, Tony and Vince pull away and head down the road.

"I sure would have liked to beat the shit out that guy for doing what he did to you," Zane said turning his attention away from the police cruisers to Andi. "And also for having the balls to come and steal you away from me like that."

Andi smiled up at Zane. "I know, sweetie, but it's all over now and he can never take me away from you ever again."

"Guess it's back to our boring lives now, huh?" Luke asked turning to face Zane and Andi.

"Damn straight it is," Andi said with a laugh

and leaned into Zane.

Zane smiled and gently squeezed Andi closer to him. He then brought his hand up to her chin and tilted it upward so he could kiss her, long and passionately.

Luke cleared his throat.

Zane and Andi slowly pulled away from each other and chuckled at Luke's obvious discomfort.

Zane smiled, let out a sigh and wrapped his arm to Andi's shoulder. "Back to our boring lives it is then. Let's go home."

Chapter Twenty-Two

A warm summer breeze gently brushed across her skin as she and Zane rocked back and forth in their porch swing. The deep blue night sky was scattered with thousands of twinkling stars and the crickets were playing their nighttime symphony. Andi sighed contently and rested her head against Zane's shoulder.

"What are you thinking about?" he asked as he rested his head onto hers.

"Just about how nice this feels," she replied quietly.

"Mmm," Zane agreed.

"What are you thinking about?" she asked in return.

"Oh, I was just thinking about that tree over there." He lifted his head and nodded in the direction of the large oak tree.

She lifted her head from his shoulder and gave him a confused look. "We're cuddling and you're thinking about a tree?"

Zane laughed and squeezed her shoulder. "I was just thinking about how nice a tire swing would look hanging from that branch. You know, for all those kids we're going to have."

A smiled tickled the corners of her mouth. "Oh, well that's a nice thought." She leaned back and curled into his side. "So just how many kids are you planning on us having?" she asked and waited patiently for his response.

"I was thinking around six or eight," he said.

Andi shot forward and gave him a shocked expression. "Six or eight! Are you crazy?"

Zane laughed even harder than he had the first time.

"Please tell me you are kidding," Andi said.

"Yes, yes, it was a joke," he replied still chuckling.

"Shoo! You had me scared," she said and placed her hand over her heart. "So what's the real answer to my question?"

"I'm thinking along the line of two or three," he told her with a smile.

"Now that I can agree with," she said and leaned back against his side. "Of course, I think we're jumping the gun a little here talking about kids. We need to be married first."

Zane nodded his head and replied, "True. And when is that going to happen?"

"I was thinking about September third," she said. "That gives us about a month to get things in order."

"Sounds good to me." Zane smiled and kissed her hair.

Andi ran her thumb over the inside base of her ring finger on her left hand and thought about how she was going to bring up the fact that she no longer had the engagement ring he had given her. "Um, Zane?"

"Hmmm?" he said.

"There's something I need to tell you," she said a bit hesitantly.

"Okay." With the hand he had draped around her shoulder be began to make lazy circles on her exposed skin.

"The night Vince found me at the bar, well, he kind of sort of saw my ring and took it away from me." She waited for his angered response and was shocked when he didn't move.

"All right," he responded in a cool even voice.

"I'm trying to tell you that I don't have it anymore, sweetie. I'm so sorry." She felt him shift around and reach into his pocket. A second later he was holding the delicate piece of jewelry between his forefinger and thumb.

Andi sucked in a shocked breath of air and clasped her hands around his.

"I found it in the dirt at the bar," he explained. He sat up from his casual position on the swing and took Andi's left hand in his. "Let me see if I can get it right this time," he said with a grin. His eyes sparkled with the light of the moon and Andi felt her heart melt. "Before I met you, my world was empty. I went through life day by day with this dark cloud hanging over my head that seemed to get bigger all the time. I thought I'd never find anyone to fill that emptiness, and then you came along. Andi, you mean everything to me. You are the reason I smile, the reason I laugh, and the reason I learned to love again. Would you do me the honor of being my wife?"

There were so many things she wanted to say in response. His speech was the most beautiful thing anyone had ever said to her. And yet all she could manage to get out at that moment was a simple,

"Yes."

He slid the ring onto her finger then gently pressed his lips against her fingertips before lifting his head and joining his lips with hers.

****

"Uh-uh. Nope. No way. Not happening." Zane stared at his mother and sister and wrapped his arm possessively around Andi's waist.

"Zane, stop being difficult. It's tradition for the groom to not see the bride the night before the wedding and up until the ceremony," Norah explained for the hundredth time.

"I don't care if it's tradition I'm not doing it," Zane protested.

"Zane Michael McKade," his mother said pointing a finger at him. "You are too going to go through with it and before you tell me you're not one more time just remember who's paying for this shindig. It's not only tradition, it's good luck. Now, Andi will stay here at the house with us tonight and you and Luke will stay at your house. You can see her tomorrow when it's time for the ceremony."

He wanted to retort with "But Mom" but held himself back from doing so for fear of sounding like a five-year old. He looked down to Andi standing at his side and let out an exasperated sigh.

"It'll be fine, sweetie," Andi said and rested her hand against his chest.

"Fine," he said and rolled his eyes. "But I'm not happy about it. At all." He leaned down and gently pressed his lips against hers for one long slow and passionate kiss.

"All right, all right, you have to leave now,"

Linda said shooing him out of the house. "Luke, you keep your eye on him and make sure he doesn't try anything."

"I'm on it," Luke said with a grin. "Come on, big brother, let's go celebrate your last night as a single man." He wrapped his arm around Zane's shoulder and shot a mischievous grin towards Andi as they walked out the back door.

Andi ran towards the back door and flung the screen door wide open. "You bring him here sober tomorrow, Luke! So help me if he's hung-over you'll be sorry!"

Luke and Zane laughed loudly as they walked towards the truck. Zane looked back to Andi and waved before stepping into the vehicle and disappearing down the driveway.

"Come on, Andi," Norah said grabbing her hand and leading her back into the house. "We've got a girls night planned and we've gotta get started. I'm gonna go grab my nail polish so I can do your nails for you." Norah released her grip of Andi's hand once they were in the living room and went to her room to grab her supplies.

"I'm gonna pop us some popcorn and get the movie set up," Linda said.

"And I've got the wine!" Belle stated as she popped the cork from the bottle. She poured a generous serving into a glass and handed it over to Andi. "Drink up, sweetie. This is your last night as a single gal, so make it count."

****

Andi sighed as she fell into her old bed. She was tired and exhausted, but oddly at the same time felt wide awake. Her night had been the most fun she had had with a bunch of women in, well, ever. Never before could she think of a time where she laughed so hard. Belle was a downright hoot when she was tipsy. Andi had to hold back a laugh as she remembered Belle dancing around the living room to "Honky Tonk Ba Donk a Donk" by Trace Adkins and going on about she'd like to grab hold of his "ba donk a donk."

She closed her eyes and attempted to force herself to sleep. A light tapping sound coming from the window startled her and she got up from the bed to see what or who it was. Taking careful steps, she made her way over to the window and pulled the curtain back just enough to catch a glimpse. A huge smile spread across her face when she saw Zane hiding in the bushes. She unlocked the window, lifted it and leaned her elbows on the frame.

"Can I help you?" she asked in a teasing tone.

"Take a walk with me," he said as he struggled with the bush that was partially blocking him from Andi.

"Aren't you supposed to be at Red's with Luke living up your last night as a single man?" she asked.

"We already went," he told her. "I told Luke I needed to get my rest for tomorrow so we headed back to the house. I snuck out after I heard him snoring on the sofa. So what'ya say?"

"I don't know," she said in the same teasing manner. "It *is* against the rules and your mother would probably shoot you if she knew you were here."

"Come on," Zane pleaded. "Neither one of us wanted this. And if we're real quiet they won't even notice you're gone." He made his way past the bush and held his hand out for hers.

"You want me to crawl out the window?" she asked raising an eyebrow.

Zane nodded. "You can't exactly stroll through the house now can you? They're like guard dogs ready to attack you the minute you try to sneak by them."

Andi pressed her hand over her mouth to keep from laughing. "Okay, let me get my shoes." She walked over to the closet and grabbed her old boots and slipped them on. She caught a glimpse of herself in the floor length mirror as she walked back towards the window. "Boy do I look a sight." She laughed as she took in the odd pairing of the old boots with her pink spaghetti strap top and polka dotted pajama shorts.

Zane reached his arms out and helped her from the window, then set her on her feet. "Hi," he said and gave her a crooked smile as he wrapped his arms around her.

"Hi." She smiled back.

"Let's get out of here before someone hears us." He took her hand and led her out of the flower bed and around the house, keeping an eye out the whole time for anyone who might catch them. They ran hand in hand through the back yard to the barn and let out a sigh of relief once they were inside.

"Why do I feel like I'm playing hide and seek?" Andi asked with a soft laugh.

Zane smiled and led her towards the ladder to

the hayloft. "After you," he said and gestured for her to climb the ladder.

Once they had both made it to the loft, Zane walked over to the wall and grabbed an old blanket and laid it on the hay. "Here have a seat," he said and then walked over to open the doors that faced the horse pasture.

Andi sat down and kicked off her boots. She pat the empty space on the blanket next to her and Zane sat down. She leaned her head on his shoulder as the two of them stared out into the open landscape.

"I'm glad you broke the rules," she said quietly.

"Me too," he agreed and wrapped his arm around her waist pulling her closer. "Are there any other rules you'd care to break tonight?"

She lifted her head from his shoulder to look him in the face. "Just what are you suggesting, Mr. McKade?" she asked with a smirk.

"Well," he said with a sly smile. "Isn't there that whole thing about not having sex until your wedding night?"

Andi tilted her head back and laughed. "I think that rule was broken a long time ago."

He gently brought his fist up and rested it under her chin, turning her face towards his. "Let's do it anyway," he whispered huskily and pressed his lips to hers as he laid her back against the blanket.

****

As the first rays of mornings light were bursting over the horizon, Zane helped Andi back through her bedroom window.

"I'll see you in a few hours," he said with a wink.

Andi smiled and was about to come back with a sweet reply when she heard muffled noises coming from the hallway. "Oh shoot, they're up. You need to get out of here before they see you," she whispered quickly.

As Zane made his way to his hidden truck, Andi ran across the room as quietly as she could and hopped in to her bed. She had just pulled the covers over her when a light knock came from the door.

"Andi?" Norah sang as she pushed the door open. She crossed the room and sat down on the edge of the bed. "Come on, sleepy head, it's time to get ready for your big day."

Andi rolled over and pretended to just wake up. "Mmm, good morning," she said to Norah as she sat up and stretched.

"Come on, you need to get up and eat something. Mom made pancakes, bacon, sausage, eggs, biscuits, you know, something light just to get you through the morning." Norah laughed. "Then you'll get your shower and I'll do your hair and makeup and... What's that?"

Andi saw Norah's intent stare and instantly became nervous. Was it stamped on her forehead that she had met Zane out in the barn in the middle of the night for a little pre-wedding night romp in the hay? "What's what?"

Norah narrowed her eyes towards Andi, then reached her hand out and removed something from Andi's hair. "A piece of hay?" she asked bewildered as she held it out for Andi to see.

"Um," Andi said flustered. Although she tried to control it, the burning heat filled her cheeks turning them crimson in a matter of seconds.

Norah sucked in a shocked breath of air and playfully shoved Andi's shoulder. "You little hussy!"

They both laughed at Andi's embarrassment as Andi fanned herself with her hand trying to get rid of the blush.

"I guess there's no keeping you two apart, huh?" Norah asked when she was able to control her laughter.

"No, I guess not," Andi replied with a smile.

"That's a good thing." Norah gave Andi a heartwarming smile and leaned in to hug her. "Thank you for making my brother happy again."

A lump rose in Andi's throat and tears blurred her vision as she hugged Norah back.

"Girls! Come on it's time to get going!" Linda called from the kitchen.

Norah slowly pulled away from Andi and stood up from the bed. "Let's go, sis. You've got a big day ahead of you," Norah smiled and held her hand out for Andi's.

Andi smiled back and wiped her eyes with her fingertips before taking Norah's hand and letting Norah lead her from the room.

****

The wedding went just as she dreamt it would. After they were pronounced husband and wife, they headed towards the side of the house for pictures while the guests made their way over to the other side of the yard where the reception was to be held.

"I do like that dress," Zane whispered in her ear as he let his eyes run over her white strapless A-line gown. The canary yellow sash around the waist was the exact same color of Norah's bridesmaid dress. "I think I'd like it better off of you though."

Andi playfully smacked his shoulder. "Stop that." She laughed.

"Well, aren't you going to tell me how nice I look," he said, tugging on his jacket to straighten it out.

"You look as handsome as ever in your tux," she told him. A mischievous smile spread across her face and she leaned up towards his ear to whisper, "But I think I'd like it better off of you as well."

He grinned and replied, "Care to sneak off to the barn for a replay of last night?"

The photographer started to give instructions to everyone about where to stand and Andi looked to Zane. "Later," she said with a wink.

Once the pictures were done, they made their way over to the simple reception area. The tables were decorated with yellow table clothes and arrangements of sunflowers in metal buckets. It was so quaint and charming and Andi had to appreciate all the hard work her new mother-in-law and sister-in-law had put in to making this whole thing happen. After the delicious meal that Belle provided had been eaten, Andi and Zane made their way out to the dance floor for their first dance as husband and wife. The singer in the band belted out a beautiful rendition of Lady Antebellum's "Can't Take My Eyes Off You" as Zane spun Andi around in a slow circle. There wasn't a dry eye in the whole place as everyone cheered and clapped when the song was over and Zane leaned down to kiss his bride. As the day came to an end, Andi and Zane made their rounds to thank everyone for coming. Hugs and kisses were given to the bride and handshakes were shared with the groom. Willy had even been able to make it, and Andi was pleased to see that he was beginning to move around better. She had made it a point on several occasions to apologize profusely for what happened to him, to which he assured her that he held no hard feelings.

"Thank you again for walking me down the aisle," Andi said to Red as she wrapped her arms tightly around him and then kissed his cheek.

"Oh you don't have to thank me," Red said. "I was happy to do it." Red shook hands with Zane and wished them both all the luck and happiness with their marriage.

The last to receive hugs and kisses were Linda, Norah and Luke.

"Congratulations you two. And Andi, sweetie, welcome to the family," Linda said.

"Thanks, Mom," she replied sweetly.

"You were the most beautiful bride I have ever seen," Norah said as she hugged Andi once more.

"Aw, thanks," Andi said.

Zane took Andi's hand in his once Norah had released her arms and stepped back to stand next to Luke and Linda. "Well, I guess we'll be heading out now," Zane said, giving Andi's hand a gentle squeeze.

"Hang on a second," Luke said stepping

forward. "Aren't we supposed to throw rice or bird seed or something like that as you run to the truck?"

"Well, that was the plan," Linda said. "But my box of rice went missing from my pantry."

"It's ok, Mom," Zane said. "We don't need to be picking rice and stuff out of our clothes and hair anyway." He kissed her on the cheek and led Andi by the hand to his truck. "After you, Mrs. McKade," he said holding the door open for her.

She went to step in but didn't need to as Zane swept her off her feet and lifted her into the truck. "Thank you, Mr. McKade," she said with a giggle.

He shut the door after she was in, careful to make sure he didn't catch her dress in the door, and then made his way around the front of the truck to the driver's side. Once he was in he shut the door and he and Andi gave one last wave good bye.

"Now," Zane said turning his attention to Andi and wiggling his eyebrows, "time for the honeymoon." With a sharp turn of the key in the ignition, the truck roared to life. Both Zane and Andi let out a surprised yell as the air conditioning kicked on full blast and showered them with an unknown substance.

"What the...?" Zane muttered and quickly turned off the a/c.

Andi reached down the top of her dress and pulled out the tiny grains of rice that had flown from the a/c vents just moments ago. She held her hand back and bit her bottom lip trying not to laugh. "It's rice."

Zane's eyes widened and he quickly rolled down the window. "Luke!"

Luke sat next to Linda and Norah with a shit-eating grin on his face. "Happy wedding day, big brother!" he yelled and waved.

"What's all that about?" Norah asked confused.

Luke continued to grin. "Let's just say I owe Mom a box of rice."

****

Later that night, in the quietness of the dark, Andi slowly and carefully eased her way out of Zane's arm and slid out of the bed. She grabbed a thin cotton robe hanging on the footboard and wrapped it around herself as she tiptoed from the room. She stopped in the doorway and glanced back at Zane sleeping in the bed. Her heart filled with warmth as she thought about how adorable he looked with his blonde hair going every which way on the pillow. She closed the door behind her and made her way over the end table by the sofa. The lamp dimly lit the room when she turned it on, and she opened the drawer of the end table to pull out her journal. With a pen in her hand, she situated herself on the sofa and flipped to the last blank page.

September 3

I am a married woman! Today was the happiest day of my life. The ceremony and reception were absolutely perfect and I have my new mother-in-law and sister-in-law to thank for that. I've been welcomed with open arms into this amazing family and for that I am truly grateful. I don't think I could've wished for a better family to be a part of.

While I'm on the subject of wishing, I might add that I don't think I could have wished for a better husband either. Zane is the perfect man. He is caring, thoughtful, loving, gorgeous, and I am thankful that I have found the love of a man as wonderful as him. I look forward to spending the rest of my life with him, knowing that from here on out I will forever be safe in the arms of my cowboy.

The End

ABOUT THE AUTHOR

In November of 2011, author Kimberly Lewis stepped into the writing world with her first original western contemporary romance novel, When the Heart Falls.

Born and raised on the Eastern Shore of Maryland, this country girl at heart caught the creative bug at an early age, doing everything from drawing to writing short stories.

After the birth of her son, Kimberly found the inspiration to pick up a pen, or in this case a laptop, and began writing her first novel. Since then she has continued to write and credits her husband, Rob, and her wonderfully crazy family, who with their love and joking demeanor provide her with the ideas that inspire her novels.

In her spare time she enjoys reading, horseback riding, and spending time with her amazing family. To learn more about Kimberly and her books, please visit her at
kimberlylewisnovels.blogspot.com

Look for these titles by Kimberly Lewis

Now Available:

When the Heart Falls

Coming Soon:

Norah: The McKades of Texas

Luke: The McKades of Texas

When the Heart Falls

When Misty Prescott moved back home to her parent's ranch after catching her husband cheating on her, she couldn't have possibly known that she'd fall for not one, but two cowboys at the same time. Nor could she have known that getting involved with both men would bring unwelcome excitement, turning her already messed up world completely upside down. As Misty's relationship with Vance Kinney begins, she can't help but develop an intense attraction to her best friend's older brother, Dylan McCoy. But just as Misty makes her choice, she indirectly becomes the target of one horrific event after another. Now, Misty must fight the very obstacles that threaten to tear her apart from the man she loves, and survive the danger lurking around every corner that threatens their very lives.

Enjoy the following excerpt for *When the Heart Falls*

The smell of alcohol on her breath was enough to make him drunk. He leaned his head away from hers and took a breath of non-alcoholic air.

"Shoo, Misty! What did you do? Take a bath in Jack Daniels?" he asked, scrunching his face up a little.

"Dylan, that's silly." She giggled. "Where are we going?" she asked as he kept his arm around her waist and started to usher her to the door.

"I'm taking you home." he said.

"But I haven't finished my show!" she protested and waved her hand back toward the stage.

"I think your show is over for tonight. That poor mic needs a rest." He chuckled.

"Dylan McCoy, are you telling me I can't sing?" she asked and stumbled a little bit.

He helped her keep her balance and jokingly replied, "Misty, you couldn't carry a tune in a bucket."

"You don't know what you're talking about. I sing like a bird," she said proudly and lifted her chin.

"A dying bird," he said under his breath. They walked past the bar and Dylan nodded to Paul. "See you in a little bit."

"I'll be there as soon as I get closed up," Paul agreed.

What should have been an easy task of walking her out to her car proved different. She kept tripping in the loose stone and dramatically throwing her arm in the air as she kept trying to prove to Dylan that she could indeed sing like a bird. Dylan was annoyed but amused at the same time. At one point she took a tumble and landed flat on her behind. Dylan could barely contain his laughter when she whined that her butt was bruised and insisted that he kiss it and make it better. When he finally got her out to her car, he leaned her against the side long enough to open her purse and get her keys. He hit the unlock button and the cars lights blinked twice. He walked her around to the passenger side and opened the door for her.

"I don't want to get in," she said like a child getting ready to throw a temper tantrum.

"Misty, please get in the car," he said softly.

"No!" she said as she stomped her boot on the ground. "Not until you tell me that I sing like a bird."

Dylan sighed and shook his head. He knew it wasn't worth arguing with her so he smiled and said, "Ok, you sing like a bird."

"Thank you," she said arrogantly with a smile. She went to push herself from the side of the car so she could take the passenger seat, but lost her balance and fell into Dylan's chest. His arms firmly wrapped around her so she wouldn't fall.

"Easy now," he said. Dylan loosened his grip a little bit after she regained her balance, but he didn't let go. He looked down at her just as she leaned her face up to see his and their eyes locked. For a moment, it seemed as if time was standing still. He could feel his heart rate quicken as she stared into his eyes. He wanted nothing more than to lean down and join his lips with hers. Caught up in the moment, he smiled a little and leaned in toward her. The scent of Jack Daniels on her breath brought him up short. He opened his eyes and pulled back from her. He could tell she was a little confused but she didn't question him. If she hadn't been so intoxicated Dylan would have taken advantage of that moment and kissed her.

"Um," he said, clearing his throat. "You ready to go now?"

She nodded her head and allowed him to help her into the car. After she was settled, he closed her

door and walked around to the driver's side. Once in, he started the car and slowly pulled out of the parking lot. Misty stared out the windshield with a blank expression. She was slowly starting to sober up and the landscape flying by was making her feel a little nauseous. It felt like her head was spinning; not only from the effects of the alcohol but from the kiss that she and Dylan almost shared. Why had he pulled away from her? She was ready and willing for it to happen. So why didn't it? She turned to look in his direction and saw a look of confusion and concern on his face. She opened her mouth to apologize for how she had acted tonight when she noticed that he kept checking the rearview mirror. Confused, she looked behind them and saw a set of headlights trailing fairly close behind them.

"What's wrong?" she asked Dylan.

"I'm not sure but I think that car is following us," he said with the sound of concern clear in his voice.

Misty looked out the back window again and asked, "What makes you say that?"

"They've been on our tail since we pulled out of the bar," he explained. "Your seat belt on?"

"Yes. Why?" she asked confused.

"Hang on," he told her as he pushed the gas pedal to go faster.

The car behind them kept up with the pace and began to tail them even closer now.

"Yep! Definitely following us," he said out loud. She wasn't sure if he was talking to her or to himself. Just then the car flipped on its bright lights

and rammed into the back of Misty's car. She let out a scream and clutched the dashboard.

"Hold on!" Dylan yelled as he floored it. Dylan drove Misty's car as fast as it would go down the dark country road but he couldn't seem to shake off the other car. The car rammed into the back of them once more and they lurched forward.

"Oh my God, Dylan. What's going on?" Misty asked through frightened gasps.

"I have no idea," Dylan told her as he continued to try and out run the aggressive car behind them.

Misty looked out the windshield and saw a sign for a sharp turn up ahead. "Dylan, you better slow down there's a bad turn up here," she quickly informed him.

"I can't," he said.

"What do you mean you can't? Slow down. We're not going to make the turn going this fast."

"I can't, Misty. Your brakes are out!"

Made in the USA
Lexington, KY
17 October 2012